The
Apostate

ASHLEY AASHEIM

The Apostate

A Critic's Choice paperback
from Lorevan Publishing, Inc.
New York, New York

Reprinted by arrangement with the Author

ISBN: 1-55547-181-1

First Critic's Choice/Bart Book edition 1987

From LOREVAN PUBLISHING, INC.

Published in association with Interpub Communications, Inc.

Critic's Choice Paperbacks
31 E. 28th St.
New York, New York 10016

Manufactured in the United States of America

To Stella Aasheim

The author gratefully acknowledges: the librarians at St. John's Gate, Clerkenwell, London; *The Knight and Chivalry*, R. Barber (1974); *The Great Siege*, E. Bradford (1961); *Malta* (Gozo & Comino), T. Cox (1969); *Golden Century of Spain*, T. Davis (1956); *A History of Europe*, Volume I, H. A. L. Fisher (1969); *The Spanish Inquisition*, Edited by P. J. Hauben (1969); *The Age of Reconnaissance*, J. H. Parry (1973); *The Siege of Malta, 1565*, Ian C. Lochhead & T. F. R. Barling (1970).

CHAPTER ONE

Tripoli, 1551

Francisco del Valle strolled with his new bride by the stream that wound its way through his small estate. The still summer's evening was scented with the lavender growing amidst the *matorral*, the scrub land to be cleared for cultivation. And as they walked the young man's head was filled with a confusion of thoughts and emotions concerning his plans for their future, his hopes and his love for Mariana, all blending to make him heady with the promise life held.

He caught Mariana's hand, and she turned, her oval face softened in the indigo light, her bright eyes clear, jet, innocent, her small figure making him feel protective. He caressed the soft skin and wondered if his hand felt leathery on her cheek.

"Are you sorry you left Seville, Mariana?" he whispered. "Life here is hard. The Estremadura yields little to man or . . ."

Her fingers on his lips silenced him.

"I am with you, Francisco," she answered, "that is enough."

"There is much to do here," he said, "lands to clear, irrigate, to make things grow . . ." His voice faded at her smile and he laughed. "I talk like a *cosechero*, a rich farmer, when I should speak like a lover."

"You speak as Don Francisco del Valle, and that is who I want to hear. His words, his dreams."

"And his dreams are that we should always be together," Francisco continued, "and that his love will grow stronger."

Her childish giggle rippled as she danced from his embrace.

"Care, Don Francisco," she chided playfully. "Love weakens resolve, and for a *brave* Knight of St. John, only courage should be your master," she raised an eyebrow, "or mistress?"

"I can have both!" he called after her as she skipped a few paces from him. "Can't I have love and courage?"

"Only if you can catch me," she teased, then hitching her skirts she ran.

Her playfulness infected him, and laughing he began to pursue her. But as he ran, his breath became laboured, his eyes blurred, and the girl faded into the mists of his dreams. Now his eyes opened to the reality of the garrison compound, its burning heat, and the tragedy of the bodies and wreckage littering the sands. The battle to save the Knights' foothold in Tripoli and its cost was strewn before him as he watched soldiers tending wounded comrades.

Mariana, whom he had married only months before, having taken her from her family in Seville, was now far away in Spain on the estate, and the memory jarred his conscience.

He had not wanted to leave her, she was more precious to him than his own life. But long ago, when he had been allowed to enter the Castilian Langue of the Knights of St. John, he had known that if the call to arms ever came he would have to go and join his Langue to fight for the Order. And after only a few months of marriage he had answered that call, his oath of allegiance to the Knights as sacred if not more so than that of any other sworn.

And when the garrison here in Tripoli was attacked by Dragut's fleet in an attempt to sweep the Order from the mainland and back to Malta, their last refuge, he, his closest comrade, Alonso de Rojas, and Alonso's brother had travelled to join their brothers in arms. Resistance to the Turkish attacks was more holy than any duty a Knight could perform. And the honour and privilege to fight in the Castilian Langue had presented itself.

"You were dreaming," he heard Don Alonso de Rojas say in a parched voice.

He turned to his compatriot, sitting like him propped against the mud wall shaded by the rushes that served as a rough shelter from the glaring sun.

Alonso's battered state reflected the pounding they had taken from the Muslim attacks over the weeks. Next to him

8

lay Miguel, Alonso's younger brother, in the same exhausted condition.

The boy, an initiate to the Order, was not yet eighteen, yet appeared three times that age with his sunken eyes, and pallor as grey as the dust caking his hair and clinging to his tattered armour, his body sprawled like a marionette.

What an initiation, Francisco thought, remembering how fresh and excited they were on the galleon that brought them from Spain. All that swagger and boast now lay buried with the dead that had fallen under Dragut's onslaughts, their pride and honour as shredded as their armour and uniforms. All that remained was the desperate will to survive the next attack.

He closed his eyes and imagined himself buried in Mariana's body, her arms wound round him as they had been on so many gentle evenings, her perfume intoxicating him.

But the stench of charring and the dead prevailed, and the embrace became the firm grasp of Alonso on his arm.

"Don't dwell too much, Francisco," Alonso cautioned as though reading his thoughts. "This god-forsaken land is no place for dreams." Francisco tried to reply, but the words stuck in his dry throat, and he felt a goatskin pushed into his hands.

"Take it," Alonso insisted, offering the water container. "It won't sustain you, but it'll free your tongue for confession."

Francisco raised the goatskin and squeezed the few drops from it, the warm liquid evaporating as it touched his swollen tongue.

"What hour is it?" he croaked.

"Early, the sun is biding its time to stoke the furnace. Even the elements support the Muslim horde," the Knight muttered.

"They know Dragut will irrigate the dust with Christian blood," Francisco answered. "How long have we been . . . besieged?"

Alonso shrugged. "Weeks, months? As an officer I count the dead, not the sunrises." He gazed at the hard, angular features of Francisco, his face half-hidden by the growth of beard. His dark eyes dull from weariness. And a pang of anguish stabbed him as he wondered if he, Miguel his brother, and his comrade were destined to be buried in these arid dusts. Men in their prime shouldn't have to die. God! How trite it sounded, he thought. He closed his eyes and leaned his head against the wall. "The Sultan Suleiman chose his leader well. That old corsair, Dragut, knows how to squeeze the life from us. You above all should know, Francisco. You slaved on the oars of his galleys when you were captured for a year."

The memory of Francisco's capture five years before pricked Alonso's conscience. He had been on a caravel when they had served in the Knights' fleet. He had seen Francisco's vessel under attack, but had not been fast enough in coming to his assistance, and as in all battles that moment of hesitation had cost the lives and freedom of the men on that caravel. Those who died would have been lucky. To have been captured as Francisco was and live in the hell of a Turkish galley must have been purgatory.

Though Francisco showed no emotion, he himself chilled at the mention of that year chained to the oar of one of Dragut's vessels. It was only five years ago that his life had hung by a thread while he toiled in shackles dragging the oar on that galley. Only his youth and strength had saved him. But he had been fortunate, he had gained release in an exchange of prisoners, when Knight was freed for Turk. It had been La Valette, the General of the Knights' Fleet, who had arranged his release and the gold of the Indies could not repay what he owed Grand Master La Valette for that mercy. It had let him live to meet Mariana on a visit to Seville and at least enjoy her courtship and love for a time. Albeit a short time if the next Muslim attack was successful.

He stared at the desperate scene of the compound and slivers of anguish stabbed at the thought of recapture. This time, he thought, there would be no release. God! He could not last another year in those stinking hulks, it would be better to die.

"I sometimes wonder," Alonso suddenly said, "if I had acted faster when you were captured, driven my caravel into the fray, would you have been saved . . . have you . . . have you ever wondered that, Francisco."

He did not answer, but many times had wondered why Alonso had stood off that afternoon instead of attacking. He had told himself that Alonso had his crew to worry about and the loss of another craft would have made no difference to the outcome. But yes, he had wondered.

"Have you ever thought about that?" Alonso probed, his eyes still closed.

"You captained your vessel as you thought fit, Alonso," he answered.

This was no time for recriminations. His only thoughts were of the present. The memory of Mariana planted in his mind by the dream and the thought of recapture dominated his emotions. How desperately he wanted to return to the *finca*, the small estate, and walk with his wife as he had in the dream. Gaze into those dark eyes that could excite, comfort and reassure him. And how fearful he was of the next attack. A novice could see the situation was virtually lost. There would be few to tell of the resistance of Tripoli.

His fear increased as in the distance he heard horns blowing and the distinctive tinkling of musical instruments that penetrated all other sounds in the compound. Even the cries of the wounded gave way to trumpets, and the cymbals of the Turks massing for the attack. For Francisco anger in previous battles had always smothered terror. Now fear was the overriding sensation. Around him, he watched men stirring, pushing their bodies from the ground, ambling in drunken weariness back to the ramparts, their weapons dragging behind them, yet he found it hard to muster himself. Don Alonso nudged his brother, Miguel, then rose slowly himself.

"Miguel, it is time," he growled.

The boy jerked from sleep.

"Don Francisco will take care of you," Alonso sighed. "As captain of the Castilian Langue, I have to join the Grand Master to fight by his side on the west wall."

The boy forced a smile. "They call for us to send more of them to their Paradise," he joked emptily as he rose.

Alonso embraced his brother tightly. "I promised our father I would bring you back safely. Help me keep that promise, Miguel. Watch for the threshing scimitars of the Janissaries, they are their most dangerous soldiers."

The boy moved uncomfortably away from his brother's embrace, embarrassed by it in front of the men shuffling past

11

them. "I have faced them, Alonso," he asserted with youthful pride.

"You have *seen* them!" Alonso snapped. "From the ramparts you have *seen* them, but not *faced* them. Now, with the ramparts blown away, you *will* face them, and learn how they gained their reputation as the best soldiers in the Muslim world!" He turned to Francisco, now rising to his feet. "We have known one another many years, Don Francisco. I am entrusting Miguel's safety to you. There is none better."

The cacophony of drums and cymbals rolled closer across the barren land separating besieged from besiegers, and as its volume increased so did Francisco's anguish. In the dream, Mariana had warned love might blunt his courage. Maybe she was right. When there was little to lose but an empty life, courage was manifest. But to lose life or liberty when the warmth of love waited for your return was a different matter.

He eyed the stragglers moving over the huge sandy compound as they quickened their pace to take their positions along the crenellated ramparts. The noise of the Turkish instruments were now being drowned in the cries of men releasing tensions in the face of attack. Salvoes of shot began to sear through the cloudless skies, thumping and thudding into the base of the garrison's walls as the Turkish gunners found range.

"Come, Francisco," the boy cried eagerly, his sword drawn and ready to move off.

"Go with Alonso!" Francisco heard himself urge desperately.

There was something strange, even fateful about the situation, and it filled him with foreboding as though the dream he had had was becoming woven into this waking nightmare. The battle was similar to others he had fought, the noises, the stench of sulphur and the dead as odious, but the sensations within him were different. It was as though his will had deserted him, leaving him with this terrible sense of not being.

Had weariness, hunger and thirst, combined with the heat created this terrible sensation or had he just lost his nerve?

Miguel urged him to join the battle as though reinvigorated by the roars around them.

"Go with Alonso!" Francisco ordered again.

"He will stay with *you*!" Alonso snapped drawing his sword

ready for the fight. "As your captain I order it! As Miguel's brother I urge it. Take care of him, Francisco, curb his impetuosity and perhaps, God willing, we will all survive to another sunrise!"

He did not wait for an answer, but rushed to the west wall to join the Grand Master directing the defence.

Reluctantly, Francisco hurried after Miguel, but on reaching the Northern ramparts a thunderous roar rolled across at them. Both stared in horror as the wall crumbled to the mining operations of the Turkish sappers beneath it.

Francisco did not know whether the cries he heard were cheers from the enemy or anguish from the men rushing to hold the yawning gap. But before the breach could be shored, it filled with the terrifying spectre of the most savage legion in the Muslim ranks – The Janissaries – Christians kidnapped at birth and conditioned to hate the infidel.

Their long plumes rose and fell above the sea of white robes as they flooded through into the compound, drowning opposition.

"Miguel!" Francisco yelled as he saw the boy rush towards the scything scimitars. But his cry was lost as a cannon shot roared into a powder barrel beside him, engulfing him in the blast.

Though conscious of what was happening around him, he could neither hear nor react. He stood immobile, his mind as incapable of thought as his body was of action. He simply gazed, stunned as the torrent raged round him.

Juan d'Omedes, Grand Master of the Order of the Knights of St. John of Jerusalem, fixed his eyes on the bowed head of the Knight kneeling before him in the dust-choked chapel where the acrid smells of sulphur and burning lingered after the Turkish onslaught. But he could not concentrate on the trial he was conducting, his mind was preoccupied with the next assault of Dragut's forces. He knew capitulation was inevitable. And as the shadows on the walls shivered in the torch-light, he wondered if they would be shown the same mercy as

13

Sultan Suleiman had demonstrated some thirty years before at Rhodes, when after battering the fortress into submission, he allowed the previous Master of the Order, Villiers de l'Isle Adam, an honourable surrender.

He looked at the six figures solemnly standing round the accused knight. Their dark ceremonial cloaks covering their battle-scarred armour might soon become their shrouds, he thought.

Each had given evidence of the Knight's disgrace, and there were more who would have witnessed it on both sides. Francisco del Valle had done nothing while the novice Miguel de Rojas was being hacked down in the fighting following the Janissary breakthrough of the early morning.

Del Valle had turned to stone, his face contorted in fear, he had become a gargoyle as the novice fell screaming for his help. It was a strange indictment for Del Valle who had served well when years before he had been with the Order. Yet, unfortunately it was not unusual for men to yield to their fears under pressure. It had happened before and would probably be repeated, with the punishment of death being as certain in each case. He sighed, this incident in some way reminding him of the onerous responsibility he himself would bear having lost the garrison at Tripoli.

"Francisco del Valle," d'Omedes said, "You have heard the evidence, what is your defence?"

Francisco did not answer. He was only vaguely aware of the counter-attack that had pushed the Janissaries back, then his arrest, the charge of cowardice, and the hastily arranged trial.

He did not remember whether he had been stunned by the explosion or fear. The witnesses had given evidence, and yet he was only aware of Alonso's testimony which described his state as one of squirming terror before the attack. That was not true! Surely that was not true! he thought. And what of Miguel? Guy de la Varre swore he stood by while the boy was cut down. But he had seen nothing, or had his terror seen nothing? Now all he saw was the oval gentle face of Mariana, and he would have willingly given his life for just one of her caresses.

"What is your defence?" he heard the Grand Master demand.

14

Francisco stared into the dust at the damp patches where sweat from his bowed brow had fallen. It was as though the room were alive with the moisture running down his body.

"His silence condemns him!"

Francisco recognised the voice of Don Alonso de Rojas as it cracked emotionally behind him.

"We are agreed," Alonso snarled. "His guilt stains us all. Let his death be an example to those who betray by cowardice!"

He could almost sense the vengeance pulsating through de Rojas and perhaps he might have felt the same in his position. But the condemnation was so total. Had his guilt been *that* obvious?

The oil flames twisted in a sudden draught blown through a cracked window, distorting the shadows around them. The room swam as though the perspiration of his body had filled it.

It was the sweat of shame, he told himself. The battle had raged round him and yet he had remained untouched, immune to scimitar, ball, and arrow that might have mercifully opened him in his stupor. Better scarlet valour than colourless salt water, he castigated himself.

"Let me carry out the sentence!" Alonso demanded. "Let me avenge Miguel!"

Francisco heard the sword scrape from de Rojas' scabbard, and panic swept through him. Lord Jesus, he prayed, am I to die without the Sacrament of the Last Rites! Without confession! My soul condemned to eternal damnation! Are past sacrifices to count for nothing!

"Let me fight!" he suddenly roared rising to his feet. "Let *me* avenge Don Miguel's death!"

"You should have saved his *life*!" de Rojas roared.

Francisco spun to see his friend's face contorted by fury, no longer recognisable as the man he had known.

"You made a vow to serve the Order, here in this chapel!" de Rojas rasped. "Soon after your release from the Turkish galleys. I was *here* with you!"

"I vowed to repay La Valette who organised my exchange," Francisco yelled back.

"Vows are not subject to semantics," d'Omedes reminded him.

15

"Then obey yours!" Francisco retorted savagely. "Show compassion and let me die with a sword in my hand!"

"You will be shown the same compassion as you showed my brother!" de Rojas snarled raising his blade.

"You were not so quick to fight on the caravel when I was captured, Don Alonso!" Francisco challenged. "I am not asking for life, but death in battle!"

But the jibe was no sooner made than a spark of steel streaked through the shadows slashing Francisco's cheek. Only Guy de la Varre's parry stopped the blade from taking his head.

"Hold your sword!" d'Omedes shouted at de Rojas now struggling between two restraining Knights. "This is a *court*! Not an execution chamber!"

He looked at del Valle. The blood streamed down the wound soaking his cloak. "You have had your revenge!" d'Omedes raged at de Rojas. "And that denies this court the right to call for more blood!" The silence created by the Grand Master's roar was only punctuated by de Rojas' laboured breathing as his fury surged. But after a few moments d'Omedes spoke. "I have decided that you, Francisco del Valle will leave this place now since we cannot execute you ourselves. You shall be stripped of any honour or recognition this Order has bestowed, and your name shall become synonymous with *el cobarde* – the coward!"

"I will redeem myself," Francisco whispered.

"None of the true faith would trust you beside them!" de Rojas snarled struggling to free himself.

"Then I will find *others*!" Francisco roared back at the dark narrow face glaring at him.

"You'll die before that!" de Rojas threatened, "I'll find you and kill you! I swear to God before this altar!"

As he spoke the Grand Master motioned to the soldiers beside the chapel doors to open them, and as they swung the evening sunlight flooded down the aisle.

"Go Francisco del Valle!" d'Omedes ordered. "Leave the garrison!"

Now Francisco realized the meaning of being cast out. He was to be thrown to the waiting Turks, to be captured or killed once outside the walls. Even if a miracle happened and he survived, those of the true faith would treat him as a leper, ridicule and shun him, vilify him as he spoke his name. Spain could no longer be his home. His own father would reject a son branded as a coward, and his life with Mariana was finished. Her family would spurn him regardless of what she felt, and if she stayed with him, she would be contaminated by his shame.

"If you live beyond those gates, I will find you!" he heard de Rojas snarl. But his words were insignificant in the face of what lay ahead if he lived. His father had once told him that *hidalgos* like them, minor aristocracy, might not have the money of grandees, but they were rich in honour. Now his name had neither.

As the soldiers escorted him along the aisle, he was filled with the image of Mariana. Those dark eyes that would never look on him with respect or affection again and that small face that would no longer express trust, only uncertainty about his courage to provide and defend her. She was as lost to him now as Miguel was to Don Alonso. It would be better if the Turks killed him as he walked through the main gates.

He made his way with the guards from the chapel across the compound, orange in the evening sun. Though only partly aware of the twisted smouldering wreckage strewn about him, and of the wounded huddled under makeshift shades, he sensed every eye on him. All was still, as though petrified by his presence.

The large gates of the fortress creaked open as though of their own accord, urging him to leave, to step beyond them and suffer his fate. His throat tightened as he thought of Mariana, and he wanted to weep as he had not done since a child. But he forced himself on through the gates, on until he found himself walking among the charred corpses of those who failed to scale the walls and those who fell from them. The decaying bodies created an evil stench, penetrating his very being, and he braced himself to join that vast army of the unknown dead, and he waited for the inevitable hail of missiles that would be hurled from the enemy.

Nothing happened.

17

Francisco raised his head. There, not 300 paces away, lining the russet hills surrounding the garrison, he saw Janissary, Mameluke, Iayalar and Algerian soldiers, all as silent as those Christians standing high on the walls above him, joining them in voiceless condemnation. He gazed at the blazing array of uniforms and pennants fringing the ridges and hoped for that merciful end. But all remained still.

No attack, nor jeering, nor derision. The silence only disturbed by the flapping robes of the dead as the breeze swept the fine dust over them in premature burial.

He caught sight of a dead Janissary propped against a block of fallen masonry, his white robes stained with blood from his wounds reminding him of his own wound whose pain he no longer felt. The Turk's eyes were wide open as though even in death he had joined the living in condemnation.

Francisco wanted to move, run, hide, yet he stood for moments, transfixed, until a voice shattered the silence; barking from the parapets above, shocking life into him.

"I will find you, Francisco del Valle!" he heard de Rojas yell.

He looked up at the awesome sight straddling the crenellated stones, cloak flaring in the wind, breast-plate afire in the setting sun.

"You will be known as *el cobarde*! And by that name I'll find you! *El cobarde* – the coward!"

His words echoed across the wasteland then resounded as soldiers took up the chant in a single voice that pulsated from the rocks until the stones themselves became alive with the roar: "*El cobarde! El cobarde! El cobarde!*"

CHAPTER TWO

Estremadura, Spain, 1565

The small boy crouched by the thin shallow stream and dipped the cracked earthenware pot into it; sparks of freezing water splashed up stinging him. The vessel filled and he placed it carefully beside him, took another and shivered as the early morning breeze cut through his flimsy shirt.

He was sleepy and wiped his wet hand over his face to wake himself. Once the second vessel filled, he set it against the other, then sat back for a moment staring across the familiar wasteland.

In the far distance, foreshortened by the clear icy air, lay a rise of blue hills. He gazed at them, thinking about the time when he would leave Santa Madre, his village, and travel to the lands he had heard the old men talk about. He wanted to see the places where the tall trees hid the sky, where there were villages with more people than it was possible to know. He wanted to see the lands across the sea that the soldiers in the nearby garrison talked of. There, they said, were mountains of gold and silver. Could there really be such a land, he wondered.

He shivered again, but this time not from cold. He sensed a strange presence nearby. Behind him. Watching him. he tensed, coiled himself ready to spring from the danger, then turned.

At a short distance, he saw an old man swathed in a heavy dark-red dusty cloak, sitting astride a large brown horse with a pack animal behind him.

His thick black beard and long hair were streaked grey, his dark skin like baked earth.

The three figures were motionless, weary, as though they

had travelled far. Maybe from the land of gold and silver mountains he thought. A soldier? No, he was nothing like the garrison soldiers in their shining breast-plates and helmets. The stranger was too heavy and sombre.

He wanted to run, warn the village about the stranger. But he remained where he was. In the moments that passed between them, only the trickling of the stream disturbed the stillness, when the stranger suddenly jerked his feet into the cob, startling the boy, causing him to jump back and knock the vessels over. He snatched at them, then turned quickly. But the stranger had moved on, riding slowly, but somehow covering the ground rapidly. The boy stood up, wanting to run to Santa Madre, but the man was now too close to the village to warn them.

Don Francisco del Valle approached the village on the small estate that had once belonged to him and his father.

It had been fourteen years since he had last seen those mud hovels but he felt no nostalgia, nor regret for the *finca*, the estate, which he had visited the previous day, and which had been left to degenerate into part of the *baldíos*, the empty lands, that stretched to the sierras of the northern Estremadura.

Ahead, he saw a few ragged figures stand gaping, held momentarily by curiosity, then scurry away.

His horses clipped their way through the quiet to the small church he had last visited with Mariana, just before he left for Tripoli. Amidst the man-made squalor and natural desolation, the cracked distempered walls seemed to protest respectability, and he remembered how at one time he had looked on this building with reverent awe. Now he saw it as just another dilapidated building. Francisco tugged the rein of his horse. It stopped, and he looked round him. The village was now deserted. Tiredly he lifted himself from the creaking saddle to the ground aching from the long hard ride through Portugal to Spain.

The animals would have to be fed and watered, he thought, but later.

His boots crunched over the broken stone and his sword clanked as he approached the church.

The icy freshness of the open air transformed into a musky dampness as he entered the church, and the pungent smell of burned candles told him that Mass had just finished. As his eyes accustomed to the gloom, he saw nothing had changed.

The same rough wooden benches faced the covered table against the far flaking wall and the same carved tabernacle stood between burnished candlesticks. In front of it stood the eternal light burning in a small oil lamp, affirming that God was in this house. For a moment the crucifix on the wall held him, demanding genuflection, a reflex from the past, he thought, but he turned away and ambled over to one of the benches where he eased himself down, propping his back against the wall and resting his leg along it. From here he could see his animals standing outside in the stark light, and they would warn him if anyone approached. He tugged off his riding-gloves and began to massage life back into the aching muscles of his shoulders.

Beyond the door nothing moved, yet he sensed he was being watched; that tongues whispered his presence. He closed his eyes and shut out his surroundings.

He remembered himself as a small boy kneeling here, with his father, in the front row as befitted their position as *hidalgos*, and how the priest in his white vestments had appeared as the personification of the wonder of Christ and his sacrifice for Man, and how the image of the simple faith and its strength had urged him to join the forces that fought its enemies – the Knights of St. John. And when he came of age, like his father before him, he went and trained, then fought on land and sea against the infidels who were trying to swamp Christendom with their barbarity, neither sparing himself, nor his loved ones in answering the call to aid the Order. But then there was Tripoli.

Even fourteen years later he could recall how he had left the garrison amidst the scorn that poured down on him from the ramparts, and how he had managed to get a ship to Portugal, and from there to the Indies and then to France where he hired himself as a mercenary. For the next fourteen years he fought for *anyone* who paid, the high principles he once held buried in the shame of Tripoli.

"Don Francisco?" a frail voice asked.

He opened his eyes.

"Don Francisco del Valle?"

He gazed at the heavy old man in the black threadbare *sotana* standing over him. The years had been as unkind to Padre Morales as they had been to him, but though fatter, with a round florid squashed face, Francisco recognised him.

"What are you doing here?" the priest hissed.

"You look like you have seen a ghost," Francisco said quietly.

"There were stories that you were dead, somewhere in France, or the low countries . . ."

"As you can see, Pedro," Francisco smiled using the priest's first name, "I am alive."

The old man rubbed his hands from nervousness and cold as though the knight had resurrected ghosts he had thought long dead. Yet for a moment the sight of him and his father riding through the village flashed through his mind. In their impoverished area of the Estremadura they were like flowers carried across the wastelands by the wind. *Hidalgos*, low aristocracy, but grand in manner and deed until the shame of Tripoli and what followed.

"There is nothing for you here, Francisco," the priest urged. "Your father, Don Ricardo, died a decade ago and . . ." his voice trailed off.

"And my wife, Mariana, returned to her family in Seville," Francisco said.

"The estate is now *realengo*, king's land," Padre Morales said avoiding further conversation about Mariana. He did not know whether Francisco knew she had remarried, and felt it would be unwise to tell him. The less he knew about her, the more remote his chances of contacting her and disrupting her life. "When Don Ricardo died," he continued, "the *finca* was taken over."

"Emperor Carlos was welcome to it," the Knight smiled wryly. "Neither he, nor his pious son Felipe have done much with it."

"Have you been there?"

"I have ridden across what was a small estate with a respectable home for a *hidalgo*, and what has now been left to become *baldíos*, wasteland."

"You contributed to that!" the priest hissed, glancing round to make sure they were alone. He wanted to say more, but stifled the words. "Enough!" he snapped. "There have been enough recriminations. You must leave here. You will bring the soldiers or the church militia . . ."

"The Inquisition?"

"If the stories I heard of you are true," he answered tightly, "they will not offer you the opportunity of the *sanbenito*," he said, referring to the yellow sack worn by penitents.

"What have you heard?"

"That you went to the Indies, then returned to France where you aided heretics, fighting for the devil!"

"I fought for pay."

The pale eyes flared in righteous indignation.

"You fought brother Catholics in the name of heresy!"

"Who told you these stories?"

"Does it matter!" The old man flicked at the folds of his *sotana* irritably. "We may be remote here, Don Francisco . . . but soldiers ride through, travellers pass . . . Your actions are what matter! Not how I know them."

Francisco looked down at the dark stained leather gloves in his hands as he spoke. "When I returned from the Indies, I took the only profession I could practise."

"Are you mad!" Morales exclaimed, "Are you so mad you would condemn your soul!" The brushing hands now gripped the folds of the black *sotana*. "Your name was listed for seven years in every church in Castile!"

Wearily, the Knight stood up and looked down at the priest. Pedro was smaller than he remembered. His hair thinner, whiter. He gazed at the puffed slits glaring up at him.

"I killed Turks for salvation," Francisco sighed, "Indiano and Catholic for gold. I fought for the Châtillons and Gaspard de Coligny because they wanted me and paid me!" He curbed the rising anger he felt for this old man, so remote from the realities of war. He understood that Pedro's isolated naivety only allowed him to see war in terms of good and evil. But in fourteen years his own perception had broadened. He had

23

seen Turk and Knight cross sides, *indiano* kill *indiano* for Spanish gold, and German Lutheran take sides with French Catholic to fight Huguenot. Pedro had never seen severed limbs, nor smelt the nauseous sweet stench of burning flesh. Nor heard men offer their souls and redemption if they could be spared execution in this life. That was *war*, dirty, squalid and savage. Not fought on the field for religious conviction, but survival.

But he said none of this as the priest would never understand. He had neither killed nor been a target. Francisco sighed as weariness washed through him, and raised his hand to rub the tiredness from his eyes. But as he did so, Pedro flinched.

For a moment the Knight held still, then smiled, realizing Pedro's physical courage did not match his moral convictions.

"I'll not harm you," he said.

"Leave!" the priest rasped.

Francisco moved, but the priest caught his arm. "Where are you going?"

"To leave."

"*After* you go from here?"

He did not reply, but the answer was obvious.

"Mariana will not see you, Don Francisco."

He shrugged the priest's hand from him.

"It's no good going to Seville . . ." Pedro sat down. "You will do no good by seeing her . . . she remarried . . . Her friend, a Cardinal arranged a special dispensation . . . we thought you were dead."

The news did not affect Francisco as he thought it might. He had long prepared himself for the possibility, and steeled himself to accept that he had no right to expect Mariana to remain loyal to a husband who brought grief.

The priest looked up at the silent figure standing over him. "Why have you returned to Spain?"

That was a question Francisco had long considered. He thought it was to travel on to Malta where the Turks were soon to besiege the last stronghold of the Knights. Europe was full of the rumours of the massive fleet being amassed by the Sultan Suleiman, and within months Malta would be struck. He had vowed to aid La Valette when he had been exchanged as a galley prisoner and his return was partly to fulfil that vow and die in defence of the Order; not for religious reasons as Pedro would understand them, but perhaps from a need to cleanse himself of his actions that day fourteen years ago in Tripoli, and maybe to cleanse his soul for those wars he had fought in. But he had not needed to come to Spain, he could have gone on to Sicily and from there to the island.

But like all soldiers he had dreamed of his home, the small *finca* he had run with his father Don Ricardo. It was the animal instinct in him to return like a wounded wolf limping back to his lair before dying. And as he had sat, the day before, looking at where he had lived, had spent his youth with his father Don Ricardo, he had relived those magic moments which all fighting men cherished in those nights when only the cold and apprehension were their companions. His father teaching him to ride, wield a wooden sword, to recognize the plants and animals that struggled for survival in the hostile Estremadura. He remembered his mother, gentle but resilient, taken so young in premature death by fever.

Yet above all, there was Mariana, blooming like the cactus flower in wastes that he had brought her to. There was and always had been Mariana, her childish naivety and teasing. Her coyness in love, her curiosity and seductive caresses that had jolted him to an ecstasy he never knew with another. Always Mariana standing before him, hands clasped in front of her, head tilted, the hint of a smile in the jet eyes and on the small mouth, as he had first seen her when he and his father had first visited Don Ricardo's friends in Seville.

And when the jungle heat made his body liquidize in the Indies, and the ice numbed him in France and the low countries, there had been the image to cool and warm him. And when the fires burned his wounds to cauterize them and stop the bleeding, there was Mariana to soothe the pain. He had not seen her since leaving the *finca* for Tripoli fourteen years earlier. But there were few times she had not been with him in heart and mind. That was why he had returned to Spain and risked the fires and tortures of the Inquisition. To see her, to translate the image once more to reality, then the worn shell of his body that he used as a war machine could be allowed to die.

But as he stood there in the sombre, dank church with Pedro, he wondered how he could ever make a celibate understand the sweet-sickly yearning of love, of longing to recapture moments of peace and happiness which so suddenly died fourteen years ago. He could no more make him understand that than the true nature of war.

It wasn't just Pedro's remoteness here in the Estremadura that would prevent the old priest from understanding, but his emotional distance from the realities of life. To him, love was marriage or religious conviction and death the natural wasting of the body.

The priest studied the broad, dark face half-hidden by the greying beard. In the moments that passed Don Francisco had been deep in thought. The dark eyes staring through, rather than at him. He looked much older than his age and the ravages of the past fourteen years showed in the creases of his weather-beaten face. Life had been hard for him since Tripoli, there was no doubt of that. But any sympathy he might have had for Francisco del Valle had been scorched away by the fires of his heresy, all he could hope for now was repentance of his sins and God's mercy.

"Why have you returned to Spain?" the priest asked.

"You seem to know."

"Is Mariana the only reason?"

The Knight shook his head.

"The call has gone out from Malta to the Langues. Suleiman, the Turkish Sultan, is amassing a great fleet to attack the island and erase the Order."

The priest shook his head sadly.

"Your redemption will not come . . ."

"I don't seek redemption!" Francisco roared. "I return to pay a debt!"

"To Alonso de Rojas?"

"To the Grand Master La Valette who rescued me from the galleys of Dragut!"

As he spoke of the galleys he could feel the overseer's lash and taste the sour wine-soaked bread which sustained his existence for that interminable year. He clearly remembered how his body had been turned into a wounded machine that strained and creaked with the timbers of the vessel.

"The Order will not accept you back," Pedro said.

"They will as a common soldier," Francisco asserted, turning to leave. "I took a vow to return . . ."

"Alonso de Rojas also took a vow!" the priest said menacingly. "And he has been in Spain while you have been elsewhere. Now you are here, he will know. He is now general to the Grand Inquisitor in Madrid, he has thousands of agents throughout the country. He will find you through *familiares*, the Inquisition's spies."

Francisco had heard the news of de Rojas' rise through the Knights and his eventual appointment to the Holy Office where he had apparently revelled in his supression of the heretic. He had brought new meanings to the concepts of savagery and torture as he himself had become a religious fanatic. If it had not been so tragic for his victims it would have been laughable that a reprobate like Alonso had been when they were young, could have now become such an arch defender of the faith. But then the Inquisition was the most unholy of Holy Offices and its members the most unpardonable of sinners. But he knew the risk he had taken in returning to Spain, and never doubted de Rojas would fulfil the promise he had shouted from the ramparts in Tripoli. He sighed as thoughts of that fateful morning returned.

"To this day," he said, "I do not know whether fear or shock from the explosion paralysed me. I suppose I never will."

"You compounded your disgrace by heresy!"

"It's no worse than horrors I've seen in France and the Indies, perpetrated in the name of the Holy Office, Pedro."

"But they spread the word of Christ!"

"They spread the word of *terror*!" he called making his way to the door.

"Francisco!"

He turned and leaned against the open doorway.

"You must confess."

"Confess?" he echoed in surprise.

The puffed slits fixed on him.

"All right Pedro, I will confess." He continued before the priest could interrupt him. "Fourteen years ago my life was destroyed by an incident, the true nature of which eludes me

27

to this day. Since then I have fought in numerous armies making snows and jungles bleed with my sword, but always in the names of God and Justice. I've razed towns, organized mass executions and created darkness to bring the light my master saw as truth. My body's a patchwork of scars from cuts and burns and I have been called every animal in the menagerie from pig and dog, to lion and tiger. Yet only here, in my native Spain, do they call me *el cobarde*, the coward. And on this dark road to redemption I have been purged of fear, compassion and belief. I have survived more than forty winters, but look fifty or sixty. I am neither good nor bad, Pedro, so when this shell dies, my spirit will enter the body of yet another soldier, and when that shell is destroyed, this spirit will inhabit succeeding generations of soldiers, and long after Spain and the Empire has fallen into decay like those extinct anonymous empires I saw in the Indies, I will still exist. But only in one form. That of the eternal soldier!"

The priest gazed at the figure blotting the light from the doorway, and trembled at the terrifying words uttered by the gravel voice. In the dusty leather jerkin, half covered by the heavy red woollen cloak, with his gloved hand resting on the giant sword, the black bearded figure appeared all he said he was.

"Heresy," the old man whispered.

"Truth," Francisco replied quietly.

"General de Rojas will get you. The Inquisition will purge you to save you from eternal . . ."

"They can do nothing to me that has not already been done!" Francisco roared.

The old man crossed himself, closed his eyes and began to pray. "*Ave Maria, gratia plena* . . ." But as he opened his eyes he saw the doorway empty. Only the bright frigid sun blazing through it.

The small boy stood in the opening of the rough grey mud hut watching the bearded stranger riding towards him. The wind whipped the dust along the central track of the deserted village and the boy folded his thin arms into his body for warmth. The stranger's figure cut sharply against the pale morning sky and as he looked at him, the child retreated into the doorway. The animals plodded on past, and the boy watched as they travelled towards the sierras.

He wondered whether the stranger was going across the mountains to the villages where there were more people than he could count, then across the seas to the green forests and the mountains of silver and gold.

But a hand on his shoulder interrupted his thoughts. It was his mother.

"Go to the soldiers' camp," she urged, "Tell them they must come to Padre Morales. Go, now!"

CHAPTER THREE

Flight

Don Francisco sat resting against a solitary tree which was the only shelter the rocky plains of the low sierras offered. His unsaddled horses stood a short distance away pulling at the *tomillar* shrubs, snorting, shaking their manes as the sharp plants pricked them.

You will learn, he thought. Whatever grows on the lower plains of the Estremadura is either inedible or hostile. He shifted and groaned, still aching from the long ride through France, Portugal, and into Spain. Yet from childhood he had learnt to ride for days, eating and sleeping in the saddle. Don Ricardo, his father, had taught him to travel longer and further than any animal with less to sustain him. But his strength seemed to have waned over the past few years, and the fever he had contracted in the Indies felt as though it drained him with each attack.

Though his lids were heavy, he forced himself to stay awake, staring blankly as his mind drifted to the *finca*, the small estate, he had visited before going to Santa Madre.

As Pedro had said, it had become *realengo* – King's land, he thought. More like *sheep's land*! The *Mesta*, the sheep grazing lands, were growing while farmland shrank; and with men leaving Castile for the gold of the Indies soon there would be no humans, only the woolly creatures nibbling the grass to its roots.

Their estate had once boasted the best lands in that poor region, and with hard work they had forced the earth to produce. Unlike many *hidalgos* from surrounding areas, they had neither begged nor borrowed. All for nothing.

"Such dreams, Mariana," he mused. "I wanted so much for us yet achieved so little. But at least you married and – " He stifled the thought of her married as a jealous passion gnawed.

The idea of her pressing her lips on another's, whispering love in his ear as they lay like he had once done with her, burned him. He tried to crush the resentment. "Reason, Francisco," he cautioned. "Reason. Better married to someone than take on the veil to shrivel in a convent. Kill sweet sentiments, kill compassion, kill love, kill the enemy, you're a soldier," he muttered to himself as he had done for so many years since that dream robbed him of courage and alacrity in Tripoli. Wasn't that the message he had given when training troops for the Huguenots? Worship your sword more than God for that is all that will save you on the battlefield. Wasn't that what he had told them? Love your horses not your memories, wasn't that the instruction to new recruits? Yet he cherished his own reminiscences, but Tripoli had taught him to separate dreams from reality. "The soldier is a savage, Francisco, and the savage knows no sentiments, only survival . . . and yet still I go to Seville."

A high pitched shriek pierced the air above him, and in the sky he saw a winged predator circling. He watched it searching for prey, then saw it swoop, dropping in the distance, then suddenly soar.

He quickly sat up. "What have you seen?" he whispered, "Something too big or dangerous for you?" He listened intently at the breeze rustling through the *tomillar* and the creaking of the dead limbs of the tree. His horses moved, pricking their ears and looking towards the north-west. "I hear them," he said, "I hear them."

Within moments both animals were saddled and packed, and as he belted on his sword, he eyed the double-handed blade strapped to the pack-horse, wondering if he should take it.

There were four or five of them in the hunting-party, and by their measured gallop were probably cavalry. He took the cob's reins, then shook his head. "Better to ride, than kill indiscriminately," he said as he swung himself up into the saddle. He took the reins of the pack-horse and sat upright, listening.

31

They would spot him immediately on the arid flat plains, so the sierras were his best choice. There in the evening light they would lose sight of him against the dark ridges.

He nudged the animals to a trot, gradually increasing their pace to a gallop. In the distance he heard a cry. He had been seen, and he spurred his horse. Soon the rhythmic beating of its hooves began to drum the pattern of the pursued as the wind cut into his face, flaring his hair like the manes of his animals, whistling in his ears, enveloping him in a freezing wild mantle, and when he looked back across the darkening terrain, he glimpsed the shadows hunting him. He bent low over his animal's neck urging it on, his eyes filling with tears from the cold blast, the reins welding to his hands, his limbs rigid, body jarring as the hooves pounded on stone ground. His cloak flapped and billowed as he drove his spurs into the cob, forcing it to give more than it was bred for, and as he finally reached the foothills, he reined the animal in, then forced it to scurry up the dusty sliding slope until almost at the top, he heard above the panting and crunching hooves, a high pitched scream; a terrible sound he knew so well from battle. He turned to see a trooper's horse pitch and cartwheel as the animal tripped in one of the potholes pitting the treacherous surface. Francisco urged his animals on to the short distance of the ridge. On reaching it, he swung round, ready to fight if his pursuers continued up after him.

"Here," he panted. "Here is where they make the decisions."

The captain of the troop pulled his horse in and stared up at the wild silhouetted figure far above him.

In the fading light, the billowing cloak and tall dark figure waiting looked ominous. He recalled the words of the priest back at the village of Santa Madre, telling him that he had seen the devil in the form of Francisco del Valle, and the threatening shadow above him gave him no reason to doubt the old man's words.

There is no need to chase Satan, he thought, he is easy enough to find; and one man had already been lost without combat. Who knew what witchcraft could be woven in a fight. Nevertheless, bravado made him curse loudly. Curse his bad luck and the incompetence of his men.

"There will be no chance of tracking him in the darkness of the sierras!" he called to the others. "When the rider Padre Morales sent reaches Don Alonso de Rojas, he will send men!"

Better the Inquisition find you, *el cobarde*, he thought. They have experience in these things; let them send you back to hell. He wheeled his mount round taking a last glance at the Knight high on the ridge, then began his way back.

Don Francisco watched the captain pull his horse round and lead the troop away.

"The officer has spared us the agony of killing," he muttered to the mount, "Let's hope others will follow his example."

He flicked the rein and rode slowly into the night.

General Alonso de Rojas stared through the grilled window overlooking the fertile lands of his *estanza* at Avila. But he did not see the rolling green hills before him, only the face of Francisco del Valle, and it took all his control to separate the emotions of hatred and revenge from those of duty to the Holy Office.

The soldier who had brought the news of Francisco's return to Spain waited uneasily beside the black *morisco* who had shown him into the spartan oak room. Any contact with the Inquisition was unnerving, he thought, but to be this close to de Rojas, the right arm of the Grand Inquisitor, was to smell the burning fascines of the stake.

In the eternity he had waited, after delivering the news, nothing had been said, and he felt thirsty and tired after the hard ride from Santa Madre through the night. But he dared not complain as he stood staring at the broad back of the general, his eye tracing the brocaded patterns of de Rojas' velvet doublet.

"This priest, Padre Morales," de Rojas said turning to him, "Is he sure the man he saw is *el cobarde?*"

"*El cobarde*, my Lord?"

"Francisco del Valle!"

He nodded.

"And would he swear to the man's satanism and heresy?"

"With . . . with respect, my Lord," he stammered, "I did not discuss that with him. Captain Gonzales, who chased the man, told me to follow the Padre's orders and contact you. I am the fastest rider in the company and . . ." he stopped as de Rojas waved his words away.

Now, de Rojas remembered the final assault on the garrison at Tripoli as heathen poured through the breaches, slicing down defenders, then the final humiliation of surrender. But more than that indignity was having to be ransomed by his father who blamed him as much as del Valle for Miguel's death.

He winced as he remembered seeing Miguel hacked down by the infidels and del Valle stand motionless doing nothing. He had been sent back by the Grand Master to check the defences as the wall crumbled and with his own eyes had witnessed del Valle's terror. Hadn't the shock of the scene stunned him, himself; rooting him so he was unable to go to his brother's rescue. But now, in the light of what Morales said about *el cobarde*, how he had stood in the doorway of the church, proclaimed himself eternal, then disappeared as the good Padre prayed, now he realized why he had been rooted that day at Tripoli. It was nothing less than witchcraft! He had seen enough of it in the years he had been on the Supreme Council of the Inquisition. He had witnessed, in trials, the face of such evil as sorcerers, illuminati, blasphemers, and heretics were brought before the Tribunals, all wearing that expression of fear that del Valle had worn that day in Tripoli.

It wasn't the torturers who had created that terror, but fear of meeting judgement before God. And that was what had rooted del Valle that day as he had woven a spell over him to prevent him going to Miguel's aid. What other explanation could there have been? He looked at the nervous soldier who shifted uncomfortably.

The man fleetingly glanced at those beads of eyes in the long narrow face then quickly looked away. It was as though the general were able to penetrate his thoughts, search out his most hidden fears and desires.

"You say your captain followed *el cobarde*?" de Rojas demanded.

"With four others in the troop, my Lord," he answered, his eyes now fixed on the timbered floor.

"Waste of time," de Rojas muttered. "He'll make for the sierras and find a way through them. A pitiless ride offering no sustenance, he knows the country."

The soldier was not certain whether the remarks were addressed to him and decided to remain quiet.

"He will have to feed himself and his horses," de Rojas continued. "In three or four days he'll have to find food and water so that should put him near Trujillo." He considered the ride Francisco would have to take. "That's where he'll rest. Trujillo. But we shall not follow him. We'll wait for him to come to us . . . That's what we'll do. We'll wait!" He glanced to the door and called. "Lieutenant Estrada!"

A young officer immediately appeared.

"Ten men," de Rojas ordered, "equipped for three days' hard ride!" With a quick acknowledgement the officer left, de Rojas slowly following him.

"My Lord," the soldier called, "I have ridden all night . . . can I have a little food, or water . . ."

De Rojas glanced round at the exhausted figure. But in his mind he could see himself handing del Valle the goatskin with the few drops of water, as they sat with Miguel under the rushes just before the attack. "Water," he repeated.

"Just water, my Lord," the soldier pleaded.

Without comment, the tall ominous figure strode out of the room.

CHAPTER FOUR

The Witches

For two days Francisco kept to the high mountain range of the sierra, riding and leading his animals through the forbidding landscape of gaunt rock shoulder, bare granite face and narrow ravines where rain, snow and wind had formed the tortuous plains into an arid moonscape. But as he mastered each crag, crevice and rise, so others appeared, demanding the same draining energies.

On the second afternoon since reaching the sierras, he found himself looking down into a grey wide clay valley below him. Only his horse, slurping the last of his water from his helmet, disturbed the desolate silence, while above them the early spring sun shone without heat as clouds unravelled into long hazy transparent blades stretching high over the relentless terrain.

And as he sat there he remembered how he and his father had ridden up here so often, on their way to cities in the south on business or visits. Landmarks brought back memories of the hard childhood Don Ricardo had put him through. The constant driving to teach him to beat the elements, the terrain, and outwit the small sparse game that scurried in cracks and crevices. He had been sick the first time he had eaten snake, but going without food for two days on one trip had taught him to be grateful for any food. And in one blistering summer, they had waited all afternoon by a dry hole they had dug, and as the cool of night came he had seen it fill miraculously with water. Then he had learnt how the trees and plants sucked up moisture during the day, only to release the earth's moisture at night so a man could drink. How many times he had fallen from his horse as a child, asleep in the saddle, the rocks jarring him awake, his father watching him remount, the derision in his eye telling him that they only slept when Don Ricardo deemed it necessary. The message was always the same. The country was pitiless, a man had to be just as hard.

But he had always had a suspicion that since his mother's early death, Don Ricardo had been determined that his only son would not succumb to Estremadura as his wife had done. It had been a hard education, but one which enabled him to survive later with the Knights, in the Indies, and Europe, when resilience and determination had taken him through cold, hunger and exposure. Thoughts of Mariana intertwined with those of his father. Their courtship in Seville, when her cousin Leonor as kittenish as Mariana herself had played chaperone to them, so amused by her role, so willing to ignore that first tentative touching of hands, willing to take a short stroll to allow the briefest of kisses to arouse but not quench the passions.

Francisco remembered the first night after that grand wedding in the cathedral, as he lay waiting for his bride to get ready, and even now, fifteen years later, his heart still leaped at the vision of the girl in the long white shift with jet tresses flowing like a silken scarf apprehensively making her way to him, a wispy intangible figure in the shadows of the oil lamp.

She had lain beside him, both so still, both so shy. How long they had lain there, until finally her whisper "I love you, Francisco," had given him courage to wrap his arms round her, so carefully, as though his embrace would break the fragile creature he had held. And gradually his hands had fumbled under the shift feeling the smooth texture and cool skin of the body curved and yielding to his touch. And as she enveloped him and the cascade of passions were unleashed, he remembered how surprised he was that a creature so fragile could explode in driving passion, absorbing him, guiding him, taking him along as if lost in the swirling current of a river.

He recalled how the following morning when Mariana's family had assembled to say their goodbye as he was to take his bride up to his estate, how her cousin Leonor's knowing smiles had embarrassed him, yet Mariana retained that controlled exterior that belied those passions unleashed by the night.

But now, as he sat staring at the bleak rocks around him, those thoughts vanished, his concern only for how he would negotiate the rest of the way down to Seville to see her one more time before leaving for Malta. And now it was the soldier, not the lover, who made the decisions.

With a mouthful of liquid a day, hard beeftack, and some oil, he could survive up there for most of the journey, he thought, until the land yielded to the fertile plains of Andalusia. He was convinced only Man could destroy him, not the elements, as he had long formed a resilience that came from the mind as well as the body. But his animals needed to be fed, so he would have to risk the descent into the lowlands.

He got up, took the helmet and wiped the few drops left in it, then mounted his cob.

"Tomorrow you can both drink properly," he said, easing the animals on.

On the afternoon of the following day he saw, far into the distance, the break in the mountain range he had been aiming for. There the rocky walls dropped away to a relief of sparse vegetation. He leaned across the neck of his mount. "Down there," he muttered, "we'll find what we need, down there."

Skirting to the south-west he found signs of an old animal track and followed it down as hard slate and limestone powdered into softer darker dust which allowed the hardy *matorral* bushes, to push through.

He travelled on through broom and scrub until the earth was coated in a thin moss indicating water. As he rode on evening began to close and he followed the thickening grass until eventually it led him to a thin stream bordered by cork trees.

Once he had eaten, he lay down beneath the trees and stared up through the coarse branches at the purple canopy above. He felt a strange weariness, and the chill of the evening had an edge that cut through him. He allowed himself to doze, but the chill began to grip in a way that had become too familiar since he had contracted the fever in the Indies. There was no way it could be fought and the fear that it would one day strike when he was vulnerable to sword or capture returned. He tensed himself to counter the trembling that shuddered through him, but he was helpless as a leaf in the breeze and he began to shiver, slowly becoming embalmed in an icy sweat that drained reality.

Only partly aware of what was happening he struggled to remain conscious, to stave off the evil visions the fever brought with it. He could hear his horses nearby and the grass by his face whisper in the night.

"Mariana," he heard a voice call in the distance, but it was an echo in his mind. He forced his eyes open as his head swam. He concentrated on the branches above him, they appeared to liquify, taking on the forms of live serpents snaking their way down. He tried to raise his arms to fight them as they wound themselves round him. Reality slipped away as the branches became crushing tendrils and his body wracked with fever.

Dreams and hallucinations returned, his ears ringing with the screams of the dead and dying in battle, one distinct cry rising above the others. That of Miguel.

In his confusion he could hear the boy calling for his help as scimitars slashed at him, and though he struggled to reach him, his body was bound. Bound by the serpent branches.

He threshed to free himself, but the broiling sun sapped him, he was soaked in perspiration, trembling from fever. Trembling from fear. No! Not fear! That had been burnt and buried leading charge after charge amidst the smoke-filled confusion of battles, amidst the flames of sacked cities, and the butchery of vanquished armies. There was no fear. *El cobarde* had been re-baptised in the blood of his master's enemies.

Fleeing shadows, black among the flames that leaped to his brain, rushed from burning cities. And all the time, there in the distance was the hazy figure of Mariana. Always there. Always beyond reach.

Hours passed as he was tortured in the flaming hells of feverish nightmares, when his sins, excesses, and savagery snatched this opportunity to return and plague him. But slowly as the hours passed, the fever relaxed its hold and other images formed in the swimming mists of semi-consciousness.

They hovered above him and he struggled to divorce the nightmares from reality. Open-eyed, he could vaguely make out their floating forms. Two people clad in rags. Thieves! Vagabonds! Robbing him! Killing him! Angels of death come to claim him!

He flung out his arms to push them away, groped on the ground to find his sword, but helpless to resist them, he was too weak to lift it and the exertions sapped him to unconsciousness.

It was still twilight when Francisco woke. The fever had run its course, but he felt feeble and dazed. He sensed there was something wrong, but could not grasp it, yet as he lay recovering, he gradually realized. He was no longer on the ground but moving; being dragged on some sort of carrier which bumped and shook as its poles bounced over rock and stone.

He tried to move, but was still bound by the serpentine branches of the trees. No. It was a harness strapping him to a litter. He had been captured! The thought terrified him.

He peered ahead in the dusky light where he could just make out two people following him, and heard others further back. One of those nearest was the hag from the nightmare. He was her prisoner!

The person with her was a boy. This was not the fever, not a dream, but reality.

He called to her. She ignored him, staring blankly ahead as she shuffled along. He could see her hair hanging like pieces of string from her head. Her gaunt face, hooked nose and sunken sockets the incarnation of evil. The youngster beside her was an olive skinned figure with a delicate face and cropped hair. It was a girl, not a boy. A fourteen- or fifteen-year-old girl.

Despite her bedraggled appearance she held herself upright, and the gentle way she held the old woman's hand denied evil, giving him a glimmer of hope.

Now he recognized the sounds that accompanied them. The footsteps were the measured tread of soldiers. He could hear the clanking of their weapons and armour as they marched. He and the other two were captives. He struggled to free himself, but the bonds held firm.

The girl was now looking at him. Her face betrayed nothing

40

of her thoughts, and hinted the resignation of a prisoner. She said something to the old woman in a dialect he could not understand, then stared ahead of her again. Francisco lay still, trying to compose himself. He was still weak and only time would tell him what chances he had of escape.

They travelled along a straight road. Man-made, he thought, and from the regularity of the fields they passed, he gauged that they were in a cultivated region approaching civilization. A city. The terrain confused him.

He had been at least two days' ride from the nearest town when the fever had struck. Therefore, he must have been travelling at least for two days, most of that time unconscious.

The troop suddenly stopped.

He heard a high voice giving orders in Castilian, followed by horses galloping off.

He tried to catch the mutterings of the soldiers, but could not make sense of what they were saying, and before he could concentrate, a clattering of hooves distracted him.

A man appeared on a horse above him.

He wore a decorated breastplate and morion, the uniform of a Spanish army officer, and the open helmet allowed him to just make out the young soft bearded face.

"Have you recovered?" he asked in an aristocratic tone.

Francisco twisted at the harness.

"Don't try to get up," the officer ordered, "We are camping by some trees over there for the night."

Before Francisco could speak, he jerked the reins of his mount and rode off shouting another order, and the litter started to move again.

As soon as they had entered the protective surround of a small wood, a dismounted soldier unharnessed the litter, dropping it to the ground with a bump.

The man then proceeded to untie the thongs holding him. He worked his way from legs to waist, Francisco wondering at the same time whether to drive his fist in his face once he had reached the last hitch. But the officer suddenly reappeared, this time with the morion, his helmet, under his arm, and looking less intimidating than he had done mounted.

41

"Lieutenant Alvaro Ramirez," he announced in the abrupt tone he had used before.

Without answering, Francisco tried to rise, but as he did so, his head swam and he stumbled, the soldier beside, catching him. Both the officer and soldier helped him over to a tree and eased him to the ground.

"You'd better stay there for a while," the lieutenant advised. "Our camp will be made there, only a few paces away if you need us."

Francisco looked up at him, still making no comment.

"You were lucky we found you," Ramirez smiled. "It was two days ago. We were out searching for those two." He indicated the old woman and girl. "We were taking them to Trujillo, but they escaped. When we caught up with them, we found them standing over you. You are a lucky man. They were going to kill you and take your animals."

"Where are my . . .?"

"The pack-horse pulled the litter, the cob is safe," Ramirez said.

"Where are we?" Francisco demanded, more confident since the officer and soldier's support when he stumbled. It wasn't a kindness that would be shown to a prisoner.

"Some leagues from Trujillo," Ramirez answered. "The road is dangerous at night. We'll leave at first light."

He turned before Francisco could ask another question, barking orders to his troopers setting camp.

Francisco relaxed more. The officer's manner was as formal and correct as most he had met. However, he was not hostile which reinforced his belief he was not being held as a prisoner. He would wait till morning when he was stronger, then get back to the high sierras.

While he was eating he studied the old woman and girl who sat against a pine some distance opposite him. Despite the fact that they had already escaped once, the soldiers seemed to prefer to guard them from a distance. Perhaps feeling, if the old one was a witch, her sorcery was less effective the further away she was. The girl chewed the old one's food before carefully placing it in her hands. They hardly spoke, but when

42

they did, it was in whispers and in the strange tongue he had heard them use on the road.

The voice of the men, to his right, drifted over, crackling like the camp fire, the familiarity of the scene reassuring him. Coarse wine, badly cooked stew laced with garlic to kill the taste, the scents of burning wood, leather and horses, tangibilities that gave him confidence.

He was indeed lucky as the officer had said. The women had not done him any harm, he had not been recognized, and news of him had not reached them. He saw Ramirez get up and approach him.

"I'm turning in," he announced. "Is there anything you need?"

Francisco shook his head.

Ramirez studied him for a moment. There were questions that needed to be asked so that he could report the incident to his superiors. but questioning this large awesome man was a task he did not relish. The long greying hair, strong features, and heavy cloak gave him a formidable appearance. His weapons and dress indicated a soldier or mercenary, and the scar that ran down his cheek and disappeared beneath the thick greying beard indicated battle experience that neither he nor his small company had had.

"What is wrong?" Francisco asked.

"I . . . I just wondered where you came from," the lieutenant ventured.

"Estremadura."

Ramirez smiled.

"That's a big place."

"It is."

"What is your destination?"

"South."

The lieutenant wanted to leave, but duty made him stay. "Are you a soldier?" He probed. Francisco shook his head.

"Have you been to the colonies?" The stranger looked apprehensive, but did not reply. "I don't mean to probe . . ." Ramirez added quickly, "but I have seen your fever before. From those who live near the swamps." He was angry with himself for offering an apology and explanation. He was an officer and had saved this man's life from the two women.

43

There was no call for timidity. Yet the more he delved, the more he fancied he would need to explain in the face of that rock-hard gaze fixed on him. It was enough, he decided. Things would be sorted out in Trujillo by those more qualified. He moved to go, but the stranger's gravel voice held him.

"What have they done?" Francisco asked, indicating the girl and old woman.

"The old one is a witch. Her granddaughter, her apprentice."

He had guessed right, Francisco thought. Her appearance was enough to condemn her.

"They were denounced by the *familiares*," Ramirez added. Francisco knew the *familiares* well. Hadn't Pedro the priest warned him that Alonso de Rojas was one of their commanders now? And the thought of them sickened him. Membership was to prove blood purity, that their pedigrees had not been contaminated by Moors or Jews, but it also gave them immunity from justice outside that of the Church. And their denunciations not only earned them praise from the Holy Office, but land or the possessions of their victims in many cases. The old woman's hag-like appearance would make her perfect for such a denunciation. However his expression irritated Ramirez.

"They have admitted their sorcery," he asserted.

"Under torture?"

"To the representatives of the Holy Office."

"The rack loosens tongues as well as bones," Francisco muttered.

"If there is a misjustice, the flames will purge them, and their souls will find eternal life."

"And what of the souls of those who misjudge them?"

The lieutenant's apprehensive expression told Francisco that he was going too far. But the fires revolted him. He had seen the terrifying ceremony of the *auto da fé* where unfortunates were led in religious procession to be judged then garotted or burnt. No human sacrificial rites nor barbarity performed by the *indianos* could match the ritual savagery of so called civilized man in these affairs.

"You speak like a heretic," the lieutenant said suspiciously.

44

"Have you seen an *auto da fé*?" Francisco asked.

Ramirez did not answer. He stared hard at the stranger sitting in the shadows of the night. The flames from the distant fire wove a sombre pattern on him creating an unreal image of movement while he sat perfectly still. A chill ran through him as he remembered that while searching for the witch and her apprentice, they came across them bending over this stranger who had appeared from nowhere. Was it possible that they had conjured him in some demonic rite? The thought frightened him.

"Do you believe in sorcery and witches?" Francisco asked scathingly.

Unconsciously, the officer's hand drifted to the hilt of his sword. Could the stranger have read his mind, he wondered. No, that was not possible. He had to compose himself, the night and his prisoners were unsettling him. At night a man was vulnerable both from the darkness within and without. Yet, where had this man come from? He had just materialized with those docile animals that stood nearby. Why hadn't they run? Because they were trained, he reassured himself. Any good cavalry man could train horses to stand by him, for days if necessary. "I believe that Man was born in sin and only by the grace of God can he achieve salvation," Ramirez said in answer to his question. "And that our Lord Jesus died for the sins of all, and that punishment awaits those who hold opinions heretical, suspect, or blasphemous against Our Lord and the Holy Catholic Faith . . ."

Francisco ignored this peculiar brand of the Creed that was recited and probably learnt to protect Ramirez himself. And as he looked over the wretched ostracized couple, he wondered who or what was responsible for their tragic situation. A vendetta with a neighbour, greed, or just ignorance? The old woman certainly appeared strange, had he not thought she was a witch himself? We are so frail, he thought. Just appearances could lure us back into the primitive. A freak rain storm, the inopportune howl of the wind or a dog could frighten us so that we would torture a woman and child. And yet we have become immune to the real terrors of starvation and death. He glanced at the young officer who had tightened his grip on the hilt of his sword.

"Do you know them?" Ramirez asked warily.

"I know them," Francisco sighed. "I know their fear, loneliness and isolation. To know these curses is to know them." He pushed himself up, "They are cold."

Ramirez stepped back.

"They will warm in the fires soon," he responded caustically.

Francisco ignored the remark and brushed past him.

"What are you doing?" the lieutenant demanded.

"I'm going to show them the Christian compassion Our Lord would have shown."

"You speak for Our Lord?"

"For humanity," Francisco answered, "For humanity, *teniente*!"

As he approached them, the young one stiffened. The old woman gripped a bony hand round the young girl's wrist staring blankly but following his movements as he crouched by their side.

"Do . . . you . . . speak . . . Castilian?" Francisco asked slowly.

The girl nodded, eyeing him warily.

"I will not hurt you," he assured them. "Where are you from?"

The girl's eyes widened as she pressed herself against the old woman protectively.

"We are *gitanos*, gypsies," the woman whispered in a harsh croaking voice. "We settled outside Trujillo a few years past when my man and her parents died of the pestilence." She spoke with her emotionless eyes fixed on him. Francisco moved his hand up to them to see if she was blind. The girl snatched it and bit him savagely. He ripped away from her, the old woman instantly thrusting a thin arm across the girl flinging her back, hissing something in their language.

"I am sorry," she blurted, "I am blind. She thought you would harm me." Again she fiercely castigated the girl in her own language, which to Francisco's surprise made the girl's expression change to one of awe.

"They say she's a sorceress," Francisco said rubbing his hand, "but she bites like a bitch."

"Neither of us are what they say," the old woman rasped.

46

"We have been beaten, starved and threatened with worse. We admitted anything they wanted to hear!"

"Why were you accused?"

"I'm blind, but have visions of the future. When we starved I used it."

"They called us witches!" the girl cried. "Don Carlos d'Arganda employed us. He believed the good yet when she warned them of the death of his son, he denounced us!"

"Enough, Sanita!" the old woman cautioned.

The girl's dark eyes gleamed as she crouched like a cornered cat.

"Did the boy die?" Francisco asked.

"In a riding accident within days of the warning," the old woman admitted.

"You should've remained silent," he said.

"It was a *warning*!" the girl spat, "not a *curse*!"

"If he had heeded it," the old woman added, "he would be alive."

"You must have known such a prophecy could invoke the Holy Office."

"It was better than Sanita offering herself to the soldiers," the blind one said in a tone neither reproachful nor contrite.

"Did she?"

"Have you ever been hungry, señor?"

The girl's expression was one of indifference, yet she was a child.

Francisco nodded sympathetically. Virginal purity was for those who could afford it, and he had seen worse in war. There were times when he wished he could have sold himself for a mouthful of water and bread. He pulled the heavy cloak from his shoulders.

"Take this. It will protect you from the cold. I wish I could do more."

"You will," the blind one asserted, "Sanita tells me you are a man with black-grey hair and a scar. You are *el cobarde*."

Instantly he turned to see if the soldiers had heard her. Five of them were lying by the fire, settled for the night, but the lieutenant sat with another watching him.

"They cannot hear," she assured him. "They do not

suspect. My ears are sensitive. They only talk of us and the bad luck we may bring them. They are frightened."

She reached out, and he felt her cold hard fingers move over his face, then trace the line of the scar.

"You are Don Francisco del Valle," she said with satisfaction.

Francisco glanced back at the officer and soldier. He was sure both had pistols in their hands ready to cut him down at any provocation. He turned as the blind woman pushed his cloak back at him. "Take it, you will need it," she said.

"It's cold . . ."

"You will need it to help us."

Her passionate trust worried him. There was nothing he could, or intended to do for her. He had been fortunate in not being captured, or robbed and murdered as he had feared. To come to their aid could be to court disaster. "I can do nothing," he insisted as he stood up. "I cannot kill sleeping men. Besides they . . ."

"There will be no killing."

He shook his head sadly, turned, and ambled back to the tree, and lay down. He drew the cloak round him and stared up at the black sky.

He wanted to see Mariana desperately before fulfilling the vow he had made when released from the galleys. That overrode all other considerations, and there was no chance of rescuing the tragic women. Besides, these sleeping soldiers had helped him. Saved his life as far as they were concerned. To attack and kill them would be an ugly act of betrayal, one that would be in the nature of a *coward*.

The women had brought the problems on themselves. They were responsible for their own salvation, not he. He had ignored many cries for mercy and pleas for help in the past. This situation was no different.

The hours passed, yet sleep would not come to release him from the dilemma. He was tormented by the fate of the women whose crime was no more than feeding the superstitions of the ignorant. He recalled how Ramirez had looked at him, as though he were in league with them, as though he were a creature they had conjured from another world. It was ignorance. Yet however innocent the blind woman and her granddaughter were, other men could not be expected to die for their superstitions. It was a choice of who should die, and one he had no right to make. Stories of knightly deeds of valour were for children, and of Christian sacrifice for the priests who sat safe in churches far from the dangers of battle. He had only two objectives, Malta and Mariana. The first to fulfil a vow, the second to revive a fleeting moment of happiness that had eluded him for almost a decade and a half. To leave a trail of dead soldiers would be to stamp a trail for de Rojas and give him sympathetic support from his cohorts. The officer that had ridden off a few days ago after chasing him, might have been more inclined to pursue had vengeance of his fellow soldiers been the driving force. Yet his conscience disturbed him, and weary as he was, he could not sleep, his mind plagued with the horrors of the *auto da fé*. Death by strangulation was merciful compared to the flames, and only those the Tribunal deemed a true repentant could hope for the first. And before repentance the most vile of human tortures would be practised until prisoners half-mad from pain were released to death. Many years ago he had seen the ugly spectacle in Madrid, and even though a believer then, the horror of it had never left him. These two were to become such victims regardless of their guilt or innocence.

But as he lay tormented by the dilemma, he heard his horses moving nervously. Looking over to them he saw the animals' heads raised, their ears pricked. He listened hard. The chirping of the insects had raised a pitch, and then, in the far distance, he heard what could be the solution to the problem.

It was possible that the old woman was right. Perhaps they could be saved without killing.

He rubbed his hand into the earth, then smeared the dust round his eyes, making them darker. If Ramirez had thought he was sinister, he would encourage his fear with drama.

Francisco waited for a time, then rose and slowly approached the lieutenant and soldier, still propped against the tree. He stopped some distance from them.

He heard the cock of the Miquelet pistol beneath the officer's cloak.

"Save your souls ..." Francisco urged in a desperate whisper, "Spare yourselves from evil." As he spoke he hoped his years of living with the elements would serve him. His timing had to be perfect.

As he spread his arms to appear larger, more menacing, and a wider target in the cloak, he heard the ratchet of the trooper's pistol click.

"Return to your place," Ramirez ordered nervously.

"Save yourselves!" Francisco hissed. "Let us go. Do not anger forces you cannot understand!"

"I'm warning you ..." Ramirez threatened without conviction.

"Release us ..." Francisco repeated, wondering how long he could keep this going.

"He is a demon, as you said," the frightened soldier stammered.

"He is no demon!" Ramirez snapped.

As he spoke, to Francisco's relief, the first flash of lightning struck, illuminating the countryside in a ghostly pallor. "Release us!" he ordered.

The lieutenant threw back his cloak and fired.

The ball tugged at Francisco's cloak as it passed harmlessly.

The other troopers had woken, but were petrified by the apparition looming in the clearing, eyes black, arms spread, unharmed by the shot.

The soldier fired as another flash crackled in the skies. Again the shot passed through the cloak, only nicking the thick leather jerkin Francisco wore.

"Help us!" Francisco called to the heavens.

The timing was perfect. A roll of thunder roared overhead. Near-by his horses whinnied dragging at their tethers. Lightning seared across the skies bathing the spectre in a ghastly white. The soldiers by the fire were now kneeling, one reciting the paternoster.

With a flourish, Francisco swept round and strode over to the women. "Come!" he roared leading them to his horses. "They will not dare defy my powers!" He might have said more, had it not been for the old woman pressing her hand on his arm as she realized he was getting carried away with his role as demon king.

50

He calmed his horses, helped the women mount, then walked the animals from the camp. Glancing back he saw the lieutenant and the soldier beside him had joined the rest in fervent prayer. And for the first time in many years he smiled.

By first light they had reached the foot of the sierras far to the south of where he had been found.

They settled by some rocks, allowing the old woman to recover from the ride, and ate the last of the food he had with him. Francisco watched the girl, Sanita, chew the food for her grandmother as she had done in the camp. He wondered how they would be able to survive. "I go south," he said "Where will you both go?"

"We have nowhere . . ." Sanita began, but the old woman interrupted her.

"We will find somewhere as before."

Sanita got up and moved over to the horses.

"It's hard for her," her grandmother said. "But she has a life and a future. She will survive. I have seen it."

"Did you see the storm as well?" Francisco smiled.

"Like you, I smelt and sensed it."

"How could you be sure I would use it to frighten the soldiers?"

The toothless grin told him much of what had happened was because of her knowledge of nature and Man rather than anything else.

"You are resourceful," she grinned.

"No magic?" he asked. "Only reason?"

"*Reason*, to the superstitious, is *magic*."

"But you knew I would come. You saw me." She did not answer, and he knew there was no point in delving into whatever powers she possessed. "I will give you silver. I will take you to Marida, get you clothes and a cart to travel in. But from there I . . ."

"I understand. It will be enough."

He watched the girl nuzzling his pack animal as he spoke. He wanted to stop her, the horses were not pets, but work animals. He checked himself. The child had few pleasures in life, to restrict one more would be callous. She called over to him.

"Why are they so docile?"

"They're trained. I depend on them more than anything else in this world."

She stroked the bay's nose.

"What's his name?"

He did not reply.

"Does he have one?"

"Neither has."

"Why?"

Francisco stood up and buckled on his sword.

"Why have they no name?" she insisted.

"You don't name something you might have to eat," he said going over to her and taking the reins.

Lieutenant Alvaro Ramirez felt that the fates had conspired against him as he watched the gaunt severe figure of General Alonso de Rojas pace the stone floor of the gloomy cavernous chamber used for trials by the Holy Office in Trujillo. The place seemed imbued with the terror of those sentenced in it, and he felt as vulnerable and desperate as the wretches who appeared there.

Not only had he let two prisoners escape, then lost them after their recapture, but had held the man the Inquisition regarded as their most dangerous enemy in Spain.

It was only in the frigid rationality of the morning following del Valle's fiasco that he realized he had been literally frightened out of his wits, and to make matters worse, the right arm of the Grand Inquisitor of Madrid had chosen this particular time to visit Trujillo.

Ramirez vowed to himself, that if he were to get through this interview, and not find himself a prisoner standing before the huge bench facing him, he would change his ways, relinquish drink, women, and anything else the true faith demanded.

De Rojas stopped pacing and turned to him.

"You say he conjured a storm from Hades?"

"He did, my Lord," Ramirez eagerly confirmed.

"And you smelt sulphur burning?"

"My troop would swear to it."

"And the shots passed through him?"

"As though he were transparent, my Lord. My troop will swear to it."

The incisive eyes, fixed on him, narrowed. "Your men are your creatures," de Rojas snarled. "You recruit and pay them yourself like every other officer in the army. They will swear to whatever you tell them!"

"Examine them, my Lord!"

"I intend to!"

"They will swear before the high altar of . . ."

"Indeed they will," de Rojas cut in, "Indeed they will."

The lieutenant's palms were sweating. He was trembling as he had done the previous night in the storm.

"*El cobarde* has learnt new tricks from the heretics," de Rojas muttered as he began pacing again. "His cowardice has been supplemented with sorcery. A demonic shield protecting his faint heart. And from the underworld he gains allies . . ."

Ramirez readily agreed. Although hardly able to hear the mutterings, he was prepared to confirm anything the general said. And since he had become a power in the Holy Office he had Felipe's religious fanaticism encouraging the King to scourge the country. What had been going on for the past few years had little to do with Catholicism or its faith. But had much to do with fanatical obsession. To many it had seemed that the Holy Office wanted to do more than just revive the days of Torquemada, the Inquisition's founder, it appeared they wanted to revive or introduce a state of royally approved atavism in the country. And de Rojas was their tool to effect it.

"Where do you think this devil will appear next?" de Rojas suddenly demanded.

"Marida," the startled lieutenant blurted.

"Why?"

"The . . . er . . . the women . . . will slow him down. He must have food for his animals . . . water . . . if he travels to the sierras . . ."

"That's what he believes we will think!" The general snapped. "But I think he will travel to Zafra to elude us!"

"Yes, yes," Ramirez agreed, " I hadn't thought of that."

"So you will take your men to Marida. *I* will go to Zafra."

"Ramirez's heart sank at the order. If fate should decide he would again capture *el cobarde*, and then lose him once more, his life wouldn't be worth a *maravedi*. And if this ominous figure glaring at him should take it into his fevered brain that he were in league with del Valle, he would find himself growing several spans on the rack in the chambers below, where he would admit to anything from complicity to heresy. "He has a day's start on us," Ramirez protested.

"The women will slow him down," de Rojas countered, "You said so yourself."

Ramirez tried to swallow in his dry throat.

"Take your men and go, *teniente!*"

"Now?"

The dark eyes seared into him warning him not be ordered again. Reluctantly he ambled to the door hearing his own footsteps echo off the grim stone walls of the chamber, knowing that even if he had to shoot his horse, he would not attempt to catch del Valle. And when he returned empty-handed, his first action would be to resign his commission and find a safer profession like working among plague victims.

As the large doors closed, de Rojas rested his arm on the high bench wondering what was in the mind of Francisco del Valle. He had told the priest at Santa Madre that he wanted to go to Malta which, as the world now knew, Suleiman would soon attack. The Grand Turk's vast preparations could no longer be kept secret. Yet it was unlikely that a coward such as del Valle would try to return to the Order that had expelled him in disgrace. Especially to fight against such a massive army whose very size indicated the imminent destruction of the island and those on it.

No. There had to be other motives. Perhaps he was an agent for the heretics of the north, trying to undermine the faith. Or even an agent of the devil himself. It did not matter. Whatever his role, he would be destroyed and the blood of Miguel avenged.

In the dank cavernous chamber of the Tribunal, Alonso de Rojas fell to his knees to pray for guidance and help to find the anti-christ who had brought with him the evils of the under-world. But his face buried in his gloved hands only saw the image of the huge Knight standing in mortal fear while his brother succumbed to infidel blades. And the thin lips moved not in prayer, but in a long acerbic curse of the man who had brought on him the anger of his own family, Miguel's death, and gnawing doubts about his own role that day. Yet since del Valle's return a convoluted logic began to work in his brain convincing him that on that day fourteen years ago, when he himself had frozen in the face of the Janissary attack, a spell had been woven by del Valle. And the explosion of the powder barrel had been nothing less than part of the web of sorcery woven by him. It would only be in a trial at an *auto da fé*, an act of faith, that del Valle could be purged and the faithful protected.

CHAPTER FIVE

Marida

Francisco and the women rode through the day, stopping only to let the old one rest in the shade from the climbing sun which burnt away the milky clouds' protection to reveal an unrelenting expanse of blue.

Rock formations and landmarks pricked Francisco's mind as they travelled. Again he recalled places where he and his father had ridden in a life so much apart from him now, that it appeared another had lived it.

It was through this terrain that he had taken his new bride, Mariana. Away from the comforts of her home in Seville to the harsh northern lands of the Estremadura. A formation of trees reminded him of where they had camped beneath the stars on their journey, rejecting the dubious comforts of the *pensiones*, and while their small party slept, they stole away to become lost in the warm embraces of the night. During the day, when the journey had become hard, he comforted her with reassurances of the golden future that lay before them, his words describing pictures of a determined young husband forging the beginnings of a great *estanza* which would flourish despite the conditions. And he would lean closer and whisper promises of a lover who would return weary from his work to the soothings of his young wife's caresses. His suggestive comments bringing feigned shock from her as she would coyly glance round at the others they travelled with and remind him that he was a Knight and gentleman, not the *wolf of the Estremadura* that her cousin Leonor had jokingly called him. But the promises had crumbled like the dust beneath his horse's hooves that Sanita's excited voice hauled him back to the present.

"Look!" she cried.

Francisco glanced over to the west and saw a huge white carpet moving slowly across the land, clouded in dust, shimmering like a mirage.

"Sheep," he said, staring resentfully at the flocks of the *Mesta* leaving their winter pastures of the plains of the Estremadura for the summer pastures of the sierras and plateaux of Castile.

"They're pretty," she exclaimed.

"They devour the land," Francisco growled. "Soon there will be no produce, no men, no grass, just the sheep."

"But to a *child* they're pretty," the old woman sharing his saddle whispered.

"We must be nearing Marida," Francisco said ignoring the remark.

"That's one of their *cañadas*, the routes they follow. We'll make camp here. It won't be safe to go into the town at night and arouse curiosity. In the morning, when people are occupied, they will take less notice of us."

They built a small fire among the rocks and ate the rabbit he had caught. The old woman sat, his cloak wrapped round her, close by the fire, gazing with sightless eyes at the flickering flames. Her frail worn body reminded him of the short dried-up trees of the arid plains, her skin as hard and wrinkled as their barks.

The girl tended her but she responded as if going through the motions of survival without interest in it. He could see she was not with them in mind. Perhaps the warmth of the crackling fire reminded her of youth, when she had sat by another fire, anticipating the excitement to come with a lover. Waiting to sneak away when the flames became embers, as he had done with Mariana. Then passions were kindled by the dark and offered an escape to a world where fear, hunger, and cold succumbed to love. Now she was old, and he had passed the first half of his life, and perhaps they both thought more about another kind of world that they had lived in so many years ago.

He looked at Sanita, her skin glowing, hair shining in the

57

reflection of the flames. Here we sit, he thought, spring, autumn and winter. All that was missing was summer. And yet the old woman and I carry summer within us, in those golden memories of loves and unfulfilled dreams.

The old woman's faint voice interrupted his thoughts.

"You are silent. Does your journey trouble you?"

"No," he said.

"There is a man who follows you. Tall, thin, a black beard . . ."

"Alonso de Rojas."

"The right arm of the Holy Office?"

"That's what they call him now."

"He waits in Zafra."

"We go to Marida."

"As we rode," she continued, "I saw him. Felt his hatred. His obsession. His guilt."

"Guilt?" Francisco mused. "Perhaps. I was supposed to look after his brother Miguel. He might feel it was his duty." He nodded, "Yes, perhaps he feels guilt."

"I have seen more," she whispered staring into the fire. "In my dreams I have seen you astride two islands engulfed in flames. . ." her voice trembled as she recalled the visions. "The place is cursed with death and disease. Invested with an armada such as no one has seen. The noise of battle thundered in my head as the eight-pointed cross clashed with the crescent. It was as though all the wars and misery of the world were centred in that one tiny place."

Sanita took her hand as she shook with the terror of what she had seen.

Yellow tongues of flames reflected in the wrinkled ochre face as they danced in the shrouding darkness.

"Will I die?" Francisco asked quietly.

"She is tired," Sanita protested.

But the blind woman composed herself as the images faded. "You died in Tripoli, more than a decade ago. You know as I do . . . what you want to know, is if you will be reborn. That I do not know. But under a crimson sky, by the dark seas you will find the answer."

"That could be anywhere."

"It is on the cursed island."

"How could you tell the death of Don Carlos' son so clearly?"

"I warned of a doomed ride, but I don't know how the vision came."

"He was riding to meet me," Sanita said.

Francisco looked at her, then nodded. It should have been obvious to him.

"Did you love him?"

"No. But he wanted me. He gave us *reales* for bread," she answered coldly.

"And you cursed him?" Francisco said to the blind one.

"His lust was the curse."

Francisco smiled as he rose. "It affects the young strongly," he grinned. "We are getting older, blind one. Age is a release."

"You are also changing, Don Francisco."

"That is also one of the benefits of age," he smiled.

"No. You are finding a wisdom that will reveal itself by the dark waters, under the crimson skies."

For a moment Francisco wanted to press her for more details. But decided not to. To know the future in too much detail, he thought, could shape you to act it out, and take away free will. It was better not to have too many details.

"I'll sleep over there," he pointed to some rocks. "Rest well, we leave at first light."

He lay between the jagged rocks and stared up at the thousands of sparks above. The old woman's words haunted him. But what she may have seen, he reasoned, was his past where many times he had stood in the furnace of sacked towns. Yet the islands she talked of, could have been Malta and Gozo, to its north. These were the last refuge of the Order.

Thirty years before, the Knights had been driven from their stronghold in Rhodes by Suleiman, the same Sultan who threatened them now. They had raided his ships and attacked his strongholds fulfilling their vows to kill the Muslim enemy. But the hosts that amassed had overwhelmed the Rhodes fortress and dispersed the Order until eventually it had been granted the bleak refuge of Tripoli and the islands of Malta. The North African garrison had fallen fourteen years ago, when

59

his life had been shattered, but even then, the Knights had plagued the Turks from their last stronghold, Malta.

In galleys under the Chevalier Romegas they had harassed Suleiman's vessels, only recently capturing the great merchantman of Kustir-Aga, the chief eunuch of the seraglio of the Sultan, and sailors said they had displayed their prize in the Grand Harbour of Malta to ridicule the Turk and boast their success. Moreover, they had joined with Felipe of Spain in capturing Peñon de la Gomera, the North African port so valuable to Dragut's corsairs – that same Dragut that had besieged them in Tripoli. There was no doubt that the order of St. John had become a canker in the body of the Turkish empire; that was why Suleiman, even at seventy, younger than Dragut himself, had to drive them from Malta in one final swoop to rid himself of them. And from the reports seamen brought in, there was no doubt that he was scouring the seas for supplies to build ships and equip an armada greater than that which had invested Rhodes.

Perhaps, he thought, that was what the old woman had seen in her visions. His final battle. It was a daunting prospect, and he wanted to turn his mind from it to thoughts of Mariana, but was interrupted by a shuffling on the stones near him.

Instinctively, he reached for his sword and waited.

Emerging through the shadows he recognized the slight frame of Sanita, and watched her approach, then stand over him as though waiting for him to say something.

The girl gazed down on the large body that appeared as hard and weathered as the rocks round it. There was a timelessness about him that made her apprehensive. He so blended with the scenery that whether he sat, rode, or walked, he appeared as part of it. As permanent as the earth itself.

"What is it?" Francisco asked.

She did not answer, but folded herself down by his side and leaned forward brushing her lips on his.

He smelt of a coarse mixture of sweat, leather and musk. The hair on his face was rough, his lips wet, his skin pliable, giving him a reality, a personality, that shocked her.

She began to pull away, but suddenly felt his calloused hand pushed under her dress, gripping her between her legs, forcing its way inside her.

There was a frightened crushing urgency about him as she struggled to free herself. But she could not move. His arm wound round her, pressing her body to him, squeezing her breast painfully. She drove her hands against him in the turmoil, then suddenly she was released. The rapacious hand disappeared, the lock round her vanished, and she sprang from the ground ready to run.

"You . . . you . . . are like . . . like the soldiers!" she sobbed.

"I *am* a soldier," he answered. "Did the old one send you?"

She shook her head.

"I came myself!"

"To thank me?" he growled. "Silver would have been better."

"You . . . you treated me like a whore!"

"You behave like one."

He rolled over on his back, no longer looking at her, but staring at the stars. "How did you expect to be treated, like a sweetheart?"

"Not with violence!"

He closed his eyes as he spoke.

"I too hire my body, but for *gold*. I expect no thanks or praise from my masters. I accept their indifference as I accept their pay. If you offer yourself in lieu of gold, expect no different."

She glared at him, but was too confused to express her anger or hatred. She had come to offer gratitude and had been treated with contempt. Even Don Carlos' son had been kind.

But in the moments that passed, as she stared at him, he seemed to transform and blend into the stone figure he appeared at a distance. He lay still, his arms folded across his chest, only his breathing indicating mortality.

She felt an urge to touch him again, smell him, even experience that moment of savagery to reassure herself that he was mortal. But she did not. Instead, she crept back to her grandmother and quietly rested beside her.

"Sanita," the old woman whispered. "He complimented you."

The girl did not reply.

"He did not offer sweetness and gentility in place of love,

but snatched at what you offered as coldly as it was given. Be grateful for the lesson."

The girl remained silent, staring at the millions of stars above them. Then she reached for the old woman's hand, as she shivered in the chill air and closed her eyes.

Francisco found them a room soon after they got into Marida. It was a sparse small place, with just a straw mattress on the floor. But was away from the stench and filth of the one large room which travellers ate and slept in below.

He left them to return later with clothes and a cart to travel in, and he now stood in the doorway of their room to take his leave of them.

He looked over at Sanita, who sat on a stool, her back to him, staring from the small window at the streets bustling with clattering carts, babbling voices and vendors' cries. The experience of the previous night had embarrassed her, the stubborn silence told him that. It was good that she had learnt a lesson that might serve her in the future, but she was still too young and inexperienced to appreciate it.

He looked down at the blind woman, standing clasping her hands. "Stay clear of the *caudrilleros*," he warned. "The police cannot be trusted."

"I have spent a lifetime avoiding them," she replied with a smile. "Now in our finery, they will avoid us."

Looking at her he marvelled how little it took to change their appearance from something as sinister as a witch and her apprentice, to something as innocent as an old lady and her granddaughter . . . Just a wash, sober linens and a comb had made the transformation.

"May Our Lord be with you when you fight in that last battle," she prayed.

The religious sentiment sounded strange coming from her. In the rags it might have appeared blasphemous, yet now it seemed part of her character.

"The Lord will be with me if my sword arm is strong," he said.

"And if you are careful," she cautioned. "Last night, in a dream, I saw you with a soldier who had no army. He is dangerous," she pulled him closer. "Beware of that man, Don Francisco."

"I have always been wary of him," he replied softly.

She looked puzzled.

"*I* am a soldier with no army," he explained.

"Perhaps." She turned to the girl. "Sanita," she called. "Bid Don Francisco farewell."

For a moment the girl stared down at the street, still confused and resentful about the incident the previous night. But slowly, she turned to see only her grandmother standing by the open door.

CHAPTER SIX

Zafra

Lieutenant Ramirez walked slowly beside General de Rojas through the shadowed cloisters of the monastery of The Saviour overlooking the small town of Zafra.

The lieutenant watched a monk swathed in a brown habit awkwardly waddle across the garden, and wondered if by some miracle the two of them could change places, if only for the rest of this interview. A monk's life was not a bad one he thought, and if God allowed him to extricate himself from this situation and the army, he might not only forswear the pleasures of life, but renounce everything and retire to the tranquil cloistered existence.

He turned to speak to the general but he was not beside him. He had stopped a few paces back and was gazing out at the garden.

Ramirez took a deep breath and walked back, wondering if de Rojas not only thought him incompetent but stupid as well.

De Rojas continued looking at the garden as he spoke. "*El cobarde* had already left Marida when you arrived there?"

"He had, my Lord, and the women could not be found."

"And you said it was your horse going lame on you, that delayed your progress."

"I had to destroy the animal myself, my Lord. My troop will witness that." He tried to look suitably apologetic, but suspected his expression only betrayed fear. It took all his resolve not to physically cower as the dark eyes of the Inquisitor General fixed on him.

"I have been billeted here, two days, awaiting your news," de Rojas said. The calm tone more intimidating than an outburst.

"My Lord, I could not get here before . . . I had to purchase a mount in Marida, and then . . ."

"You were right about Marida," de Rojas interrupted.

"A guess, a fortunate guess. But your logic . . ."

"Was confounded by demonic rite," de Rojas continued, "which would also explain the lameness of your animal."

"I was about to say that." Ramirez readily agreed. "This power is beyond human comprehension."

"My own words to my men, general."

"It can turn a Spanish officer into a lying, babbling, sycophant who would say anything to save himself from the rack."

"It can, my Lord, it ca . . ."

Ramirez's knees buckled as he realized the implication. He stood silently under the withering glare of contempt.

"You could have had him," de Rojas muttered. "You could have caught him in Marida, *teniente*, and no animal's lameness, but your own gutless cowardice prevented you!"

Ramirez forced his eyes from the dark brands that held him and stared at the stone chapel in the garden.

"The Holy Office can deal with lying officers, just as it deals with heretics," de Rojas snarled. "You will confess your fear of this man, and regret your deception!"

"I did not fear him," the young officer muttered, now looking up at the dark face. "I feared not capturing him would result in examination by the Inquisition . . . and I was right."

"No Christian need fear the Holy Office!"

"True believers fear it more than the Turk," Ramirez countered, his hopeless situation engendering, if not courage, defiance. "We fear the *familiares*, the denunciations and the torture, not as Christians, but mortal men."

"I will pray for your soul," de Rojas said sweeping round and walking away.

"Pray for your own!" Ramirez called after him. "Pray for your own," he whispered.

De Rojas hurried through the gates of the monastery and mounted the horse his captain held for him.

"We go to Seville," he snapped. "There will be no more waiting in towns on his route, we will wait until he reaches his true objective. His wife in Seville!"

65

"What of Lieutenant Ramirez?" the captain asked.

De Rojas wheeled round his horse.

The captain did not ask again. The silence was enough to tell him that the unfortunate lieutenant would join the thousands of other faceless ones held in the Inquisition's dungeons.

CHAPTER SEVEN

The Deserter

Francisco led his animals along the broad natural path that edged the mountain in the high sierra Morena. Far beyond he could see a green patchwork of *matorral*, broken by a thin sliver of steel. A river.

By nightfall, he thought, he would reach it.

Satisfied with the time he had made since leaving the blind woman and Sanita two days before, he had managed to cover half his journey in just over a week.

He stopped his animals, took his helmet from the pack-horse, filled it from the goatskin, then let the bay drink. To the right of him the mountain climbed precipitously and to his left, fell away in a chasm of sharp ridges. The path would have to be followed all the way down to the foothills.

But as he stood considering his position, the splashing slurping noises of the bay drinking became intermingled with more familiar threatening sounds.

He rested his hand on the muzzle of the animal and listened intently. The metallic clinking of metal was accompanied by shuffling and the clipping of hooves. "A party of men," he muttered, "with an officer on horseback. Moving slowly, wearily. Should be able to outpace them."

He wondered if it were a troop sent to track him, or just a cavalry patrol in an area notorious for bandits. Either way there was no choice but to continue.

He finished the water himself, then gently tugged the reins of the animals and led them on, hoping the men would be lost in the sounds of their own footsteps and not hear him. If he were lucky, he mused, and they were as tired as their shuffling suggested, they might just miss his tracks.

He glanced around for some brushwood to tie to his animal's tail to sweep the tracks clean from the dust. There was none. He would have to try to outpace them and as he reached the lowlands, outride them.

He moved quickly along the shoulder, keeping his horses close to the mountainside to avoid leaving an obvious central track. "Less than two leagues," he said, "then we'll be safe."

Francisco looked dismally at his shadow as he sat on a rock. The position of the sun told him an hour had passed since he first heard the party behind him.

He had easily doubled the distance between them and the twists and turns along the escarpment, shielded from their view, by bulging corners, but rounding a ledge he had been confronted by a massive boulder lodged by a rock fall.

He had tried to move it, but it stuck firm and he estimated it would take three men with leverage to shift. To scramble over it would have meant leaving the animals, and on foot weighed down by equipment he would be as slow as the men following. There was no choice, he had to wait for the troop to catch him up and hope they would believe the story he had concocted.

The sun was reaching its zenith when he heard the trampling boots echoing off the mountainside, getting louder with each tread. Moving at a marching pace, he thought, no longer shuffling, the knowledge they were reaching the lowlands probably putting a spring in their pace.

The first man edged round the jutting ridge, and Francisco stood up to greet him, but the startled soldier stopped, raised his arquebus, and gaped at him, his horses and the boulder.

"I mean no harm," Francisco quickly declared. "I'm stuck here as you see."

The man ignored his comment, training the musket on him and quickly looking up at the side of the mountain obviously worried about an ambush.

"It's no trap," Francisco assured him.

But the soldier called a warning to the others following, and within moments the rest of the troop appeared taking positions strung up the mountainside, their faces wet and flushed from their march, and betraying their apprehensions.

68

Something must have befallen them, Francisco thought, for seven men to be so nervous of one. Either they knew who he was or had been in a skirmish on the trail. And the clipping hooves, of a horse being led, would soon give him the answer.

Their officer appeared, easing his horse round the same precipitous edge as he had done. But to his surprise, he saw tethered by a long rope from the saddle, a bedraggled figure following.

The officer immediately gave charge of the prisoner to his sergeant and demanded to know who Francisco was.

He explained that his name was Ernesto Cortes, a traveller visiting his sister in Cordoba and had chosen the trail through the sierras because he knew it.

"Hands behind your back!" the officer roared.

Francisco glanced at the nervous men on the mountainside. They were wary of an attack, he thought, and it would take little for them to fire at him. Even if he could draw his sword, three or four balls from the arquebuses would hit him at that range. He forced a smile and tried to explain, but the officer's glare convinced him that putting his hands behind his back, as ordered, would be the better policy for the moment.

"We know who you damned well are!" the officer snarled. "You are the one who calls himself el –" he broke off as Francisco's stomach knotted at the imminent revelation. "This is the one we've been looking for," the officer announced to his men. "This is *el chacal*, the jackal!"

The words stunned him into a mixture of relief and disbelief.

"You killed half my troop yesterday trying to rescue this bastard deserter," the captain raged. "But not this time! No traps this time!"

"I am not *el chacal*!" Francisco protested.

"Prove who you are Señor Ernesto Cortes," the officer sneered using the name he had given him.

Francisco knew it was useless suggesting he look at the *ejecutoria* in his saddle pouch, so that the pedigree would prove he was an *hidalgo* with the right to certain privileges; the *ejecutoria* would only confirm he was Francisco del Valle, wanted as much by the Inquisition as *el chacal* was by the military.

"You hesitate *el chacal*," the captain snarled. "Prove who you are!"

Francisco eyed the deserter with the leash noosed round his neck, and the man shook his head sympathetically as though telling him he was dealing with an idiot.

"Make your signs to one another!" the captain yelled drawing his blade, "they're the last you'll make!"

"Wait!" Francisco urged desperately, appalled at the idea of dying at the hands of an incompetent captain who had mistaken him for a bandit. "My sister in Cordoba will prove who I am," he shouted. "She'll offer *gold* for my deliverance!" It was all he could think of to give him time, but he had never met a soldier who could resist the temptation of gold. It was their only release from poor pay and harsh conditions, and the word worked its magic.

"Captain!" the sergeant called, dropping the rope from his prisoner and rushing between them. "Captain! If he is *el chacal*, there is more glory in taking him *alive*!" . . . Think of it, captain," he insisted. "Think of the *advantages* in taking him alive!" He eyed the sheer drop into the ravine below.

Francisco noticed the beard on the captain's face was as sparse as his experience. A youth who had purchased his commission as he purchased men from the villages. His rewards were glory, theirs booty, and he was on the verge of depriving them of it.

"Think, captain," the sergeant urged. "Your whole *future* could be changed by this event!"

The implication of what might happen to him, high on these lonely ridges, if he got in his men's way was obvious. And Francisco saw the pride of inexperience give way to the young man's better judgement as reluctantly he sheathed his sword and cast a venomous glance at both Francisco and the mutinous sergeant. "Tie him up!" he ordered.

The sergeant nodded to a trooper who produced a rope. "Shall the men move the rock with their arquebuses, sir?" he asked.

"Use the stocks," the officer snarled as he strode back to his animal. "Don't damage them!"

Francisco watched him mount his horse outraged by his sergeant's betrayal and his own helplessness. But he would learn, Francisco thought. An officer could get his throat cut for his horse in the right circumstances, or sold to the enemy for a hundred *reales*, such was the price of glory in Felipe's army.

His hands were bound behind him and a noose placed round his neck while three men heaved and shoved at the boulder which only slowly gave ground, crunching loose, then rolling along the path until with a roar it released its hold and plunged into the chasm dragging earth, dust, and debris in its wake.

Francisco was placed beside the other prisoner, and with the officer holding both tethers they began to head for the plains below them.

"I'm Pepe Santano," the prisoner announced as soon as they moved off. "Are you really *el chacal?*" He did not wait for a reply, but shrugged. "That's your business, I suppose. This one," he indicated the captain, "he thinks everyone's *el chacal*. He thinks I am, probably thinks the sergeant is because of the incident back there. This lot would've have had him over the side in a moment. Could've collected his wings on the way down!" he coughed a throaty laugh. "They hate him. Who wouldn't. They laid a trap for us yesterday, the vagabonds, I mean. It was so obvious. No birds sang, no insect moved. Silence. You know how it is, you look like a fighting man to me. Obvious ambush. But this one took as much notice as a eunuch in a *putería*, a brothel, you know . . . we lost eight. Eight! He thought they were after me. Didn't realize it was the weapons and clothes. When you're rich, you don't think of that. But I just wanted to return to my village. He couldn't see it. He thinks everyone's waiting to die for that religious maniac in Madrid. I've fought for an *idiota* like this one many times . . . France, low countries, Barbary . . . twenty-five years of it . . . I'd just had enough!"

The man chattered like a parakeet, Francisco thought, and despite their danger, his eyes were twinkling as though he were part of a festival procession.

He had the short stocky build of a Castilian, with a nose squashed against the face, and coarse thick black hair that crept down his sweating forehead like a tight-fitting cap. What was left of his uniform was tattered, yet he still wore a dusty,

71

dented breastplate which for a reason Francisco could not think of, he had not discarded.

"I fought the Turk," he continued, "with Captain Cordillo. Brave man. Eighteen when they buried him, *requiescat in pacem*. Then there was Captain Osvaldo. Served with him in France . . . or was it the Barbary?" he shrugged. "Cowardly man. Led from behind. I think he's a general now. Jesus!" He yelped as his foot twisted on a stone.

"Shuttup!" the captain shouted back at him.

"Why?" Pepe countered, "You going to hang us, *general?*"

The captain ignored him.

"Us walking behind him like this," he continued, "reminds me of a story of King Felipe . . . you're not fond of Felipe, are you?" he did not wait for a reply. "Well, no matter. Felipe was riding with the Duke of Alba in procession in a carriage behind two white horses . . ." his grin broadened. "In Madrid, of course . . . anyway, one of the horses farted . . ." he guffawed, ". . . and Felipe turned to the Duke waving away the smell and said I am sorry about that . . . That's all right your Majesty, the Duke replied, I thought it was the horse!"

The second guffaw attracted the captain's attention again, but he did not bother with a reprimand, both would be hanged anyway.

"That one," Pepe went on, "that one is completely mad. I joined him as soon as I deserted my last outfit. But it was a continuous round of drill and polish. That's why I've kept my breastplate," he announced proudly. "It's filthy. Look at it. But it aggravates him. So I keep it on. It makes me sweat but it makes him sweat more. Can't abide a dirty breastplate. His wet-nurse probably had polished nipples!" Again he coughed a throaty laugh and spat. "Only been in action with him once. And then he lost half the damned troop. Oh, I told you that." He glanced round at the other soldiers. "This is no life," he complained. "Look what it's got me. I think I'm about forty. I've a bad back, bad feet, bad teeth from rotten food. I swear I've eaten more maggots than meat. The quartermasters and captains keep the victual allowance, don't they. And it affects your sex life. I can't like I used to. Once or twice in the afternoon, a couple of times in the evening, and then it hangs like a nag's tail. Eunuchs could do better . . ."

72

The deserter continued prattling as they moved closer to the lowlands where it got warmer and the land responded to the spring sun, thrusting shoots through the soil. Conifers in the distance indicated the valley was wetter than where they had come from, and Francisco, though a prisoner, sensed the peace of the place.

Thoughts of how he could escape, possibly with the aid of the deserter crossed his mind, while Pepe talked. With the broad sword and Pepe's help, he could probably take the seven troopers. Provided the deserter was willing to risk a fray. But they would have to pick their place. Perhaps when they stopped he reasoned, then he might get his chance.

Yet here, in these grasslands, it seemed almost a paradox to think of killing. It was idyllic with only the sounds of their marching interrupting the silence. But as they moved into the long grasses, he began to realise it was *too* quiet. No bird songs, no insect chirps, nothing but the breeze through the thick *matorral* rustling the bushes.

Pepe continued complaining about the army and had gone on to recounting amorous adventures. But Francisco silenced him. The deserter continued undaunted.

"Quiet!" Francisco hissed.

"Why," he protested. "It helps me to talk. You don't have to answer."

"Listen to the silence!"

He did not need to be told a second time, and bad soldier though he was, experience told him that as before, the inexperienced captain was leading them into another trap.

"Too late to warn him," Francisco said sensing the impending danger. He noticed the other troopers nervously glancing at the thick bushes around them. "If there's an attack," he warned the deserter. "Run!"

"As if the devil held this noose round my neck," he retorted.

Francisco noted the bushes between them and the river. While the others fluttered in the breeze, those remained still. Too still. "I see them." Pepe whispered without being told, and his words were no sooner spoken than the vegetation began to come alive.

Human forms emerged, swathed in rags, partly protected

by scraps of armour, brandishing sabres, pikes and farm implements.

The captain's steed whinnied, rearing as the creatures lashed at the officer, dragging him from the horse, hacking at him as he fell.

They swarmed round the soldiers, now panicking, ignoring their sergeant's orders to stand their ground; wild shots fired from the arquebuses, then the men ran, and offering no resistance they succumbed easily.

Francisco and Pepe had bolted the moment the attack was launched, bursting their way through a shapeless flurry of rags making for them, tugging on their ropes to free themselves. Suddenly, Francisco was beset by two of them. He rushed one butting him in the face, the man screaming as the hammer force of his head split bone and skin. Instantly he swung round on the other, then checked. It was a woman.

But his hesitation lasted an instant as the prongs of her pitchfork thrust like the horns of a bull. He swerved, lashing out with his boot, catching her, doubling her in a contortion of pain.

Beside him, Pepe kicked at another, and in unison they charged, butted, barged, crashing into anything in their path.

If Pepe was the worst soldier in the Spanish army, he was also the meanest brawler, and at that moment, he became a snapping threshing weapon.

Both ran, fought, tripped and stumbled through and from the mêlée forcing themselves on until the sounds of fighting faded in the distance, then they pitched and rolled into the reeds by the river's edge, until their panting heaving bodies could move no more.

They lay gasping for breath, listening to the final cries of men being stripped and murdered, far out of sight, then finally the rippling waters shrouded the sounds of death.

"The last . . . time . . . I was in a brawl . . . like that . . . was in Calzada . . ." Pepe panted.

"My boot," Francisco snapped. "There's a knife in the top . . . get it . . . cut the ropes!"

The deserter twisted round, grinning toothlessly, a red smear gashed across his mouth.

"They didn't search you?" he sneered. "I told you that captain was . . . incompetent!"

"Get the knife!" Francisco ordered.

They remained in the same place for a few hours, their hands freed, but too exhausted to move and wary of any other vagabonds that might still be lurking around.

Pepe noticed the rope burn round Francisco's neck. "You will have to wear a ruff when you dine with King Felipe in future," he grinned, "or our pious king will think you escaped the garotte at an *auto da fé*."

Francisco did not reply, but sat listening, still wary of anyone creeping up on them. The only sounds now, though, were those of peace – the washing of the river, the flutter of birds as they hunted down its banks for the evening insects buzzing along them. Cautiously, he rose and peered through the dusk. It was difficult to make anything out, other than the long dark ridge of the sierra Morena.

"What will we do?" Pepe asked sitting up. "No horses, no weapons or food."

"My horses are trained to run and return to the spot where I left them," Francisco replied. "We should hear them by first light." The deserter's disbelief was apparent.

"No horses can be trained . . ." his voice trailed as he gazed up at the broad dark bearded face above him in the shadows.

In the darkness, the man appeared larger, more menacing than when they had been roped together. He stood as though planted on the spot.

"Why do you stare at me?" Francisco asked.

For once the Castilian had no words. He merely rose and made his way to the river where he splashed himself and drank. When he returned Francisco was lying down, his eyes closed.

"Will those horses really return?" he asked. The huge figure did not reply. "If we wait through the night one of us will need to guard," Pepe suggested. "The water has refreshed me, I can take the watch for a few hours."

"Wake me when it's my turn," Francisco muttered.

He could hear the wind rustling through reed and branch,

and smell the soft wet earth, and it reminded him of his escape from the disaster of Dreux in Normandy, when the Huguenot armies of Coligny and Condé with whom he had fought had been crushed. Shadows of men in hand to hand combat flitted through his mind. He could still smell the stench of powder and burning that intensified, choking him with the ferocity of battle as the Catholic armies rolled on setting the torch to all resistance.

He and others had fled to the river where they hid among the reeds for days, while cavalry patrolled and stabbed with lances to capture those they missed.

The victories had been so ephemeral, he mused, the defeats so crushing, and the solutions so temporary. All in the name of what? Certainly not faith. More Lutherans had fought on the side of the Catholics than on the side of the Huguenots for pay. And had not Gaspard de Coligny changed from Catholic to heretic himself? There was no reason to any of it. But then he had not sought reason. He had long been divorced from the ideals and faiths of those he had fought for and against. Since Tripoli his faith had been placed in his sword, and his objective was to practise his profession. To become a craftsman of death.

Pepe sat up watching the giant man for hours as his breathing relaxed into the heavy regular pattern of sleep. He lay straight, not curled like so many sleeping soldiers he had seen, his eyes covered by his arm.

He had changed much since he had first seen him in Tripoli fourteen years before, his beard streaked grey, the eyes set deeper, the skin leathery and weather-beaten, the years stitching lines in the broad forehead, with the scar Alonso de Rojas had cut still showing above the thick growth of hair on his face. But his back was as straight, and his gait as purposeful as it had been then when he had first noticed the giant on his arrival at the garrison. Tall, slim, and as arrogant as most of the Knights there. There was no longer an arrogance about him now, more a dark formidable presence. The cub had turned into a lion, the dark mane, broad nose, and steady eyes a warning that the beast had learnt skills, his claw having grown from sabre to double-handed broadsword, that now lay beside him.

It was unlikely that Francisco del Valle would recognise him as one of the soldiers who had brought him, stunned, into the chapel for the hasty trial the Grand Master held. The Knights of St. John never noticed the *common* soldiers, they were too busy strutting, parading their aristocracy to notice anything. But he remembered *el cobarde* and his humiliation. He remembered him scurrying away below the ramparts with the blast of men's derision tolling in his ears like a death-knell, neither Turk nor Christian giving him the satisfaction of dying in battle.

Where did being such a grand Knight get you, Don Francisco, he laughed to himself. As a common soldier you can desert, swear allegiance to the enemy, join them, then desert them as you did the Christians. But as a peacock, there is nothing but glory or death. You and your kind can keep those kinds of privileges Don Francisco. And now you ride, hiding your shame from other men, a fugitive in your own country, despised by anyone who hears your name. You know the *comedias*, the players who tour the villages, they have performed a *comedia* about you, *The Shame of Don Francisco of Tripoli* is one title I saw it acted under. You are famous, lying there in deep sleep you don't realize how famous you are. And to Pepe, you're valuable. Alonso de Rojas would pay anything for that huge carcass of yours, there is no doubt his vows still hold good.

The deserter composed himself then called softly.

"Hey, Don Francisco del Valle . . . hey, Don Francisco . . ."

There was no response.

He picked up a pebble and tossed it near him. It clicked along the ground. The man lay still.

Courage, Pepe, he urged himself. The time will never be better than now.

He felt beneath his breastplate for the long thin poniard he had hidden to aid his escape, grasped it, then crept towards the sleeping Knight.

I have to strike for the throat, firmly, swiftly, there will be no second chance.

He stopped close to the Knight, aware of the sounds of his

own heart thumping, straining to hear a sudden change in the man's breathing. It was safe.

He raised the dagger and plunged using his full force.

His ears exploded with his own screams as his wrist caught in the vice snapping it. Simultaneously an arm wound round his, transforming the limb into a blurr of white pain as it twisted and wrenched snapping his shoulder. And through the blurr he saw the Knight rise, a sombre shadow, blotting the sky above him.

"In the name of Jesus!" Pepe screamed clutching the dangling arm. "I have done nothing!" His words severed by the pain searing through him. "I . . . came . . . to wake you," he hissed. "As God is my witness. I came to wake you!"

"With a *knife*?"

"There . . . there was . . . a movement . . . I thought . . . I thought it was a snake."

"It was," Francisco muttered. "How do you know me?"

"I don't, my Lord," Pepe pleaded. "On my mother's grave, I don't know you!"

"You should have been more curious," Francisco growled. "Someone as talkative as you asks questions. Yet you asked nothing!"

Pepe's eyes were wide with terror, feeling that the menace straddling him would crush him like an insect at any moment.

"Please, my Lord," he begged. "Have mercy on a comrade . . ."

"Comrade?"

The game was up, Pepe knew, only an offer could save him now.

"I was in Tripoli . . ." he stammered. "*I*, Pepe Sanchez told them stories of . . . the stories were lies!"

Francisco nodded, the reason for the attack was clear. The deserter had been a soldier at the garrison and wanted his body for de Rojas for the reward. It was only to be expected that something like this might happen. It was amazing that it hadn't happened before.

"I told them all," Pepe blurted. "I told them it was a lie . . . your moment of . . . of hesitation was a ruse . . . to draw fire from Don Miguel de Rojas beside you . . . Even Alonso de Rojas hesitated when he returned to that breach in the wall . . ."

"What do you mean!"

"De Rojas was ordered back when the wall collapsed . . . But the blast, the attack . . . the confusion . . . he froze like others . . . no one knew what was happening . . . even I ran!"

The remark that *even* he ran, as though it were not in his nature, would have been funny, Francisco thought, had it not been for the situation. But the deserter's words made de Rojas' outrage more understandable, made his quick and utter condemnation of him clearer. De Rojas' own doubts, more than hatred haunted him, twisted him. Twice he had capitulated to fear, once on the seas when he had been captured as De Rojas failed to intercept the Turkish galley, and then in Tripoli where he failed to save his own brother.

Francisco gazed down on the squirming man. It would take only a moment to crush him, but in a way he should be grateful. The information, if not vindicating his action in Tripoli, as least told him he was not alone there in his confusion that evil day. Yet the man at his feet had tried to kill him, and there would be others. Would he kill all of them? This time he had a choice, and fate could decide what would happen to Pepe. His right arm was useless, and in this dangerous place where eight had already been killed, he could take his chances.

He bent down to pick up the dagger and Pepe rolled into a hedgehog ball. But Francisco ignored him, took the weapon, and threw it into the river.

As he began to walk away he heard Pepe call his praises for sparing him and laud his courage. At thirty paces he heard the man plead not to be left alone to the vagabonds who attacked them before; and at a hundred paces the wind carried his curses and invective, blowing them with the darkness across the grasses.

". . . despised by Christian and Turk! Soldier of the devil! *El cobarde . . . el cobarde . . . el cobarde!*"

Francisco watched the first threads of light streak through the skies in the greyness of early morning, and as the veil of night

79

lifted, he realized he had been sitting only a short distance from where they had been attacked.

He stood up and looked around. Not thirty paces from him he saw the swollen naked body of the young captain, stripped by the vagabonds. Yet he felt no resentment for them. Bands like them roamed Europe, many from villages that had been razed by men like him. These bandits were no different to him other than they wore no uniform other than the rags of the peasant, and killed for a fraction of what he charged for his services.

"Francisco, Francisco," he muttered. "You are becoming enfeebled by sentiment. First you risk yourself saving two women, then you spare an assassin. Are you becoming weaker, or is it the proximity of Mariana that mellows you?"

His eyes were drawn to another soldier some paces from the captain, and in the same state. Soon all would become prey to predators, and the thought filled him with despair. It was the continuous cycle of Man destroying Man and whether in war or peace there seemed no end to it.

He turned from the corpse and gazed at the low banked cloud stretching back to the sierras, and there, in the far distance he spotted the cob, grazing. He was relieved that he had trained it well, to run from the fray then return to the spot where he had left it. If only Man were as dependable, he thought, as he left the scene of carnage.

On reaching the animal, he saw it had not been harmed, and once mounted he set off to find the pack-horse. It was possible the thieves had caught or injured it, all he could remember was it galloping away with the other when the attack began. Within an hour, he found himself following a trail of blood confirming the animal had been wounded. The spoor soon led him to the injured bay, and on dismounting he saw its back legs had been slashed.

It whinnied as he approached, kicking weakly, and the wine pool it lay in told the story of how it had managed to drag itself to this deserted spot and the pain it must have suffered throughout the night.

He spoke softly to it as he walked towards it, then dropped beside it, stroking its neck as with his other hand he eased the broadsword from the scabbard strapped to the pack.

He rose and stepping back steeled himself.

The bay had become docile, lying on its side, its eyes open, almost aware of what he must do.

In his mind he could see himself as a child with his father on their estate, standing as he did now over an injured horse.

His father pressed a sword in his hand ordering him to put the animal out of its misery. But he had raised it from a foal and could not do it.

Don Ricardo insisted, instructing him where to strike so it could be done cleanly, minimizing its pain. And closing his brimming eyes, he lunged. The animal screamed and threshed, then lay in agony. The sword was snatched from him by his father who finished the job.

For weeks later Don Ricardo refused to speak to him, only to break the silence by castigating him and cursing fate for giving him a son with the disposition of a girl.

The bay, now at his feet, snorted, and he drew back the weapon to a thrusting position.

This time there was no mistake.

"You asked me why I never name my mounts, Sanita," he muttered, remembering how the girl asked the animals' names. "If you were here now, you would understand why they had no names."

CHAPTER EIGHT

The Actors

Francisco sat quietly and inconspicuously by the corner of a
large rough communal table in the noisy *ventorro*, the cheapest
inn he could find.

Though the small town of Constantina offered alternatives,
the *venta* was patronized by the *pícaros*, the colourful characters
of towns and roads. Muleteers, vendors, and servants sat
alongside vagabonds and cut-throats on their way to and from
Seville, less than two days' ride off. If there was gossip, this
was the place to hear it.

He gazed at those cramming round the table shovelling
food into their mouths, drinking, laughing, talking, indifferent
to the filth and smoke that belched from a huge black iron
pipe hanging above the open stone stove.

At the far end of the room lay those who had paid a *real* for
some straw and a place for the night. None slept, but tossed
and scratched at the fleas and bugs attacking them.

He began to think about Mariana and how he would
contact her when he arrived in the city.

If she had remarried, he mused, as the priest said, then his
only hope would be to contact her through her cousin Leonor.
She had been a good friend when he was courting Mariana.

Mariana and Leonor had been more like sisters than
cousins, and it was Leonor who teasingly christened him *Lobo
de Estremadura*, the wolf of the Estremadura, because of what
she called his lack of social graces. But in those innocent days
of courtship when she had acted as chaperone, he had become
close to her, when in the countryside, by a ruined Mosque, she
and Mariana had taught him the superficial behaviour of
urban life. What to say and when, how to dance, bow, and

play the courtly lover. But they had all been so young then, so untouched by the affectations of Sevillian society. Now Leonor might have changed. His disgrace at Tripoli had brought shame on her family's name as well as his own, and contacting her might be prompting disaster, but it had to be risked, there was no other way. He could only hope she had retained some of that girlish sense of fun which led her to neglect her duty as chaperone, and walk away, while he and Mariana made those first tentative moves as young lovers. But if he contacted his wife, then what?

He could speak to her, apologize for having brought shame to her family's name. Ask her forgiveness. See her one last time, and that was all. Yet that was all he really wanted anyway. Just to see her. Be with the only person he had ever loved. Be with the only person who had made him feel part of the world, not alien to it. She understood when he told her that his thinking, his actions, his being, were as though he were not part of what existed around him. Understood when he told her he felt as though he were watching an *auto*, a play, and what happened only concerned him as an observer, not participant. It was exactly like that in Tripoli when Miguel had been killed.

It was a strange sensation. He felt part of the mountains he rode through in the Estremadura, yet not part of the people who lived in them. Part of the grass he lay on, but not of those who walked on it. Part of the water he drank, but not of those who shared it with him.

It was a strange isolation only mitigated by her presence in that golden interlude of their courtship and marriage. And before Malta, he wanted to experience that sense of being and belonging again.

His thoughts were disturbed by the *taberno*, the innkeeper, shoving a plate of hash in front of him. Francisco looked up at the fat greasy man who beckoned a girl in rags. She came over and poured some wine from a pigskin into his wooden cup.

"Three *reales*," the man grunted.

"I'm not staying the night," Francisco replied indicating the price of a bed on the *arancel*, the tariff board, on the wall.

"Three *reales*!" the innkeeper insisted.

He shook his head but handed over the money. It would be stupid to have trouble this close to Seville, he thought.

The inkeeper swearing ambled away.

Francisco was revolted by the solidified hash on his plate. It could have been anything. He pushed it from him and sipped the wine. It tasted of vinegar infused with hide and pitch.

"You must be used to better, soldier," someone said.

He looked up to see a straggly haired man, next to him, sitting with a glazed amused expression on his pale thin face. The maroon velvet doublet he wore was balding with age and covered a frayed woollen shirt.

"Not the victuals for a hero of Felipe's *tercios*, heh?"

There was no malice in his tone, just a teasing playfulness.

"Why do you think I am a soldier?"

"Your military bearing," he grinned. "That dour expression is not one a merchant wears. They present the mask of integrity. And you're not a muleteer," he nodded towards a group of them sitting at the far end of the table. "Their long-nosed simplicity is of their *burros* . . . and you don't bear the hungry mask of an actor. No. Your mask is of the warrior . . . seeking truth . . . not conviction . . . but . . ."

"Diego!" A small man next to him cautioned. "I am sorry about my friend," he apologized. "The wine makes his brain lag behind his mouth. I am Lopez de Rossa," he said introducing himself. "And this drunken wreck is Diego Ferra. He means no offence."

"I mean pleasure," Diego smiled loosely, his lids drooping. "Entertainment . . . for now Lent has passed like a dry hag's embrace, we leave the *pasiones* and welcome the *comedias* like the lover welcomes the soft breast and dew of the virgin's . . ."

"Quiet!" Lopez hissed looking round nervously.

"But I refer to the untouched girl, not the Mother of Chri . . ."

"He is drunk," his companion quickly cut in. "He means no blasphemy."

Francisco shrugged, "I am not a *caudrillero*, a policeman, nor a *familiar* of the Holy Office. You have nothing to fear," he assured the nervous man.

"But there are others," Lopez whispered leaning close enough for Francisco to smell the garlic on his breath. "On the road from Cordoba we heard they have proclaimed the Edict of Faith in Seville and other cities. There will be denouncements to the Holy Office. It is not a time to invoke the interest of the Inquisition."

"Why are you going to Seville?" Francisco asked, hoping to get news of what was happening.

"Holy Week," he answered. "The festival of *Semana Santa* is over and the rejoicing of *feria* begins. There will be an *auto da fé* where heretics will be judged. The city will be crowded with the curious . . ." He took a sip of wine. "As you can see we are a *gangarilla*, a company of actors . . . three of us. Me, Diego, and the boy sleeping on the straw over there."

"We have a repertoire of three *autos* and four *comedias*," Diego mumbled staring at Francisco through dazed eyes. "For the price of five *maravedís* you can see a performance." He shook his head dismissing the thought. "Still let's not talk of work and *auto da fés* but of the ladies of Seville, clad in taffetas, silks and brocades which hide perfumed bodies. Of those who offer kisses as sweet as the Madonna's . . ."

"As I said," Lopez interrupted in a loud voice, "we came from Cordoba where we played the *pasiones* . . ."

"And I played the *Saviour!*" Diego asserted spilling his wine over the table.

"Can you save us from your rotten mouth!" A man sitting the other side of Francisco snapped.

"He means no harm," Lopez apologized again.

"I have just returned from the Indies," Francisco said trying to quieten the situation and divert the conversation. "On my return I heard that the Grand Turk . . ."

"The Grand Turk?" Lopez repeated vaguely.

"I heard he is amassing an army."

Lopez nodded. "A soldier in Cordoba said something about it."

"Did he say help was being sent to Malta?"

"Malta?"

"The Turk will attack Malta. That is what I heard."

Lopez considered for a moment, then shrugged.

"The Grand Master, La Valette, is getting in stores for a long siege," the man who had threatened Diego shrugged.

Francisco turned to him.

He was as tall as Francisco, the same age, but wiry, with the face of a ferret, and a snapping voice.

"I'm a sailor," he said. "They say La Valette has requisitioned all he can get from Sicily and Naples and the Great Carrack, his flagship, is loaded with provisions which will be useless in the face of the Sultan's forces."

"What forces?"

"Everything," the ferret answered, "from Dragut's corsairs to Iayalars from the islands, Spahis, Janissaries ..." he shrugged, "Maybe 30,000 or 40,000 men."

"And the Knights?"

"Only 600 and 10,000 Maltese, if they decide to fight ..."

"They'll fight," Francisco asserted. "They're Christians."

The sailor laughed derisively.

"The Maltese have been treated with contempt by the high and mighty Order. I've been there and seen it. The island's nobility, the Inguanez, Sciberras and the rest have retired to Mdina because they want no part of it."

"You speak like a Turk," Francisco threatened on relfex as his old Order came under attack.

"I speak as a common seaman," the ferret rapped.

"If Malta falls Christianity will be threatened," Francisco said.

"That's what they said about Rhodes, and it fell. That's what they said about Tripoli. It fell. Yet here we are. Still not threatened by the Turk, more by the heretics in the north!"

"Malta is the key to the seas, and the Turk attacks better from the seas than on land," Francisco retorted.

"Don't talk to me of sea warfare," the ferret snarled. "I've fought more Turkish galleys and corsairs than you've had women!"

"What of the women of Malta?" Diego cut in hearing his speciality mentioned. "What of the women there?"

"They'd suck you in like a piece of string and spit you out!" the ferret sneered.

"A sweet death," Diego slurred, sipping his wine, "and better than succumbing to the Moorish pox that scourges all seamen!"

Without warning a knife materialized in the seaman's hand and flashed across the table, only prevented from ripping Diego's throat by Francisco grabbing the ferret's wrist. "He's drunk," Francisco snapped.

The sailor wrenched free then lunged at him.

"In the name of God," Francisco yelled springing from the table. "I don't want to fight!"

The blade flashed again.

"Get your friend and the boy out!" he yelled to Lopez who needed no encouragement and was already heading for the door dragging Diego after him.

In an instant a crowd had formed a human arena.

The seaman now faced Francisco, legs astride, body swaying like a cobra's, the long blade glinting in his hand.

The room blurred, the shrieks and yelps of onlookers urging both to kill, faded in Francisco's ears. All he was conscious of was the blade and his assailant. He turned sideways narrowing the target and raising his arm to deflect a blow. "I don't want to fight over such a trifle, sailor." The blade darted like a serpent's tongue in response. "Please!" Francisco pleaded. "I apologize for what he said."

The plea was greeted with hoots of derision as spectators pressed for blood. From the man's stance and the way he held his weapon describing small circles before each thrust, it was obvious he was a skilled knife fighter, brawling for enjoyment and to enhance his reputation, rather than gain. The worst of all, Francisco thought, the man who took pleasure in killing. And once that steel poniard was drawn only the taste of blood would satisfy it. From the guffaws and sneers of the spectators, he could tell that the seaman had already earned something of a reputation, here, among the mob.

The tiny black eyes facing him blazed like coals, and still the dagger circled, trying to mesmerize him, distract his attention from the steel tongued thrust. The seaman's tactics as obvious as the outcome of the contest would be.

The man lunged, Francisco's cloak deflecting the attack. "Do you want to die!" he roared.

"Try!" The sailor rasped as his long arm whipped out. But this time his wrist was caught, its impetus being carried round in an arc and turned in on himself.

He screamed as the blade tore into him.

Francisco instantly stepped back, watching the half-doubled figure, bony hands outspread still trying to grab him. The sailor gaped in stunned amazement. The hilt of the poniard sticking from the seeping scarlet wound. Now Francisco became conscious of those round him. The room fell silent as the sailor staggered a few paces, then pitched forward.

"Murder!" someone yelled.

"Get him!"

"He's killed him!"

A montage of faces began to close on Francisco who had already drawn his sword and was backing to the door. He felt behind him for the heavy block latch and pulled it. From the darkness he heard Lopez call. "Your horse is here. Take it!" The call was accompanied by the clattering of the actor's cart rapidly moving off.

Francisco swung round, leaped on the mount and spurred it, riding hard through the dark streets until the shouts from the *ventorro* dissolved in the distance.

CHAPTER NINE

Seville

Francisco looked out of the window at the busy street below. He had now been waiting for four days to get a reply to the note he had passed to one of Leonor's servants. As Mariana's cousin and his friend she was the only person he dare trust.

He had spent the first two days in the city watching her house, and had once seen her drive out in a carriage, but could not approach her in case she was being watched, so he had decided to risk writing a note and handing it to one of her *morisco* servants.

In it, he had told her where he was staying and that he wanted to see his wife just once more, before leaving for Malta. He had signed himself *Lobo d'Estremadura*, the wolf of the Estremadura, the nickname she had given him.

He felt safer, in the two days since passing the note, reasoning that if she had decided to call the authorities they would have attempted to arrest him. Therefore, whatever the reason for her not answering it was not betrayal.

However, it was impossible to wait too long and he decided that if he did not receive any reply within the next two days he would go on the streets to ask questions. He dare not go to Mariana's house, where her father or family would certainly have him arrested, if only for the shame he had brought on their name.

Despite the breeze from the window, the room was hot and uncomfortable, reminding him how much he hated cities and their claustrophobic atmosphere.

Below him the street thronged with the commercial activity that had made Seville the hub of the Empire. Importing gold and silver from the colonies and exporting necessities for the colonists' survival.

He remembered how overawed he had been by the Giralda, the golden minaret steepling the cathedral, when as a boy, he and his father had first travelled down to the gleaming white walls of the city. It had shone like a beckoning beacon in the sun. And as they had got closer he marvelled at the Arenal, just outside the walls, where a cornucopia of goods were loaded and unloaded from tall masted ships by their berths on the Guadalquivir, the waterway which brought galleons, galleasses, galleys and caravels up to the city.

Inside those walls he had been impressed by the piety of its citizens who expressed their faith in a plethora of churches, monasteries and convents.

To his child's mind on that first visit, he could see how God materially rewarded those who dedicated themselves to the faith. It was only on subsequent returns, as he got older, that the impression jaded as he began to realize that slavery was rife with Moors making up almost a quarter of the population. That it was the merchants and their shops which predominated, and the procession of buying and selling seemed to continue forever through the narrow tortuous winding streets, beyond the Alcaicería quarter which abounded in silversmiths, jewellers, wood-carvers and traders right up to the steps of the Orangery, flanking the north side of the cathedral, and on into the remains of the ancient mosque where bankers and dealers discussed their business under the bas-relief of Christ throwing the traders from the Temple. Moreover, you did not have to go far to see streets stalked by deprivation and squalor, infested by a man-made darkness which drove the most wretched on to the *corral de los naranjos* by the cathedral, where within ecclesiastical jurisdiction, gamblers, thieves, killers, and prostitutes, the so-called *pícaros*, thrived, beyond the powers of lay justice. And from there it was a short step to Sierpes Street and its notorious prison. Amidst the abundance of a city that boasted ostentatious wealth and piety, life was the cheapest and most expendable commodity. But he had never visited a city whose values had been different.

He looked beyond the street to the small flotilla of tartans, shallops, and feluccas making their way along the murky waters of the Guadalquivir to supply the forests of masts down the river. It would be on one of those that he would have to make his way to Malta. But it would be difficult, if as the sailor back at the *ventorro* had said, Suleiman's galleys were on the seas in force.

He shook his head sadly. The memory of the seaman depressed him. "What a waste," he muttered, "to throw one's life away in a brawl that could so easily have been avoided." Humans were strange as individuals, he thought, and unbearable *en masse*, with no more than a score being able to assemble without friction. Yet they contrived to live in these stifling honeycombs like Seville where proximity created pressure and conflict.

He ambled from the window to the mattress on the floor and lay on it staring at the flies swarming.

"Two more days, Leonor," he muttered. "Then I must go out and search myself."

A soft persistent rapping on the door woke him.

It was dark and he realized he must have fallen asleep in the afternoon. He listened for a moment. The street outside was quiet, the traders having long disappeared.

The rapping continued.

Francisco took the knife from his boot and cautiously approached the door, opening it a fraction. In the shadows he could just make out the dark face of a Moor.

"*Lobo d'Estremadura,*" the man whispered.

Francisco did not reply.

"Doña Leonor de Cortinas sent me." He pressed on the door. "I am Kassim, her servant." Francisco studied the gleaming skin and dark eyes for a moment, then let him in.

The man was tall and powerful with a mahogany flat face. He might have been imposing had it not been for the exaggerated Moorish costume he wore beneath a plain dark hooded cloak. One of the sad fashions that their Spanish masters insisted on as though to stress the servitude of those who had once ruled the land.

"My lady has asked me to take you to her," Kassim said. "We must leave immediately."

He spoke Spanish without the trace of an accent stressing the incongruity of his dress.

91

"Why has she taken so long to contact me?"

"She is married. Her husband, Don Dominico de Cortinas is a member of the twenty-four, a municipal magistrate. It was impossible for her to contact you while he was in Seville. Today he left for Cádiz." As he spoke he focused on the knife in Francisco's hand. "You will not need that," he said. "You can trust me."

Having had little contact with Moors except in battle, he did not like the idea of trusting one, especially in this situation.

"Where is she?" Francisco probed.

"Outside the city walls. I will take you."

Francisco picked up his cloak hesitantly. Though despising the idea of ridiculing Moors by dressing them up, he had no love for them, and had not forgotten the year he had spent in the galleys under their lash.

"I give you my word it's safe," Kassim insisted.

"The word of a Moor," he said in a controlled voice.

"I do it because Doña Leonor urged me, and from your bearing I thought the risk worth taking. You do not do yourself justice."

Francisco had regretted the words as they had been uttered. "I'm sorry. It was stupid."

Kassim ignored the apology, pulled his hood up and disappeared through the doorway into the shadows.

Within an hour, Francisco found himself following the Moor through tall cypresses in surroundings that prompted images from the past.

Soon they approached a clearing where the remains of a ruined mosque immediately brought back memories of the warm evenings he spent with Mariana and Leonor who came with them as chaperone. It was there he expressed endearments and made promises as Leonor turned a blind eye to his caresses and kisses. Here he had teased Mariana's cousin with talks of snakes and scorpions that lurked to frighten her away and leave them alone with one another. Here he had first touched his wife, stroked her face, brushed her lips with his, pressed her to him in the strained passions of youth.

92

The Moor stopped, dismounted, indicating he should follow him. As Francisco trailed through the moonlit shadows,
the scents of the night fed images of the past and he left the
shell of the scarred warrior to become a young man again
infused with the excitement and expectations of love. His
caution was swallowed by the yearnings of so many years, and
though he tried to check himself, memories crowded in until
they formed a vision of a hooded figure standing amidst the
silhouette of the mosque. For a moment he wondered if the
dark and his mind were playing tricks. But no, the image was
real!

"Mariana!" he called.

The shadow turned.

He rushed forward throwing off the restraining arm of
Kassim and the figure threw back the hood.

It was *Leonor*!

He stopped, stunned, and the ghost of youth vanished.
"Leonor," he said quietly, curbing his disappointment with a
smile.

"*Lobo d'Estremadura*," she grinned. "The wolf of the Estremadura."

Apprehension returned and he looked round warily.

"There are no wolf traps," she said taking a few steps closer,
"Did Kassim explain why I could not answer your note?"

"He told me," Francisco answered relaxing. "You are
married now."

"To a magistrate."

"You've done well," he answered, stifling the urge to ask
where Mariana was.

"Better," she smiled, "I've three children."

The superficial comments seemed out of place under the
circumstances of their meeting.

"You should say I haven't changed," Leonor prompted, as
though teaching him courtly graces as she had done so many
years before where amongst the ruins, she had played at
turning a peasant into a gentleman. "You should tell me that I
am still as beautiful as you remember me," she chided.

He studied her. Her face was only slightly fuller than when
he had known her, and the right eyebrow still arched in that
mocking disapproval he remembered. She had Mariana's

93

narrow patrician nose and small mouth, a family characteristic inherited from Mariana's father's side of the family. And despite the touch of colouring on her cheeks, her skin was as pale and smooth as it had been so long ago.

"You haven't changed," he commented thoughtfully.

"You have," she sighed gazing at the grey bearded face once so unlined and tanned. It was a face that reflected the harshness of the years since they had met, the dark eyes no longer mirroring the aspirations of youth and love, but experienced and steady like those of the war-torn warrior.

Her throat tightened as if the figure before her confirmed the death of the young Knight she had so loved when he had courted her cousin.

"The years have been hard," Francisco admitted.

"I've heard," she said. "From my brother, father, and Dominico my husband." She paused, "They said you've become a heretic."

"I've become a survivor."

"Has your soul survived, Francisco?"

The question implied a new found piety which he had never associated with Leonor, and his apprehension returned.

"Have you become religious?" he asked.

"I attend Mass regularly."

"You sound like a matron."

"You still growl like a wolf."

"Perhaps my growling will save you from the snake behind you."

She leaped from the spot into his arms and he hugged her affectionately. But instantly she pushed herself away.

"You even smell like a wolf," she said quickly checking to see if there was a snake. "You would tease me like that when I chaperoned Mariana . . ."

Her voice tailed off as she mentioned the reason for their rendezvous.

"How is she?" Francisco asked.

She did not reply, but carefully straightened her cape. "Why did you come back, Francisco?" she suddenly said.

"To see Mariana, I explained in the note . . ."

"Your note was fourteen years too late. Why didn't you come for her after Tripoli?"

94

"In the name of Christ you must understand that!" he exclaimed.

She shook her head. "No Francisco, I don't understand, nor did Mariana."

He released an exasperated hiss. "Leonor, you call me *Lobo d'Estremadura*, the wolf. Do you know what they called me after Tripoli . . .?"

"*El cobarde*," she answered flatly. "The coward. I did not believe it, nor did Mariana . . ."

"But did your brother believe it?" he demanded passionately. "Did your father, did Mariana's father?"

She shrugged.

"Why must women be sacrificed on the altar of Man's honour?"

"I don't know," he sighed. "But she couldn't have come with me. She'd have died in the Indies, and she couldn't have lived with those who bought my sword."

"And now you go to Malta in penitence."

"To fulfil a vow."

"A vow!" she exclaimed contemptuously. "Such chivalry! You should wear shining armour and ride a white stallion, not a cob!"

"I might do that!" he snapped.

"But be careful you and your stallion aren't burned at the *auto da fé* to placate the vengeance of Alonso de Rojas." She noticed the instant wariness the name provoked. "He is here, Francisco, here in Seville. I told you my husband is a magistrate. A meeting was held in the general's honour, its main topic, you! There isn't a church where your name hasn't been posted as a heretic. Will you ride on your stallion through the streets shouting for de Rojas to meet you in mortal combat!" she cried angrily. "And will Mariana give you her colours to wear!" She bit back the tears. "Oh Francisco, there were no two people in the world I loved more. Now look at yourself. Gnarled from fighting, a decade older than your years . . ."

"Don't torment me Leonor," he snapped. "Will she see me?"

"She was married . . ."

"I know."

"She has two children . . ."

"Can I see her?" he pressed desperately.

"Why? Is it vanity? Do you need to confirm that your long lost love has spent years in yearning only to find true happiness on your return? And then with a farewell you ride to Malta in a blaze of glory!"

Her words stabbed deeply. Vanity was a motive he had never considered. But it may have lain dormant behind the confusion of reasons he had for making the journey. It was a strong enough emotion. And the *honour* she mocked, consisted in a good part of vanity.

"Do you realize what Mariana risks if she meets you?" she continued. "If the Holy Office associates your names!"

"Your families are too well known."

"It has not saved others!"

The outburst stunned him into silence, and for a long time neither spoke as they stood in the moonlit ruins of the mosque.

To Kassim, waiting with the horses, they looked like ghosts risen from the debris of his ancestors' temple. The woman, still, her long satin cape rippling in the breeze, the man motionless, head bowed as though in prayer. There was a desolation about the scene that chilled him. But eventually, the Knight came to life, and approached him.

"It was not from vanity," Francisco called back to Leonor. "And I was too selfish and too stupid to realize the risk she took."

He took the reins from the Moor and hauled himself up into his saddle.

"Francisco!" Leonor called, hurrying over to him. "Wait!"

He held the mount.

"Why do you want to see her?"

Francisco glanced at the earnest face staring up at him, then around at the peaceful landscape that rolled beyond the trees in dark silver waves.

"Perhaps she represents all this to me. Its peace, tranquillity ... I never realized how much until tonight ..." he paused searching for the words. "I was brought up to be as hard and savage as the land I lived in. The Estremadura is not soft like Andalusia. My mother died giving birth to my brother. It was the harshness of the land that took them. My father, Don Ricardo, determined I would be as unyielding as

96

the rocks that bred us. Only Mariana lifted a curtain to show me a glimpse of a sunlight that shone with warmth, that did not destroy what was beneath it, but nurtured it . . . it bore through me, melted a part of me to become human. Perhaps it weakened me, I don't know. Yet for the first time I think I felt what others did. Reacted as others reacted. Feared what others feared . . . returning here might have been selfish . . . but isn't that another human trait? Perhaps I only wanted to recapture moments of respite from what I essentially am. A war machine."

"You damn yourself," she cried.

"It's not what I chose, Leonor. I would have been a farmer, a *cosechero*. It was fate that . . ."

His voice wavered as the emotions boiled in him, and he found himself trembling as the face looking up began to swim. A chill gripped him; perspiration trickled down his face as the fever struck again.

Leonor held on to the bridle.

"I'll take you to her!"

"No . . . the risk . . ."

But his words were incoherent resounding in his head as though spoken by another. He could only vaguely make out Leonor's voice, but there was no reason to what she said. The sentences were confused and distant. He tried to steel himself, but it was useless as the fever wracked him, swaying him in the saddle until the ground rushed up, swallowing him in oblivion.

The first thing he was aware of as he opened his eyes in the dimly lit room, was the scent of rosewater that came from the sheets he lay between.

He tried to rise, but was too weak, and as full consciousness gradually returned and his eyes grew accustomed to the dim light he realized he was in a spacious room with whitewashed walls half covered by esparto matting. Opposite, a crucifix hung above a massive carved oak chest, the simple symbol of a faith he no longer had. A crackling came from a metal brazier burning olive stones, and mounted on a wooden stand in one corner.

The oriental rugs strewn about the polished floor, gave the place a Moorish atmosphere. He was relieved to find that at least he had not been captured while unconscious, but he felt vulnerable in this weakened state, and the grandeur of the room did nothing to ease that sense of helplessness.

Concentrate, Francisco, he urged himself. You were talking to Leonor before you succumbed. You were on the cob, she was looking at you . . .

But before he could completely collect his thoughts, the heavy door at the far end of the room creaked open.

He braced himself. To his amazement a small figure with long fair hair, dressed in a tight satin bodice and ballooning farthingale entered.

More a miniature adult than a child, she took petite steps as she approached him and despite his apprehensions, he grinned. The small face expressed irritation at the smile.

"What amuses you, señor?" she asked pertly, stopping some paces from him.

He looked beyond her at the bright lights outside, but could see nothing.

"Where am I?" he asked.

It was the child's turn to be surprised.

"You smile, yet you do not know where you are. I do not smile, and I know exactly where I am."

He wondered whether the room and child were part of the hallucinations he suffered when the fever struck.

"Am I in a villa?"

"You are not in a field," she replied, each word carefully enunciated.

"Who is my host?"

"It is rudeness not to know your host."

"What is your name?" Francisco asked, wondering if despite the child's serious face, she was playing a game with him.

"I am María Teresa Elena Caterina Ruiz d'Olivera."

"A long name for one so small."

"It has been said before," she said irritably.

"Where do you live, Maria Teresa?"

"In the *solar* de los Rios."

The name meant nothing to him.

"Is that where I am?"

"That is where you are, Francisco." A voice he knew so well said. He stiffened to counter the explosion of his senses as passion, regret, love and resentment coursed through him. For moments he dare not look in case his ears had tricked him into believing that the impossible had happened. Mariana was there. And in those fleeting seconds the anguish and violence of the years disappeared. He was no longer *el cobarde*, no longer a fugitive, but a respected Knight. His body as unscarred as it had been then; his soul was cleansed. He was Don Francisco del Valle husband of Mariana del Valle. Lover, protector, provider. Mariana!

His heart lept as she came over to the child.

"You should be in bed, María Teresa," she said. "Go to your room."

He did not notice the child leave, nor her apology for the girl disturbing him. He was only aware of her presence. The oval face and dark clear eyes that had eluded time. The jet hair, no longer loose, but swept back, still as silken as he remembered it. The satin dress flattered her slim figure, her bearing was not of the flowing movements he recalled, but straight and firm, creating an impression of assurance and control. Yet she melted the years of shame and bitterness, and he released a sigh pent up from the moment he had ridden from her that afternoon in the Estremadura.

Mariana appeared to hover in the shadows of the flickering oil lamps and he wanted to reach out and catch her before she evaporated into the memories of the past. But her voice shattered the illusion as she echoed the same distant formal tones of the child.

"Have you recovered, Francisco?" she asked curtly.

"Mariana," he whispered.

"Leonor and her servant brought you here," she announced. "They told me you were afflicted by a fever. It seems to have passed. Your horse has been stabled, and I will arrange for some food."

He gazed at her, shocked at the matter-of-fact tone. He had spent years with a dream of a warm tender girl who had infused him with her own compassion. He had ridden across countries, risked himself just for this one meeting, and yet was confronted with someone wearing Mariana's mask, yet acting the stranger.

"Do you know me?" he said.

"Of course I know you, Francisco," she answered in the same icy tone. "You have changed much, of course, as I have. But we recognize each other."

He tried desperately to curb his resentment.

"You married well," he commented, the emotions rapidly fading.

"I had no choice, Francisco."

He eased back into the pillows suppressing the bitter feelings that it had all been for nothing. The journey, the hopes, all for nothing. He cursed himself for having put both of them at risk. For having been so stupid as to have imagined she would fly into his arms and they would recreate the magic of that summer together. God, had he really expected her to lock her love in a gilded cask only to open it on his arrival and bathe him in its glow. He had been her lover for half a year, her husband for less. It was a fraction of his fourteen years' absence, and yet in his ... what had Leonor called it ... *vanity*, yes, in his *vanity* he had expected more than he had a right to. How could you have been so stupid, Francisco, he castigated himself.

"I must leave," he said without thinking. "I put you and your husband in danger."

"The Marqués has been dead four years, so you do not endanger him. As for myself and the children, we are safe so long as no one knows you are here. You were not followed. We can see far across the valleys from this *solar*." She turned to leave, but he called her. She stopped, her back to him.

"I was wrong to come here," he said. "I shouldn't have tried to see you. I wanted to take you with me after Tripoli. It was impossible." The words poured from him faster than he was able to think. "I wanted to send word to tell you where I was, but the battles were fluid, there was no one I could trust. I didn't want you associated with my shame ..." His voice trailed. The excuses sounded empty. Sentiments he could never express. In minutes he was trying to explain the emotions of years. It was impossible.

For a moment she was silent, then spoke.

"They say you turned heretic," she still did not look at him. "Is that true?"

"I lived by selling my sword, not my beliefs. There was no alternative."

"You could have changed your name . . ."

"I did and fought until discovered. Felipe's *tercios* are spread throughout the globe. Few had not heard of *el cobarde*. I covered the stigma of the scar with a beard, but it only half concealed my identity. I went to the Indies and was denounced. I returned and joined those who cared as little for my past as I did for my beliefs."

"I would have come with you if you . . ."

"Come with me!" he exclaimed. "Where? To the Indies where you would have been wasted by disease. To another city in Spain, where you would have been reviled as the wife of *el cobarde*, the coward. Or to the wars, razing towns and villages. Have you seen what we do in God's name? Rape, murder, offer human sacrifices on the pyres of faith. By the tenth or twentieth battle I cared little for the nature of the war or its reasons, and even less for myself. I would have gone on to join Egmont in the low countries had it not been for the news that Malta was going to be attacked!" He no longer looked at her as he spoke, but stared at the flickering flames of the oil lamp. "And when I heard I felt relief. Euphoria. Because deep within me I knew this would be the final onslaught I would have to drag myself through. But as I wept with relief I knew I wanted to see you. To see the only person who had ever meant anything to me on this planet. Perhaps just to relive the tranquillity of those days before it all putrefied . . ."

He turned from the flame to see her now standing over him. She looked down on the hardened scar tissue on his body, and the eyes once so alive now dulled. His face was worn without a trace of the hope it had once reflected. She sat on the bed and gazed at his calloused hands.

She had been so sure that she could resist this moment if it ever came. That she would be able to look into the self-assured eyes of the man who had left her in the Estremadura on his saintly quest, then silently turn and without explanation turn away. But whatever anger she had felt could not translate itself into icy silence or frigid comments to the war-weary man who lay in Francisco's shadow. And she heard herself tell him

101

how she would have followed him anywhere, but had returned to Seville after he had not come back. And in the years had a marriage arranged to the Marqués, a kind man who gave her the tranquillity she needed so desperately. As she spoke her fingers wrapped round his, as they had done when they talked in that summer so long ago.

"I needed that warmth and security so badly, Francisco," she finally said.

"I understand," he began.

"You don't!" she snapped releasing his hand. "I am not asking for forgiveness. You should be asking *me*! You left me in a wilderness to fight a battle that you could have avoided . . ."

"I had made a vow!"

"You made a *vow* to *me*!" She pushed away his hand as he tried to comfort her. "I was an unworldly girl, taken to a desert and left alone with your father. You spoke of the glory of defending the faith, obligations to the Order of St. John, and I was a gullible, gullible child! Her eyes brimmed. "Tripoli is over, yet the fighting continues. No one has won. *We* have lost. And in the years you wandered, your beliefs waned. But to sustain you, you kept an image of an innocent girl. Passive and pliant!" Tears now rolled down her cheeks. "That girl is dead, Francisco. She died alongside the man she loved in Tripoli . . . and the two people in this room no longer resemble them or their dreams . . . one is a mother and widow, the other a scarred fugitive seeking a lair in which to die." She moved from the bed, wiping her cheek. "Stay as long as it is safe. But don't try to recapture . . ."

The door suddenly opened.

In the light Francisco saw a tall slim boy in a dark doublet, his hand resting on a short dagger hanging from his belt.

Mariana tried to compose herself.

"I'm coming, Ruiz," she said.

He shot a hostile look at Francisco.

"Are you all right?" he asked Mariana still watching the stranger.

"Yes," she replied taking a deep breath. "Your cousin Fernando has recovered from his fever. You feel better, don't you *Fernando*," she said.

Francisco nodded.

"This is my son, Ruiz," Mariana said trying to smile, "Leonor and I have mentioned him to you in our letters to the Indies.'

Francisco acknowledged the boy whose hostility was still evident.

"How is it in the Indies?" the boy asked.

There was an arrogance about him which irritated, Francisco felt. And whereas the stiff formality of María Teresa was amusing, it was pompous in her brother.

"You help spread the glory of the Empire and God," the boy stated as though patting a soldier on the back for doing a good job.

"I did," Francisco agreed. "You should have been there when we garotted *indianos* after they converted to the faith, you would have been proud, master Ruiz."

"Marqués," the youth corrected.

"I beg your pardon, my Lord," Francisco apologized, the mocking tone not lost on the boy.

"You look weary, mother," he said coldly, "you should retire."

"I will, soon."

Without another word he spun round and left.

"He was young when his father died," Mariana explained as soon as he had gone. "His formality compensated for uncertainty."

Francisco did not answer, but stared at the crucifix opposite him. He heard her dress brush the floor as she went over to the door. Then closed his eyes as the door closed on the only dream he had ever valued.

Although early morning, the air was warm and moist. Francisco sat on a stone wall some way from the *solar* looking out across the groves of the estate, the Andalusian sun shining on the rich textures of the gentle countryside.

Mariana's words had haunted him through the night. He had expected too much when he could offer her nothing. Had he really believed she would sit in a tower, chaste, waiting with her tapestries for him to return on a white stallion as Leonor had said? It was the arrogance of an impoverished *hidalgo*, so satirized in the *comedías*. If he ever met Lopez and Diego, the actors, again, he could tell them his story and they could write a tragi-comedy about it.

He had considered himself a realist and yet had engineered nothing more than a romantic *auto* casting himself in the main role, not the lover, but the fool.

What right had he to take a bride to the *baldíos*, the wastelands, then ride off to fight the Turk. The enemy he should have fought was the elements and the land. They, not the Muslims, had taken his mother. But perhaps that battle was too arduous, and he had thought it easier to meet a more tangible enemy and die in the glory of fire rather than wilt in the endless battle against an arid plain.

"Stupid, Francisco," he muttered, "So stupid."

"It's not good to talk to yourself," a voice said behind him.

He turned to see the child, María Teresa.

She was in a long smock more suited to her age than the adult attire of the previous night.

"My father always said that talking to oneself was a sign of madness, do you agree?"

Despite her dress, the tone retained the practised formality.

"He was right." Francisco agreed.

She stood beside him and looked out across the valley.

"It is beautiful at this hour," she said.

He agreed.

"My father said the orange of the sun transfers to the fruit of the groves and that is how they get their colour. Do you think so?"

"But what of the olives?"

"Their colour is from the grass," she asserted.

"And the different flowers?"

"From the rainbows."

"Your father was wise."

She was thoughtfully silent for a moment, then spoke.

"My father said none of these things to me, of course. My mother told me that these were the things he said to her."

"Then she is wise too."

"My mother told me much of what my father had said after he died. Perhaps I was too young to understand his words when I was small."

"And now you understand."

"My brother Ruiz," she said climbing the wall to sit next to him. "He understood all my father's words."

Francisco did not reply, his mind wandering to the journey he would take back to Seville to get a vessel to Malta.

"When we visited Seville," the child continued, "my mother told me how my father hated cities. How they closed people in."

The words penetrated his thoughts, and he looked at the small round, earnest face gazing out at the valley.

"What else did your father say, María Teresa?" he prompted tentatively.

The child picked up a stone from the wall and lobbed it down the hill in front of them. "My mother told me what father said. I was too small to understand."

"You told me that."

"My brother Ruiz, he understood all that our father taught him."

"Yes," Francisco sighed.

"My father believed that the deserts and wastelands could become gardens. Do you believe that?"

Francisco's throat tightened. "I once did," he muttered.

"María Teresa!"

They turned. It was Leonor.

"Go into the house," she ordered the girl. Without hesitating she pushed herself from the wall, but waited a moment, pensive. "Will you take me riding?" she suddenly asked, looking at Francisco intently.

"Perhaps."

She ambled off picking flowers as she made for the house.

"How long have you been standing there?" Francisco asked when the child had left.

"I heard her," Leonor replied joining him. "When the Marqués died, the emotions of the years flooded from Mariana."

"When we were young, I used to tell Mariana where the colours came from and that deserts would one day bloom . . ."

"She said many of the things you told her, after the Marqués died. Ruiz was too old to listen, and had been drilled by his father, so she used María Teresa to tell her all those

105

things that had remained with her." She put her hand on his shoulder. "She cared, Francisco. But you told me that one had to survive. She had to as well, and couldn't survive on yearning. But there is no point in you mentioning what the child has said. Neither of you can gain from it. You are wanted for heresy, and you intend to go to Malta. Finish what you set out to do. Let the ghosts rest."

"I will leave today."

"No. You will leave in a few days. You are our cousin, Fernando, visiting from the Indies, not a sick animal we have stabled to nurse. A few days will not interfere with your plans, nor arouse suspicion. I will stay here . . ."

"As chaperone, as you did in the past."

"As your cousin!"

"And the boy?"

"Take no notice of Ruiz. He is young, the son of a Marqués. His father taught him the stiff formality of the aristocrat, you must have noticed traces in María Teresa . . ."

"She is more flexible, like my own . . ."

"She is *not* of your blood, Francisco. She is seven. You have been away fourteen years. Her flexibility is because of her age. Ruiz is older, possessive over Mariana, and suspicious of strangers." Francisco thought for a moment, wondering whether staying might create more problems than it solved. But there was no escaping the fact that he desperately wanted more time with Mariana. If his life were to end in Malta, there were few things in the past he could cherish. The peace of his surroundings with Mariana was something he wanted to carry with him.

"I will stay two days . . ."

"Three or four," Leonor insisted. "Today I will show you over the estate. When we return you will comment on how well it is run, how it contrasts with the plantations of the Indies where you intend to return after your business in Seville." She gazed at him making sure he understood the instructions. "The conversation will be *cordial*," she warned. "Not of love, poetry or the past, but the trivia of everyday life."

The instructions were reminiscent of her role so long ago when she tried to transform his crude country ways. But this

106

time, he felt, there was no amusement, or playful chiding in the tone. It was firm and assertive, and he could not resist commenting that she had become harder.

"Practical," she answered. "Men can dream, women have to be practical." She eyed his clothes. "You will also change from these clothes into more suitable dress. I can have something brought from Seville. This is not a battlefield, but a *huerta*, with groves and woods."

"Shall I shave for you, as well?"

"If not for that scar, I would insist on it," she replied turning and starting back for the house.

CHAPTER TEN

Sierpes Prison

Alonso de Rojas sifted through the reports submitted by soldiers and *familiares*, the Inquisition's spies, that had come in over the past few days. But none was clear enough to allow him to follow a course of action.

There had been numerous stories of men fitting del Valle's description, and it appeared as though every *matón*, killer, had been presented as del Valle, each having long, dark hair, a beard, and scar.

With the *feria*, the festival, in the city, the place abounded with *valentonas*, criminals, each clad in leather doublet with sword. It was as if the devil himself had conjured an army of suspects to protect the Antichrist, del Valle, he thought bitterly.

He rose from the table and went over to the window. Through the bars he watched the procession of ragged wretches flowing through the large gates of the prison from Sierpes Street; a shuffling army of degenerates picked up by the *caudrilleros* for committing every conceivable crime in the crowded narrow cesspools of Seville. And though watching the bedraggled men and women herded to the cells below, his mind was on the measures he had so far taken.

He had the city house of del Valle's wife under observation, but no one of his description had been seen there. Men had also been sent to scout the *huerta* of her dead husband, the Marqués, but again there were no reports of interest. The place was too large to cover thoroughly with a few men, and he dare not send a troop to the lands of a Marquesa, at least not without evidence to support him. Her family and dead husband were benefactors of the Church, and he would risk his own position if he began to accuse them through the Holy Office.

The feud between him and *el cobarde* was well known. If his suspicions of the Marquesa proved false, he himself could be indicted for misusing the powers of the Inquisition to satisfy personal revenge, and that would find him joining the procession in the courtyard below.

He would have to be patient, he decided. His *familiares* could remain on the estate inconspicuously. Something would develop. It had to. The forces of evil had always succumbed to those of good in the end. Didn't the *auto da fé* demonstrate just that fact? Hadn't all heretics recanted before being garotted? Hadn't what happened in the past fourteen years to *el cobarde* been proof that punishment existed even here on earth for those who sinned?

Once caught, *el cobarde*'s confession would be made along with other heretics before he faced the flames. It would be rent from him on the rack or *estrapada* while he hung by the wrists. Burned from him with coals, or choked out with the *bosteza* clamped in his mouth while the *toca*, the wet rag, was forced down his throat, expanding as water dripped on it.

He looked down at his hands, they were shaking. The man's evil had invested his own spirit by just thinking about him. "He will be caught Miguel," he muttered to his dead brother. "You will be avenged. His confession will vindicate my action in Tripoli and you will hear it, Miguel. You will see, it was his satanism that checked me from coming to your aid." He gripped the bars of the window, pressing his head hard against them, tightening his hold to stop the trembling. "You will see, Miguel," he rasped hoarsely. "I will prove his cowardice and heresy to you. I'll prove it, Miguel!"

CHAPTER ELEVEN

Betrayal

As Francisco walked with Mariana in the cool evening by the river that wound through the estate, he had the strange sensation of *déjà vu*. It was as if all this had happened before in a dream. And though he reasoned that in the days before they married, they might have taken similar walks in the Andalusian countryside, he could not rid himself of the feeling that this walk had once preceded an awful event. Only Mariana's voice turned him from his preoccupation.

"You have looked better, these last two days," she commented stopping by a tall cypress by the bank. "You no longer have the hunted look of the wolf Leonor used to tease you about."

He did not reply, but stared at the elliptical reflections in the water. "Do you remember how she used to call you *Lobo de Estremadura*?" she smiled. "The wolf of the Estremadura."

"I carry another name now," Francisco murmured.

"The doublet Leonor got suits you," she said raising her voice, not wanting to dwell on the subject. "I prefer you like this, with shorter hair and trimmed beard."

"And the scar?"

"I also prefer you with a collar rather than a ruff," she answered ignoring his comment. "The ruff is courtly, like the *caballeros* who parade in the Alcazar in Seville. Most of them are *buhoneros*, pedlars or *valentonas*, common criminals who have stolen a few ducats and parade as courtiers."

"Mariana," he sighed, catching her arm. "There is no need for trivialities now. We are alone."

She pulled away, checking the passion his touch aroused. The sight of him the past few days, shorn of the look of a fugitive, the weariness bathed and rested from him, had rekindled memories of the love they had shared before. And as

110

he had dined with them, played with her children, talked to her of those superficial things Leonor had instructed him to speak about in company, she began to yearn for the life that might have been. And at night, as she had lain awake, roused by the passion she no longer thought capable of, it had taken her all her control not to slip from her bed and hurry those few paces across the hallway to him. And now as they stood in the warmth of the evening, for the first time alone, she determined she would keep that control.

"There is more need to speak of trivialities when we are alone, Francisco, than when in company," she replied tartly.

"Perhaps you are right," he agreed, gazing at her in the shadows. In the tight brocaded bodice, ballooned sleeves and high collar, she was almost the image of María Teresa when the girl had entered his room on that first night. But Mariana wore a pink cerise hue painted on her cheeks and a thin layer of wax to moisten her mouth, making her doll-like and somehow unreal in the light. "You never used to paint your face," he said reflectively. "I remember when you were happier in billowing skirts and blouses than in satins." Only a flicker betrayed her anger, and he himself became irritated by the strain of being with her, yet not being able to touch her. "You wanted to talk of trivia," he challenged. "We have talked of men's fashions, now we speak of women's."

"I remember when you wanted to push a plough, not wield a sword," she countered. "I remember when you spoke of planting and not reaping, and of the future, not the past!" She pulled at a small twig angrily and crushed the leaves in her hand, then dropped them. The shoots left a stain on her fingers. "My lips are red, my cheeks pink, and my hands green," she murmured.

Francisco gazed at the soft face that so earnestly uttered the words then roared a bellowing laugh that echoed through the velvet night sweeping back on a wave that carried Mariana's rippling laughter with it until the sound intermingled in the evening and their arms folded round one another, and lips pressed the salt taste of tears which melted the scar tissue of separation. Sinew enveloped satin skin as they fell to the grass, the dew bathing them, the scents of the earth swallowing them in an embrace as old as time itself.

* * *

111

Francisco woke to her caress as her finger traced the line of the scar that ran down his face.

Around them, the night pulsated with the chirping of insects and gurgling of the waters. Now he had found the tranquillity he had sought wrapped in her arms, lost in her aroma. "Are we young again?" he murmered.

"As only passion can make us," she whispered.

"And the past?"

"There wasn't one," she said running her finger across the crease in his neck. "You have slept and dreamt . . . we are to ride to your father soon, up to the Estremadura . . . there we will make the earth green."

"Like your hands," he smiled catching her wrist and pressing it to his face, drinking the ambrosia scent on her. "Which is the dream, Mariana?" he asked. "Which is the reality?"

"Now is the dream," she sighed. "Your leaving, the reality."

Both lay silent for a moment, her words drawing them back to the present.

"When are you going?" she asked, bracing herself.

"It's not honour, nor glory, this time," he said thickly. "It's safety. I have stayed long enough and the risk for you and the children grows each day."

"That was not my question," she said.

He released her hand and pushed himself from the ground, offering to help her up.

"When are you going, Francisco?" she insisted.

"First light tomorrow. The Holy Office will be hunting me, if you come, they will hunt you and the children as well."

"Spain is not the only country," she said, not moving from the ground.

"The world is ablaze with religious wars and the Inquisition's arm reaches beyond here." He closed his eyes as emotion swept through him. "If there were just two of us . . ." the rest of the sentence stuck in his throat as she took his hand and he pulled her to him. "If I acquit myself in Malta, maybe I can return."

She knew he was lying and that de Rojas would never give him peace. But it was on such lies that the threads of hope hung and it was better to believe the lie than suffer the truth.

His arms wound round her, pressing her to him and he buried his head in her neck in a desperate embrace of love and need and she caressed him, no longer a lover, but a mother.

"If it were different," he began.

"The dream cannot be changed, Francisco," she whispered. "We sleep while it happens and it runs its course through our minds, feeding our emotions, making them bloom, sometimes inundating them."

He pulled back from her. "Yes," she said, "your words, Francisco, the words you used when you left to go to Tripoli."

"The hollow words of a young man."

"But they comforted his young wife."

"If only I had not left."

"Then you would not have been Francisco del Valle," she replied, choking back the emotion. "And I would not have been your wife, and we would not be standing here."

"In grief."

"In anticipation of where the dream will take us."

She took his hand and began to walk to the horses, desperately trying to check her emotions so that she could return to the *solar* and her children composed. She was no longer a young girl, she told herself, she was a mother and could not afford the luxury of being overwhelmed by sentiment, but as they reached the animals, he turned her to him.

"I love you, Mariana," he said softly.

"And I love you, Francisco," she answered now more controlled. "Our love has never been in doubt, just as it never solved our problems, but created them." She understood the disappointment he felt, although as if she spoke the passions by the river had not happened. "Oh, Francisco," she sighed. "You still want to carry the image of that girl into your battles. I don't want you to hold that image any more. Francisco, men can lose themselves in the glory of wars, but we have to bind their wounds, mourn them, feed their orphans. I love you," she protested, "but as a woman, not as that girl you knew." She shook her head sadly, then put her foot into the stirrup and mounted as he helped her. "María Teresa likes you," she said looking down at him. "In time she would love you because she sees in you the romance I did when I was a girl. Ruiz resents you, because the scar you carry threatens his manhood and represents valour. Yet he does not

113

see the pain that scar caused, or the web of codes created, which you broke, and which became a tragedy for both of us." She sighed, "Would you prefer me to pine for you as a love-sick girl?" She anticipated the shake of his head.

"You would, Francisco," she asserted. "But your own peculiar code even prevents you from admitting it." She tugged the rein of the mount, the conversation becoming too painful. "Let us go back," she cried. "The words cannot replace life as we are living it!"

As they rode back through the undulating silhouettes of the night, the sensation of remoteness filled him again. It was as though he were not merely riding through strange country-side, but in a world he was not part of. Except that now Mariana was beside him, yet the feeling lingered. Time appeared to have escaped him. His fourteen-year absence had matured Mariana, yet somehow missed him. Perhaps as time passed and they stayed together he could revive that sensation of being she gave him. But time was something he had little of.

A light burning in the main reception room greeted them as they walked through the garden to the house. Neither spoke, but both sensed danger and they hurried through the dark-ened hallway up the stairs.

Francisco opened the door to see Leonor with María Teresa on her lap and Ruiz relaxing in a high backed chair.

"The soldiers have been," Leonor said as he entered.

Instinctively he put his arm round Mariana and saw the flicker of jealousy in Ruiz's eyes. "How many?" he asked ignoring the boy.

"Two," replied Ruiz coldly. "A sergeant and captain. I spoke to them. They asked me if there were any strangers on the estate."

"And what did you tell them?" Mariana said apprehen-sively.

"That our cousin Fernando was visiting us from the Indies," he smiled frigidly. "That is so, isn't it?"

"What description did you give," Francisco pressed, sen-

114

sing that the boy may have taken advantage to exploit his antipathy towards him. Since they had met, he had shown nothing but a contempt bordering on hatred for him. He knew it was something to do with his relationship with Mariana, though he had never seen them do anything other than talk. But a child of his age was perceptive and what he could not perceive, at thirteen or so, he would imagine. And given Ruiz's spoilt arrogance in his treatment of servants, and his fierce jealousy of Mariana, it was possible that he had told the soldiers exactly who was staying there, revelling in giving them a detailed description.

"A description?" the boy repeated.

"Yes," said Francisco. "Did they ask for one?"

"No," Ruiz lied, "Why should they? You're not wanted, are you?"

"They'll be back," Francisco said ignoring the comment. "If there is any trouble you must tell them I forced you to let me stay. I'll return to Seville now and arrange a vessel. My horse is saddled."

"Why do the soldiers want you?" María Teresa asked, struggling off Leonor's lap and coming over to him.

He crouched down and took the small shoulders in his hands, but the round serious face gazing at him in wide-eyed trust robbed him of words.

"I'll explain later," Leonor said.

"Will you come back, cousin?" the child asked. "I like you," she blurted discarding the formal tone she usually used.

"You must let our cousin leave, María Teresa," Ruiz asserted acerbically. "He is in a hurry."

Francisco stood up, but the child caught his hand, her brown eyes fixed up at him. "Thank you for riding with me," she suddenly said.

Ruiz's voice cut through the affection reminding them that Francisco was in a hurry, and Francisco eased his hand from hers as he glared at the pompous youth resting back in the chair, legs crossed, hands resting on both arms. There was an uncanny familiarity about him. The narrow face, dark brown wavy hair, ruff and doublet all reminded him of someone he could not place. Perhaps an overbearing officer he had served under, he wondered. The triumph at his leaving was so evident in those self-assured brown eyes, but it was understandable. He must have suspected something, with Francisco turning up as he did without warning, and now he was getting rid of someone who was a rival to his mother's affection. Yet that face, so reminiscent of someone he had known well, and so unlike the little girl's that gazed up at him.

"Forgive me rushing you," the boy said in mock apology. "But you seem to want to leave quickly, though I cannot see why two soldiers should hasten you."

Francisco dismissed his thoughts and taking his hand from María Teresa's hurried out of the door with Mariana following him.

It took only moments for him to gather his few belongings and get to the courtyard where his horse was waiting.

He pressed Mariana to him and she wound her arms tightly round him, her face pressed into his chest, trying to blend her body with his so they could become one. And in the darkness they moulded to one another, no longer exchanging words, but clinging in an embrace that would need to last them an eternity.

In his arms, sensing this would be the last time she would see him, she now wanted to make a revelation for which she had been waiting for the right moment. Yet there was a chance Francisco could be captured and worse might follow. No, she had to check herself. She could not throw away fourteen years of silence in a few fraught emotional seconds, as she herself had reasoned before, she was no longer a love-sick girl, but a responsible woman.

His lips found hers, pressing desperately on them, then suddenly pulling away as he turned to mount his horse.

For moments they stared at one another in silence, then he wheeled the animal round and rode through the darkness into the night.

Through the mists of her tears Leonor stood by the window above watching the scene, aching as she felt Mariana's pain, and closing her eyes as Francisco mounted, his horse's hooves clattering across the cobbles as he rode away.

She turned and walked over to a chair, staring blankly

ahead until eventually she heard her cousin's footsteps along the hall as Mariana went to her room and shut the door.

She wanted to go to her, comfort her, but there were no sentiments she could express to ease Mariana's pain, only time could do that.

She leaned back, biting on to the emotions that wanted to flood from her, but which she could not let flow in front of her cold-eyed nephew and bewildered niece. And she closed her eyes, shutting out the night.

Leonor woke with a start two hours later. She shivered from the cold, and as she became aware of her surroundings she realized someone was sitting opposite her. Through the gloom she saw Ruiz. He was as rigid as he had been when Francisco had left.

"I had a servant put María Teresa to bed," he said accusingly, "you and mother were . . . preoccupied."

"How long have you been sitting there?" Leonor asked ignoring the remark.

"For some time, mother's sobbing disturbed me," he smiled. "So many tears over one we have hardly known. Our cousin must have been very dear to you both."

His expression was complacent, Leonor thought, more than that, it was smug. "You don't understand Ruiz," she said.

"I understand!" he snapped. "You think I have the intelligence of a child like María Teresa!"

A sense of foreboding gripped her. "What have you done?" she demanded.

"Done! What *should* I have done!"

"I was not here when the soldiers came. What did you tell them?"

"The *truth*, of course," he replied to her mounting uneasiness. "I told them our cousin from the Indies was here, gave them his description . . . and would you believe it," he said now leaving his chair and moving over to her, ". . . that description matched a man called Francisco del Valle, a heretic they were looking for. Of course, I told them that the man in this house was not the same. How could it be. This is

117

the *solar* of a Marqués, not a refuge for filthy heretics. I told them . . ."

The words were slammed into his mouth as Leonor's hand cracked across it, leaping from the chair, whipping it back again, staggering the boy.

"My father's house has been desecrated!" he yelled.

"By your treachery!" she hurled back, her hand ready to strike again. "The Marqués would never have betrayed a guest!"

"He would have twisted the garotte round a heretic's neck himself!"

"Then you never knew him!" she cried, "he was loyal to the faith, not the Inquisition. Your stupidity and jealousy have blinded you!"

"No *you*! You brought that filthy heretic to this house. Do you know what they call him *el cobarde*! Do you know his story?" he raged. "Did you know they perform the *auto El Cobarde de Tripoli* in the squares. I have seen it myself! I have seen his cowardice acted out by the players. Seen him cringe as the brave Miguel died at the hands of the infidel. And you brought him here!"

"I must warn him," Leonor muttered shoving the youth aside.

"It's too late," Ruiz shouted. "He has been gone two hours, they will have caught him, and I will watch him burn at the stake!"

Leonor spun round to the face disfigured by hate and jealousy, no longer able to contain her fury. "Francisco is your *father*!"

The boy gaped in disbelief, not at the revelation, for he was sure that was fiction, but that his aunt should go to such lengths to protect his mother's lover. But in the moments that passed, Leonor was able to control herself.

"It is true," she said quietly, relieved that the fifteen years of deception and the pain it had caused Mariana had now been brushed away. And the incredulous expression on her nephew's contorted face only gave impetus for her to continue. "You were born on a *finca*, not here, but on a small estate near the village of Santa Madre in the Estremadura. Your father was an *hidalgo*, Francisco del Valle, a Knight of the Order of St. John. You were brought here when a few months old."

118

"Why do you lie like this!" Ruiz hissed in disbelief.

"The Marqués accepted you as his child," Leonor persisted indifferent to his incredulity and the consequences of what she was saying. "The Marqués was a kind man, unlike many aristocratic ostentatious prigs, and he accepted the child his young bride brought to him, and he loved him as he loved his mother. And he gave you *everything* Ruiz. His name, title, but most important, his love. But his indulgence turned you into a strutting autocrat who can barely dress himself or saddle his horse."

"Get out of my house!" the boy exploded. "You and your merchant husband always envied our blood, our . . ."

"Ruiz!"

He turned to see the apparition of his mother, her face as white as the long shift she wore, drawn, her eyes red, hair straggled.

Leonor hurried over to her, but she pushed her away.

"I'm all right," she said.

"You heard?" Leonor asked, now aware of the consequences of what she had told her nephew.

Mariana stared at her son, the disdain and outrage scarring his face. And a steel band of emotion tightened round her throat as memories of the long journey back from the Estremadura returned. She could still see that tearful farewell to Don Ricardo, Francisco's father, who had insisted she make a new life for herself and her child in Andalusia, where the climate was not as harsh as it was in the Estremadura. The old man seemed to have died when he heard of his son's shame in Tripoli, and for months had urged her to leave, change her name, or remarry and forget Francisco ever lived as he intended doing. So reluctantly she took Ruiz, only a few months old, and made the tortuous trek back over that terrain that had promised so much when first she covered it with her young husband.

And only their baby kept her going, giving her the will to live for him. Even her marriage to the Marqués had been based on the security and position he offered her child, the chance for him to shed the name of del Valle and assume a pride that men seemed so desperately to need. But now as she looked at him bathing in his sanctimonious indignity, challenging her to deny Leonor's words, there seemed no reason for showing the caution she had when saying goodbye to Francisco hours before.

"You have betrayed your father, Don Francisco del Valle," she said in a controlled voice.

The boy shook his head, a twisted smile of uncertainty on his mouth.

"What *is* this conspiracy?" he whispered.

"There is no conspiracy," she answered. "The only lies you heard were the ones, God forgive me, I led you to believe before tonight."

He gasped in horror and instinctively she moved to him.

"Stay away from me!" He threatened, his hand flying to the hilt of his dagger.

"Ruiz!" she cried. "You will accept it, as the Marqués accepted you, without shame or reservation. He was an aristocrat, but not too haughty to accept the son of a *hidalgo*, that's why I married him. He was a sensitive, kind man, but the dignity he tried to instil in you has become arrogance. We knew if this were ever revealed you would need courage and bearing to withstand it. But we failed, Ruiz. We failed!"

"My father was a Marqués!" the boy protested, tears streaming down his cheeks. "He was not an *hidalgo*, a *coward*, a *heretic*, he was a Marqués!"

"Francisco must be warned," Leonor urged.

"I sent Kassim, your servant, as soon as I heard," she said slowly approaching her son.

"I *am* a Marqués," he sobbed.

She put her arms round him and hugged him tightly, her pent up tears now flowing as freely as his. "You are the son of a man who sacrificed his lands, love and himself for the true faith . . . and no man was worse rewarded for that sacrifice."

From the corner of her eye, Leonor saw María Teresa wander in sleepily and she caught the child, transfixed by the emotional scene, and lifted her.

"Why is Ruiz crying?" the child asked bemused. "Ruiz never cries."

"He has learnt the truth," Leonor whispered.

"The truth does not make us cry."

"It does, María Teresa," Leonor sighed. "More than deception."

CHAPTER TWELVE

Auto da fé – Act of Faith

Francisco leaned back against the cold stone wall and watched the sleek rodent scurry over the wet slabstones of the cell, then stop by some straw. Its oval body glistened in the gloom. It looked at him, then continued on, unhurried, unafraid of the human who had temporarily invaded his dark slimy world. The walls round him were etched with the misery of others who had shared his fate until the executioner had released them from the nightmare. He closed his eyes, the scratched names and dates only increasing his despair. But the images that assailed his mind were those of his capture by the soldiers outside Seville as he had ridden into the trap.

He vaguely recalled the short flurry of fighting before what seemed like a mace, felled him, and emerging from the whirlpool of blackness he woke to find himself in the dungeon.

In the first hours of consciousness, as he had lain listening to the desperate cries of other prisoners punctuated with the screams of the insane or tortured, he sifted through the possibilities of who had betrayed him. It must have been a *peón*, or servant, he told himself, who probably approached the soldiers when they came to the *huerta*, any other answer was unthinkable.

He glanced up at the narrow barred window, it was too high to reach, and the walls and iron door too solid to break. Even if he overpowered a guard, what lay beyond the door? The pitiful cries indicated other cells, the shrieks, a torture-chamber, and what might await him there frightened him.

He had tasted the lash as a galley prisoner, searing wounds in battles, but he had never known the slow calculated infliction of pain by torture.

He tried to force his mind from the terror. Focus on Mariana, their moments together, the tender embraces, the passions, her gentleness. But the prisoners' shouts, clanking doors, and the tramp of boots penetrated to remind him of what might lie ahead.

He wanted to sleep, escape in his dreams, but he ached from the blow he took in arrest, and the cell was infested by every creature that could plague man by feeding on him. In the centuries since Torquemada, the Inquisition had perfected instruments of mental and physical pain, and here, nature's creatures seemed to conspire with them in torment.

"Sleep Francisco," he urged himself. "Make dreams reality, and reality the dream. Lose yourself in the memories of sunlight, rivers and trees. *My hands are green.* He heard Mariana say as she stared at the stain the leaves had left. She laughed. He embraced her tightly. *Is this a dream?* He asked. *The dream cannot be changed*, she answered, *it runs through our minds, finding its own course. Feeding our emotions. Making them bloom, sometimes inundating them . . . Your mouth is soft*, he said. *Your breasts and belly warm. I sink into them. Into you. I want to slide into your body, your mind, your being, so we become one. Drink me. Swallow me into you.*

The door crashed open.

Yellow flames flared, piercing his eyes as they opened, but as soon as he focused, he saw two guards, their breastplates and morions ablaze in the reflection of the torches. They were flanked by the tall gaunt figure of Alonso de Rojas. Francisco looked up at him. He had changed over the years, his face narrower, the high cheekbones more prominent, his eyes deeper set, but they displayed the hatred he remembered from Tripoli.

"*El cobarde*," de Rojas said almost inaudibly.

Francisco went to push himself from the ground, but one of the soldiers pressed his boot into his hand, holding him.

"Call your dog off!" Francisco hissed.

The soldier pressed harder.

De Rojas motioned the soldier to release him. "Well you have some spirit," he said. "A pity it was so absent in Tripoli."

"Am I here to pay the debt of Tripoli!" Francisco retorted. "I thought Grand Master Juan d'Omedes had passed judgment then."

"You have been arrested in the name of the Holy Inquisition," he answered quietly. "The charge is heresy, satanism, profanity, blasphemy, denying . . ."

"It's enough. Bring a confession and I'll sign it."

He had involved Mariana and her family, he decided, better to confess to anything, than risk breaking down under torture and implicating others.

"You demonstrate the same cowardice as at Tripoli," said de Rojas.

"And you, the same thirst for revenge. I'll not quench it. I paid fourteen years of my life for that incident."

"Miguel paid for eternity."

"So will I."

Del Valle's resignation infuriated de Rojas. It bordered on arrogance. He wanted to see repentance, regret, and fear. Above all, the fear he saw in Miguel's eyes as he fell. Resignation was not enough! "There is no remorse in you, is there?" he challenged.

"For Miguel, yes. There is remorse for Miguel."

"And your sins!"

"I sinned against myself."

"Against Man and the Holy Church!"

"That is for God to decide. Not you."

"Man decided that long ago!" de Rojas roared, his body shuddering as he remembered his brother's death. "All in the garrison saw your terror that day. Your hand hovering over your sword without drawing it. The stench of sulphur as the devil's explosion wrapped you in a shield that protected you from the infidel! You became his creature, and Miguel his victim!"

The stark glaring eyes chilled Francisco. The man had become unbalanced. He had seen it among obsessives in the religious wars where fervour bred hysteria and the hysteria madness. And the spectre hovering over him now was certainly insane.

"You could not be touched!" snarled de Rojas. "No Janissary blade could harm you in that evil blue mist. Any Turk who attacked you was felled by a missile. I saw you protected by that . . ."

"You *saw* me!" Francisco exclaimed. "*You* saw me! You were with d'Omedes on the west wall. How could you have *seen* me from across the compound!" His words prompted vague images from that afternoon. "What else did you *see*, general! Did you see the power barrel ignite. Did you see it blow up!"

"It was Satan's hand!"

"Did you see the *tercios* counter attack! And did you hear Miguel's screams as the scimitars and axes felled him!"

"I heard him plead, Don Francisco help me, help me!"

"From the *west* wall. Above the sounds of battle you *heard* Miguel's cries!"

Once again Francisco saw the battle rage, saw himself immobilized by shock, and yet identify a shadow rushing across the compound. He had always told himself that the image was not who he had once thought it was, Alonso de Rojas. He had assumed his own guilt was such that he had created that shadow in his memories to reduce his culpability. But now, in the flickering flames of the torches, the figure became clear.

"You *saw* everything, and *heard* everything because you came back from the west wall on d'Omedes' orders," he whispered, "and maybe the panic, or the explosion which had immobilized me, stopped you. Just as you were paralysed when my galley was taken all those years before when you should have rammed the Turk that overwhelmed us. I spent a year in the galleys as a slave for your hesitation, and fourteen years in hell for your fear!"

Only the trickling water running down the stone walls and the crackling torch flames broke the silence. The burly sergeant who had trodden on Francisco's hand shifted uncomfortably as he and his comrade avoided looking at either man.

"Your hatred of me," Francisco said finally, "comes from your own sense of guilt. Only you know whether you could have saved Miguel by rushing into that attack. Just as only you know if you could have saved my galley by ramming the Turkish vessel."

As he uttered the words his only relief was that of a man

whose crime had been shared. "You are as guilty as I," he said quietly.

"I am no heretic!"

"That is not the issue."

"That is why you are here!" de Rojas roared.

Francisco shook his head. "I'm here because of your contrition and the accusations you made so convincingly at my trial. I'm here because you left me no alternative but to survive as best I could."

"You will admit to the crimes, and to being aided by the Marquesa Mariana d'Olivera . . ."

"De Rojas!" he roared, "Your revenge concerns *me*! Not the innocent!"

But he continued indifferently.

". . . to her family's aid and their participation in your crimes."

"Have you arrested them?"

"On your confession, the family will be . . ."

Francisco was checked by the soldiers grabbing him as he leaped forward, tripping and pinning him to the ground. From outside two others rushed into the cell adding their weight, while de Rojas looked down at the threshing figure.

Now he had the reaction he wanted. He would get del Valle's testimony admitting the family's complicity.

"Chain him," he ordered leaving.

Walking through the dark passages of the dungeons from the cell, de Rojas was absorbed in the problem of how to break del Valle, his preoccupation making him indifferent to the stench and the pleas of those he passed. The lash and *bastinado* would not break him. He had survived beatings in the galleys and his skin was tougher than hide. Hanging by the *estrapada* would take too long. He wanted a confession before the *auto da fé* so that he would suffer the humiliation of public denouncement and his execution would be a warning to others. He would need something that worked quickly, but left no sign of torture.

He stopped as he came to another long dark passage and

now became aware of the moans of the incarcerated, but he also was aware of something else. The steady drip of water on the slimy flagstones. He smiled. He would have his confession.

The features of those surrounding Francisco were distorted by the twisting flames from the torches lighting the chamber. As previously when he had been brought there, the three guards, de Rojas, the hooded torturer and the monk were present. Yet it was the monk who disturbed him most.

The guards were indifferent, and de Rojas masked his feelings, but the monk looked compassionate, and in the presence of what was happening, that pink pained face frightened him.

To watch Man at his most bestial, his most primitive, yet condone was terrifying. To sympathize with the victim, while being part of that bestiality was beyond his reason. This was not just a confession of heresy they wanted, but complicity, involving the innocent. Francisco stared up at the sad eyes and wondered what the man believed in. Perhaps like those savages in the Indies who thought human sacrifice appeased their idols, this man believed this ritual appeased something. But what!

De Rojas began, as he had done so many times before.

"Will you sign a confession implic . . ."

"No confession," Francisco hissed the words forced through his swollen throat.

De Rojas nodded to the hooded torturer.

The man jammed the *bosteza* into Francisco's mouth, the instrument forcing it open. The *toca*, the linen strip, was pushed down his throat, then water poured down rapidly expanding the material. For moments, Francisco gagged, choking, but at the point of unconsciousness, the rag was pulled out.

Again the demand to name Mariana and her family as conspirators was made. Again he refused. Again the treatment was applied. De Rojas gazed at the body lashed to the rack, realizing that few men could last long on the water torture and it would be unlikely *el cobarde* would live to confess anything if

126

it continued much longer. Moreover, he wanted a confession at the *auto da fé* that would ring like the bells of the cathedral. In his present state he could barely speak. In the past few weeks since he had been there, he himself had been under pressure. The *alcalde*, the mayor, had already made enquiries about the Marquesa's implication, and her son, Ruiz, had sworn that del Valle had threatened to kill them all unless they hid him. Hadn't he himself, the boy maintained, warned the soldiers as soon as he had a chance to escape. And Leonor de Cortinas had made the same statement under oath, and her husband, a magistrate, had made threatening noises about forcing false confession which would harm the name of a prominent family whose support of the Church was exemplary. Only the Marquesa had refused to give any testimony, which people saw as a noble gesture to protect the husband she thought had died so many years before.

He looked at the convulsing body and wondered just how long he could last. Then, as many times before, del Valle lost consciousness.

De Rojas' eye caught the sergeant's who shook his head indicating the man would be neither broken nor last many more sessions.

"Torturer!" de Rojas called. "How much more can he take?"

"Few more treatments, my Lord," he shrugged, "but he'll have no voice for confession or recantation."

"Take him to the limit," de Rojas ordered as he turned to go. "But don't lose him. I want him in that procession!"

The sergeant watched the dark figure of the general slowly mount the stone steps to the rusting iron door of the chamber, then disappear into the blackness beyond. He glanced back at the racked figure stretched like the cord of a ballista. He was pleased unconsciousness had released him from his agonies. The exchange between de Rojas and del Valle in the cell had disturbed him. In fact, prison duty and these tasks in particular sickened him. This one wouldn't crack, he thought. The granite face, scar tissue on the leather skin bore witness to that. He looked at the monk muttering prayers for the battle-hardened soul that had long relinquished belief in the spiritual, then turned to the masked torturer returning with a bucket of filthy water to revive the prisoner.

"Leave him!" the sergeant heard himself say. "Return him to his cell. He's had enough."

"General de Rojas ordered he should be taken to the brink!"

"Look at him, man!" the sergeant rasped. "He's beyond that!" Not waiting for an answer, he motioned the soldier beside him. "Untie him, take him back to his cell." He watched the man untie del Valle, pull his body from the rack, then drag it across the stone floor like a carcass. "Wait!" he ordered. "I'll help you." As he lifted the prisoner's legs, he heard the torturer call after him.

"You are weakening, sergeant. The man's a heretic. He has no soul. He believes in nothing!"

He glanced over his shoulder.

"And what do you believe in, master torturer!" he growled.

In unconsciousness Francisco relived the horrors from the past. Old battles were refought, wounds inflicted again, enemies cut down, and cities razed. Fractured faces of the dead and living returned in a montage without sequence. Only the acute pain was clear in the flurry of experiences that passed. Not only his own pain, but that of others, a sharp all-embracing agony that racked him physically and emotionally. The pain of loneliness, deprivation, fear and helplessness. And in his desperation he prayed. He was a child again in Santa Madre, on his knees in the old church, praying that the agony of his mother would cease. Tears stung his eyes as he concentrated hard, so his words would be heard and she would be saved. But on his return home, his father told him she had died. Now he was alone. Alone in a bleak, hostile world.

He opened his eyes to darkness. His face was wet, and his throat felt as though it were encased in a steel band. The dreams had vanished. He had woken to the nightmare.

Now he was frightened.

In the clammy darkness he had lost track of time. Lost his sense of resolve. Lost his perspective. He could no longer relate that what was happening to him had any relevance to the confession they were trying to extract. He felt pangs of terror as he realized he could be lost for ever in the dungeons of the Inquisition like thousands before him. Losing freedom, and identity, gradually slipping into the madness that had overtaken those he heard screaming from other cells. It must not happen, he urged himself. He had begun with a purpose, it had to be maintained. But what was that purpose? To return to Malta, that was it. Repay a debt of honour. Why? Release from the galleys! That was the debt of honour. That was his objective. But Malta could have fallen. The debt never paid. All would have been for nothing. A mindless barren wilderness.

No! He silently castigated himself. There had been Mariana. He had seen her, held her, loved her. Her tears had infused him with a compassion long discarded. Her smile rekindled passions he thought were dead. She had reawakened life and purpose, not just objectives. Pressed against her body he was a man like any other, not a sword-wielding machine. She was his existence, and that existence endangered her, but he would willingly sacrifice that existence if he could. But there was no weapon near to release him. And if his sanity went God knows what he might say or sign.

He listened to the faint noises round him as rodents scurried. He pushed himself from the floor. "Walk, Francisco," he muttered. "Walk. Keep your sanity. Hold on to sanity!"

But in the blackness he could not be sure whether he was standing or lying on the floor. His stomach curdled as he realized he did not even know if his eyes were open. "Yes. They're open. But there's no light. Blind? No. Transferred to another cell." He reached out. He was standing. There was space either side. "I am standing! I must be!"

A blinding light scorched his eyes as the cell door crashed open. "Get on your feet!" a voice ordered. He screwed his eyes up at the torches.

"Francisco del Valle,' someone said. "You have freely confessed your heresy and aid to the demonic powers that have fought the true faith . . ."

"I confessed nothing," he whispered hoarsely.

"You have admitted to satanism. Sacrilegious actions and blasphemy. From here you will be taken before the Holy Office of Seville where you will again freely confess your crimes and sins and be judged accordingly."

Before he could answer the figure vanished, and in the glare of the torch he could just make out the shape of a soldier, breastplate and morion gleaming.

"I admitted nothing," Francisco muttered.

The man did not reply.

"I did not . . ."

"You implicated no one," the sergeant said sympathetically to the dazed figure on the floor. "But you confessed heresy."

In the weeks he had watched the man go through the hell of torture and disorientation, he had almost come to feel his pain. Perhaps it was the sight of this powerful figure gradually being reduced to a shell while his strength was choked from him by the *toca* forced down his throat, and the starvation and darkness intended to make him lose his senses. "Those you wanted to protect are safe," he said quietly.

Francisco struggled off the floor, and the soldier stretched out to help him. The act of kindness filled him with tears as he reached out and clasped his hand.

"Your ordeal is over, Don Francisco," the man muttered hauling him up. "The mercy of Our Lord awaits you."

"The *auto da fé*?"

"If you . . . if you have gold . . ." the sergeant said in a low voice glancing over his shoulder, "perhaps . . . perhaps I could bribe the executioner to put gunpowder on the fire . . . death would be quicker . . ." Francisco said nothing. "Then confess," he urged, "Show true repentance. The garotte is better than the flames."

And the sword better than the rope, Francisco thought, as he stood swaying on his feet, and the missile better than the blade. But the end is inevitable.

"Appeal to them," the soldier pressed. "You have suffered enough."

He broke off as he heard de Rojas returning with an escort and the monk.

In the cavorting shadows thrown by the torches, Francisco stared at the general, wondering if he were thinking about Tripoli and Miguel. Wondering if the torture and his imminent death satisfied his vengeance or resolved the guilt that obsessed him. But the grim face betrayed no emotions.

"How long have I been here?" Francisco croaked.

"Nearly a month," de Rojas answered.

"Malta . . ."

"Has been invested by the Turk," he asserted. "But that is no longer your concern."

"But it is *yours!*" Francisco hissed, "You should be there, fighting . . ."

"I fight evil in the name of the Holy Spirit whether it is infidel or traitor who poisons the teaching within society!"

"And there is less danger here," Francisco added.

De Rojas' gloved fist crashed across his face; he staggered, but steadied himself.

"Wait by me until the flames consume me, Alonso," he hissed. "For if I ever see you again, you'll die!"

His burning anger smothered the pain, the dejection and self-pity he had felt, renewing his strength.

Despite the general's attempt to ridicule him, the powerful figure of del Valle stood with a dignity that denied contempt. His eyes reflecting the loathing they felt for the gaunt dark figure opposite him. And the general himself seemed uneasy under their glare.

"Now, *el cobarde*," he heard the general say. "Now you wear the true colours of *your* Order!" But the prisoner did not answer as the sergeant thought he would, and he realized that of the two the wrong one was dressed in the ridicule of the Inquisition, and despite his velvet doublet and long cloth cloak, he sensed de Rojas himself knew it. And those dark eyes, which so many had come to fear when brought before the general, now lost their intensity in the face of the prisoner's derision.

De Rojas shifted uneasily.

"Take him," he ordered. "Take him to the procession. Let him know the consequences of his evil!"

But the sergeant noticed how the voice had lost that total conviction it had always had, as if the glare from del Valle's eyes was sapping the will of de Rojas as a furnace melted metal.

"In God's name, take him!" de Rojas finally roared. "*Take him!*"

* * *

131

As he was led from the darkness of the cells up and out into the huge dusty yard of the prison, Francisco winced as brilliant sunshine pricked his eyes. And as he became accustomed to it, he could see a group of about thirty dishevelled people, herded together by the large gates, all wearing the hideous yellow sacks of the *sanbenito*, all with the same haggard glazed expression of those who had existed in terror.

He was shoved among them and adopted their silent anticipation as they waited for the procession to pass the prison to take their place in it.

The early morning sun burned down, and he felt dry, withered, and exposed, like a carcass in the wastelands.

The whitewashed buildings opposite the open gates were crowded with spectators at their windows, and he heard a babble of expectation beyond the prison as the curious massed along the narrow street. But it was not the excited hum associated with a festive event, more an awe-stricken muttering of those about to witness a terrible deed. Like *indianos*, he thought, waiting for their gods to be appeased.

The noise was gradually replaced by the steady thump of drums pacing chanting men as the procession approached.

He was pushed towards the gates and felt as though he were about to join the fury of battle. A sense of isolated unreality took him, drenching him in the cold sweat of apprehension. The drums slowly beat their way closer, and through a crack by one of the huge gateposts, he saw the massive green satin-banner of the Inquisition held high against the cloudless sky, emblazoned with the herald of the Inquisition. It hung limp in the still air, but seemed to be approaching him personally, moving onwards, ready to envelop him in its folds and smother him in the ignorance and superstition it stood for.

But it passed.

Behind it, followed the gold cross, effulgent in the sun, once a sign of purity and hope to him, now debased in this most sacrilegious of processions.

Bearers of the sword and olive branch followed, symbolizing justice and mercy, and as they passed, he saw the army of *familiares*, clad in their finest, the cohorts of the Inquisition. Each bore either a cross or banner, and amidst the finery of their velvets and brocades marched the priests, Franciscans in their rough brown woollen habits, Dominicans, stark in black and white, their simple garments contrasting with the spectacle of the flamboyant clothes of the militia. The procession and drums stopped.

He was herded on until he found himself pushed between two *familiares*, one shoving something in his hands. It was a long yellow candle. He wanted to throw it down, but the nullifying atmosphere, the awestruck silence of the thousands watching in the thin street, the overwhelming solemnity, embalmed him, anaesthetizing him to that simple individual action; and blindly he began to follow the prisoner ahead as the drums resumed that steady hollow thump, accompanied by the chanting of the Creed.

The eerie procession made its way through crowded streets silencing onlookers outside closed and shuttered shops, when they fixed their eyes on the prisoners heading the lines of magistrates, judges, administrators, clergy and members of the Holy Office winding their way through the snaking dusty claustrophobic roads that led the way to the cathedral.

His ears echoed with the steady throb of the drums and he could see himself once again leaving the silent garrison at Tripoli as Muslim and Christian witnessed his humiliation. This was Tripoli again, but more elaborate and ritualized. This was why de Rojas had not continued to torture him until he implicated Mariana. Only this ultimate condemnation would satisfy him, and he did not want to risk killing him to let him avoid this public exhibition.

He prayed Mariana had stayed away. To see him die would have been painful to her, to see him despised and ridiculed in the *sanbenito* and *coroza* would have been intolerable.

Soon they entered the cathedral square which had been transformed since he had last seen it.

A huge platform had been erected and to one side tiers of wooden seats. The *familiar* beside him motioned him to move towards the tiers and without thinking he obeyed.

"Top row!" the man ordered. "Go to the top row."

From witnessing previous *autos*, he knew that this was the place reserved for the condemned. But the apprehension he had felt was replaced with resignation. Once he had wondered why prisoners in these ghastly exhibitions had not resisted, run, let themselves be cut down by the soldiers rather than submit to the ritual. Now he understood how the spirit could be squashed and drained of any action other than reaction.

He climbed the ladder, and from his high perch watched blankly as the Inquisitor of Seville, the bishop and other functionaries assembled themselves to commence proceedings.

The leading dignitaries of the city now approached the dais on which the bishop and Inquisitor sat and began to affirm their faith and take the oath to defend it.

As the sun climbed, Francisco was lost in the drone of those who confirmed their beliefs with a passion motivated more by fear than conviction.

Morning blazed into the heat of noon, and he began to feel sick as the smell of the other prisoners on the benches drifted up. It was as though he were on the galley benches again, immersed in the stench of human misery, his fate wholly in the hands of others. But in the galleys, the nostrils could be plugged with tobacco, and chances of survival depended on the strength to pull an oar. Here, salvation rested in the hands of the wizened arid prosecutors of the Holy Office who had decided your fate long before you ever reached the torture chambers and confessed. He gazed down at the preacher on the rostrum bellowing up to them to repent, confess freely, indulge the Holy Office's mercy.

But his eyes drifted away to the packed spectators behind the human barrier of steel breastplates that held them back with pikes.

It was for them that the *auto da fé* was being held. Not in the name of justice, but in the name of spectacular terror. The ritual staged to threaten every one of them and convince them of the totality of the power of the Inquisition. As he stared, he became aware of the prisoner next to him. The swollen disfigured face was familiar, yet he could not place it.

The man gazed back, then nodded to himself as he, too, recognized Francisco.

"You are the soldier," he muttered with a whistle as the air was sucked through missing teeth.

Francisco tried to remember.

"At the *ventorro*, the inn," the stranger prompted. "I am Diego Ferra, the actor. Do you remember?"

He did, but the face was hardly recognizable.

"What happened to your face?" Francisco whispered.

"What happened to your voice?" Diego retorted.

Francisco did not answer.

"The *toca*, the water treatment?"

He nodded.

"I was fortunate," said Diego. "I confessed everything. Their torture took the form of beatings . . ." he indicated his face, "Here . . . and in more painful parts."

"Why?"

"Blasphemy, profanity, insulting the Holy Office . . ."

"Shshshsh . . ." A *familiar* at the end of the row hissed.

Diego glared at him.

"Señor, I don't need to hear what they say," Diego hissed, indicating those on the dais. "They say if you play with yourself, you'll end up here. And if you leave it alone like that dried cucumber, you'll end up with them down there!"

A few prisoners laughed and the bloated face turned away. His comments reminded Francisco of how careless he had been in the *ventorro*. But the punishment was out of proportion to his crime.

"Why are you sitting with the condemned?" he asked. "Your crime only warrants wearing the *sanbenito* and recantation?"

"Blasphemy does," Diego answered sadly, "not adultery." He shook his head dejectedly. "Lopez, my friend from the *ventorro*, warned me. But I took no notice. She was the wife of a dignitary. He was old, could not give her the little pleasures of life. So Diego supplied what was missing in their marriage. And for this charitable action I am here."

"I'm sorry," Francisco sympathized.

"So am I. She was as dry as autumn leaves. The breasts of the Madonna in the church of San Pablo, the lips of the cherubs in St. Theresa's. But no real inclination or interest. I think she just did it to spite her husband." As he spoke he gave an acrimonious look to the *familiar* at the end of the row. The florid face turned back to the proceedings. "I wish it had been *his* wife," he muttered. "But then I might have had her last time we were here." He studied Francisco for a moment. "Why are you here?"

"Heresy," he answered.

"That's bad," the young man muttered thoughtfully.

"We are both condemned, Diego."

"But I'll go to heaven after confession. Will you?"

Despite their situation Francisco smiled.

"Still, your heresy might stand you in good stead down there," Diego added by way of compensation.

"You don't seem worried about what's to come," Francisco observed.

"Nor do you," he shrugged, and considered the proposition for a moment. "When they arrested me I was worried," he admitted, keeping his one good eye on the preacher exhorting them to repent. "When they took me to prison, I was scared, and when I thought of what they could do to me, I was terrified. I messed my breeches when they took me before the Inquisition. But then the beatings started and I became acquainted with pain and the fear abated. The pain remained of course, but I could no longer distinguish between its degrees and my fear subsided into simple misery . . . and misery is the companion of all actors."

"And death?"

"I've been crucified hundreds of times in market squares all over Spain, and killed a thousand times in the *autos* we performed. This is like a final performance." He turned from the preacher, "But I am scared. Are you? . . . Scared I mean?"

"Of the unknown," Francisco replied.

Diego nodded. "I should thank you for helping me out of the *ventorro*, when that idiot sailor attacked me." He shook his head. "But then, if you had not helped me I might just have been wounded in the fight and not met the magistrate's wife, then not ended up here alongside you on the condemned bench."

His tone was matter-of-fact rather than provocative.

"Do you believe that?" Francisco asked.

"No. But I am still not going to thank you." He gazed back at the black-frocked preacher ranting. "I could do better than that," he muttered. "Do you know today's date?" he suddenly asked.

Francisco shrugged.

"It's not the tenth of May is it?"

"Later I think, maybe the twentieth."

"How can you tell?"

"By the position of the sun."

He glanced up.

"It's my birthday on the tenth," he said, "I'm pleased it's not the tenth."

They lapsed into silence as crimes were read out to each prisoner brought before the dais, the readings going on for hours, until eventually Francisco was brought before the Inquisition where he was charged.

Throughout the elaborate condemnation he kept his eyes fixed on Alonso de Rojas standing beside the bishop. The general returned his look, betraying neither satisfaction, nor recognition.

The sun burned into the back of his neck as he stood, bound, before them. He said nothing of the charges, consoling himself that he would die without implicating Mariana or her family, which was more important than death. His salvation would soon be decided by a force more vast than that assembled in the square around him. But it was something he had long resigned himself to. Death was the soldier's constant companion, relieving the pains of wounds, eliminating his enemies, its imminence cautioning him when a comrade fell. As inevitable as sunset, it was as necessary a part of life as birth. Only the regret of never seeing Mariana again weighed heavily. She was life. Brighter than the midday sun, more vivacious than the greens, yellows, scarlets and golds that blazed from the dais above him. There was no death, he thought, only pain, the pain of losing someone.

His thoughts were interrupted by the *familiar* next to him, who indicated he should return to the benches. He glanced up taking one final long look at de Rojas. He could no longer even muster the loathing that had welled up in him back in the dungeon. At least what befell him next, would offer the consolation of release. But for the gaunt, dark, drawn figure that stood so emotionlessly beside the bishop, the hell he had condemned him to, would continue. You do not frighten me, Alonso, he thought. But your studied indifference reflects a terror within you that plagues you even more than those you condemn.

The *familiar* tugged his sleeve, and slowly he turned, following the man back to the benches, where a priest mumbled inaudible words of comfort as he had done to others alongside him. Francisco ignored him and watched Diego led down, the actor maintaining a dignified gait as he approached his accusers. Twice during his short trial he interrupted but was silenced with a roar from the Inquisitor's Secretary. Then he too was led back to the upper tier.

"You are *el cobarde*," he said sitting down, apparently impressed by his experience.

Francisco nodded.

"You should have told me at the *ventorro*," he whistled through the missing teeth.

"Why?"

"We were thinking of doing your *comedia*, "El Cobarde de Tripoli.""

Francisco was puzzled.

"It's a play about you and the death of a Knight's brother."

The revelation left him unmoved, his emotions exhausted so that even such a damning fact no longer had the significance it might once have had.

"You don't appear the coward they said you were in the *comedia*," Diego observed. "But then I don't appear an actor," he added as if by way of conciliation.

The long shadows that had stretched across the dusty cathedral square vanished as the sky changed from turquoise to purple and the proceedings wound to a close.

A black-cloaked secretary took his place on the pulpit before the assembled lay and ecclesiastical bodies, and in a voice that resounded off the cathedral walls began to pronounce sentences. The crowds round the perimeters pushed closer, fascinated by the macabre spectacle of men being sentenced to death.

The lists were read out and some led away to be condemned to wear the *sanbenito* for a period, others were condemned to the galleys, and some to prison. Finally, Francisco heard his name and Diego's called. Both were to be released to the secular courts.

"We are free," Diego whispered in amazement.

Francisco shook his head.

"But we have been released to the secular courts. We are *relajados*, those *released*!"

"To the *secular courts*," Francisco stressed. "That means we are condemned to die."

The badly bruised face contorted, and the one open eye filled with a tear as if the enormity of the proceedings had suddenly caught up with him. He trembled and Francisco gripped his arm with his manacled hand and squeezed it.

"Have courage," he whispered, "don't let that fat pig at the end of the row see you weaken," he indicated the *familiar* whose jaundiced expression had turned to pleasure. "You have been magnificent through all this, Diego. A little longer and both of us will be true *relajados*, really free."

"I . . . I am frightened," the young man sobbed.

"So am I," Francisco comforted. "But they won't see it, will they? We won't give them the satisfaction. We'll walk out to the pyres in one last great performance." He helped him up as they waited with the other ashen faced prisoners. But Diego's chains rattled as his hands trembled. "Diego," Francisco said quietly, "I have hidden a gold piece in my lining. Pull it out. Give it to the executioner. He'll put gunpowder on the flames. It will be quick. Take it." He guided his hand to the lining of his *camisa* where the coin was hidden. "Take it," Francisco urged. "It will be quicker."

"And you?" Diego asked thickly.

Francisco grinned ruefully.

"You said yourself before. I am a heretic. The fires can only be a preliminary to where I'm going. Take the money!"

They shuffled back along the benches and made their way down the steps to the square. As each man got to the bottom, he was unmanacled, his hands tied behind him to the large green cross of the Inquisition.

For a moment the process was held up as one man threw a fit of hysteria, screaming for mercy, but the soldiers beat him unconscious then dragged him off behind those who were to meet their fates.

"Where . . . where will we . . . be, be taken?" Diego stammered.

"Beyond the city walls to the Arenal, by the Guadalquivir . . ."

"The trading-place?"

"Beyond that."

The ten who had been sentenced to death marched in
the shrouding darkness, a small crowd following at a distance.

"Francisco," Diego said, "I am sorry."

"Sorry?"

"For not thanking you for saving me at the *ventorro*."

The escort with them was small, the clergy and lay people
having already gone on to the place of execution, only those
lingering behind remained. Stalking them like jackals trailing
a wounded animal. The escorts' torches threw spiralling
shadows on the whitewashed houses they passed in the
narrow dark streets. Francisco felt as though he were being
transported through a dark tunnel to another world. The
world he should be inhabiting perhaps, he thought. Maybe he
had been placed in the wrong world at the wrong time, and
what followed was not death, but a means by which he could
be taken from here to the other.

"Have you any regrets?" Diego asked in a resigned tone.

"I'd have preferred to have died in battle," he said unconsciously, "and I'd have liked to have killed the man responsible for this."

"The dark one on the dais? With the sharp beard. The
general?"

"How do you know?"

"I saw the way you looked at him, and the way he watched
you when we sat on the benches. No man has a right to enjoy
another's plight like that."

"What regrets have you?" Francisco asked, getting away
from thoughts de Rojas provoked.

"I regret not believing in the next world as much as I
believe in this one."

"Do you believe in God?"

"I'm trying to," Diego said seriously. "But I'm wondering if
he believes in me."

140

Suddenly they stopped as the street narrowed. A large cart blocking their path.

"Move it!" a soldier called. "Move it, you sons of bitches!"

The soldiers beside Francisco looked warily at the dark abyss of a narrow side street near them.

"Damn them!" the soldier swore as he began to approach the cart to organize its removal. but he had not taken a dozen steps when a flash followed by a roar shook them as the barrels on it exploded.

Screams rent the street as the jackals following fled, while the escort panicked, firing blindly. The air filled with explosive chemicals. *Sachetti*, small pots, were hurled down on them from the rooftops, and burst into a clinging incendiary liquid.

"Francisco del Valle!" a voice yelled from the darkness of the side street.

Grabbing Diego, Francisco ran towards the voice, their speed hindered by the crosses tied to their backs.

Three soldiers padded after them, swords drawn, closing quickly. But from the slanting roofs of a building two lassos were dropped, and without needing to be told, Diego followed Francisco in working his body into one of the loops.

The ropes tightened, gripping them. Slowly they were drawn up the side of the house, the soldiers gaping in the darkness as if by magic the condemned men were being raised by some awful spirit.

Once on the roof they were jostled by cloaked helpers to the other side, and before either could speak, were pushed off, dropping through the blackness, falling on soft straw sacks, then covered by a tarpaulin.

For the next two hours they rattled on through the night, into the city and out to the countryside, oblivious of who had rescued them and where they were being taken. But Francisco had a shrewd idea that Kassim would have had something to do with it. *Sachetti* was the favoured incendiary of the Muslim.

CHAPTER THIRTEEN

The Holy Office

Alonso de Rojas sat watching Mariana who stood by the grilled window of the large main room of the *solar* bathed in the orange of the afternoon sun. He was taken with her quiet dignity which belied her ever having any association with Francisco del Valle. Her bearing indicated all the qualities of an aristocrat, yet her claim to their ranks was only by marriage to the Marqués, and he wondered if the years she spent in his family and among his friends had encouraged her to adopt their distant reserve. She was certainly much changed from the young girl he had visited so long ago on del Valle's small estate in the Estremadura.

She had not spoken to him since he entered her house, but that was to be expected. It was the third time he had led a search here in the past three days since del Valle's escape, and though there was no doubt in his mind that she had organized it, it would be difficult to prove.

Neither had spoken for the past hour, and he listened to his soldier's boots tramping up and down the parquet floors outside in the corridors, and across the cobbles in the stables, as systematically they went over ground that must have been familiar to them after persistent searches. He still seethed over the outrage of the escape which challenged the authority of the Holy Office itself, but Mariana's cool hostility somehow made him restrain himself when dealing with her.

A knock interrupted the silence, but Mariana did not bother to answer it.

"Come!" de Rojas called.

A captain entered, reporting as on previous searches, that there was no trace of del Valle, and he waved him out, then spoke as the door closed.

"You are being foolish, Mariana."

She did not reply, but continued to look out of the window at the men's horses below. She was irritated by de Rojas' familiarity in using her first name; she had only met him twice before the searches began and that was long ago as Francisco's bride.

"We'll find him," de Rojas continued. "You will be implicated in his escape. Your family will suffer. You have young children who will bear your guilt and face the consequences." He paused, hoping for a response. There was none. His eyes were drawn to the gold cross round her neck which blazed in the sun's lowering rays. In profile, against her blue satin dress, sparks appeared to fly from the plain gold object. He broke off his gaze, returning to the issue.

"Your position, your rank, will be no protection," he pressed. "The Holy Office is only responsible to King Felipe himself. You know that, and you know what happens to those who shield heretics. Don't you feel any responsibility to your children!"

She suddenly turned, her small mouth tight, her dark eyes afire, and for an instant her vivid beauty stunned him, and he could understand how del Valle would risk everything to return to her. But the scintillating cross around her neck reminded him of his duty.

"Don't tell me about responsibility," she retorted. "In three days you have searched and found nothing. You have questioned me, my son, and threatened María Teresa, a small child." Her nails dug into her palms as she spoke. "You have no evidence that I, nor any of my family are implicated in Francisco's escape, and for all you know it could have been friends of the man who escaped with him! Yet still you come, cajole, menace and accuse. I have told you, we know nothing of what happened in Seville three days ago, but you choose to persecute us because I was once Francisco's wife!"

"And because he has hidden here before!"

She sighed impatiently. "You were told, he threatened us."

"That's a lie!"

"Then, in God's name, arrest us!" she shouted.

De Rojas restrained himself from getting lost in the heat of the argument and saying something he might regret. What he was doing had to be done in the name of the Holy Office, not for personal revenge. To arrest her, a Marquesa, her son, a Marqués, or any of her influential relations, might look as though he was pressing his vendetta regardless. And the Marquesa was well known in Seville for her philanthropy and piety. To imprison her without concrete evidence could trigger a riot.

He glanced up at the small flushed face glaring at him. "You press fortune hard," he said quietly.

"No, general; you do!"

For a moment, she seemed unreal. Perfectly still, set against the crimson of the sky, framed in the arched window, she appeared a character in a painting. Only the soft breeze ruffling the high collar, brought the image to life.

"I want you to swear an oath you had nothing to do with the escape," he demanded.

"My children and I have done so."

"I did not like the wording of that oath," he snapped. "I will arrange the wording of the new oath. "The original wording was ambiguous, I want you to swear you neither financed, nor planned, nor . . ." his voice cut off as the door behind him opened. He turned to see her son, Ruiz, enter.

"Your captain asked me if the men should search the house again," the boy said as he came in.

De Rojas eyed the stern-faced youth, then called him over. He rested his hand on his arm. "We have spoken before, haven't we, Ruiz?" he said. The boy nodded. "And you know how dangerous this man, del Valle, is to the Church and your family." The boy did not reply. "And if you knew anything about him, you would tell us, wouldn't you, Ruiz?"

"I am loyal to the Holy Church," Ruiz asserted indignantly.

De Rojas sighed. It was the same answer he always gave.

"But you would help us in any way you could," he demanded, his fingers tightening round the boy's arm.

There was no reply, but the sincerity of the youth's expression angered rather than reassured de Rojas and unconsciously he tightened his grip.

Ruiz did not flinch, but stared back hard into the taut face.

"It could go badly for your mother, sister . . ."

144

"You do not take the word of a Marqués!" Ruiz challenged defiantly, pulling his arm from de Rojas.

"He wants us to swear another oath," Mariana said going over to them and drawing Ruiz away. "He wants humiliation. If he cannot have Francisco del Valle, then he'll revenge himself on those close to him. Isn't that so, general?"

"I want what the Holy Office wants," de Rojas declared, "I want a self-confessed heretic, a traitor, an Antichrist!"

"Then find him!" Mariana cried, "And leave us alone!"

De Rojas stood up, "I'll be back," he threatened.

"I helped you capture *el cobarde*," the boy called as he strode to the door. "Is it likely I would help him escape?" But his words were silenced by the door slamming.

As the horses clattered away, Ruiz turned to his mother.

"Did you help him escape?" he challenged bitterly.

Mariana did not answer, but walked slowly to the door, her heart pounding from the tension de Rojas infused by his presence.

"Did you help him?" She heard her son call after her. She stopped and turned to the angry figure standing in the misty light of early evening.

"You renounced the right to know anything about your father when you denounced him," she said quietly.

The words savaged him. He had remained quiet to protect his family, and through feelings of shame at betraying a guest as Leonor had so clearly pointed out to him that night del Valle had left. He had born his mother's indifference to him over the past weeks when del Valle was held captive and had secretly hoped that if he escaped the Inquisition she would talk to him again. He had even begun to have a grudging admiration for del Valle himself, when he had sneaked away and seen him at the *auto da fé* dishevelled, ragged, yet defiant in the face of his accusers. But he would not accept the lie that del Valle was his father. Whatever conspiracy motivated his mother and aunt to make him believe it, he would never yield. The heretic would never be his father, just a glance at himself revealed his aristocratic heritage. And now as his mother began to close the door behind her, he stifled the tears and called "He's not my father! *He's not my father!*"

Mariana closed the door on his denials and took a deep breath to compose herself as a servant hurried past with a tray.

Restricting conversation with Ruiz to necessities over the past few weeks had rent her as never before. From a baby she had lavished all her affection on him, perhaps, she now thought, transferring that love she felt for Francisco to him. And until María Teresa came along, she had allowed no one to impinge on the love she shared with Ruiz, and God had been kind in giving her a husband, though twenty years older, who had never made demands nor intruded on that special affection she had for her son.

But Francisco's sudden appearance had shattered the comfortable security of the world she shared with Ruiz and María Teresa, as he brought with him the violence and passions of their youth. But he had also brought the outside world to their *solar*, the reality of the despair and uncompromising harshness that existed beyond the lands of their estate, and what she had seen that first night, when he was brought back, sick, hunted, and wary, like an animal, had disturbed her.

Ruiz had been protected from all this, and when confronted with a man like Francisco, he had reacted with a disdain that was the only protection he knew. But when being told this outsider was his father, it was obvious that his reaction would be one of bewildered violence. Yet that was not why she had not spoken to him. It was his betrayal through jealousy and his contempt for Leonor and her husband, who he called *the merchant*, that cut so deeply. Though he did not know it, Ruiz looked, walked, and in many ways acted like Francisco when he had been younger. But somehow the boy had adopted an overbearing arrogance that was supported by nothing other than the wealth and title he had inherited. And that contempt for other men she would not tolerate. After this was over, her son would learn that honour and respect cannot be inherited, but have to be earned. Just as Francisco learned that the cost of war and glory was a far higher price than most men would finally be willing to pay.

She steeled herself against the sobs she heard in the room behind her, curbing her instinct to go, as she had in the past, and comfort her son. Ruiz would accept Francisco as his father long before she ever showed that special affection she had showered on him again.

She closed her eyes, wondering if Mendoza, the Jew, who had played such an important part in aiding Francisco's escape had been discovered. The old man had shown a courage that went beyond what one could expect from friendship. How would Ruiz react to that, she thought, if he knew a Jew, one from such a despised race in Spain, was sheltering, not merely a Christian, but one who was once a member of the Knights of St. John, an Order they had no reason to love.

Ruiz was still young, but he would soon learn compassion and respect for all his fellow men, regardless of who they were. Of that she was certain.

CHAPTER FOURTEEN

The Jew

Francisco stared at the bright candle flame glowing in the darkness of the cold, dank cellar they had been brought to three days before. Food had been left for them at the top of the long flight of stone steps at its entrance, but their rescuer had not revealed himself. From the distance they had covered in the cart, he estimated they must be somewhere on the fringes of Seville. He had thought of jumping the Moor who brought them their food, waiting for him just near the door then grabbing him; but then what? There had to be a reason for keeping them here, in ignorance. Probably because, if the house were searched, and they were caught and tortured, they would not be able to reveal who was responsible for their escape. Possibly it was better they were left like this for a few more days.

Their conditions were grim, but his throat was healing, and he could feel himself regaining some of his strength. Diego too, looked better than he had. The bruises and cuts from the beatings he had taken in the prison were less obvious.

In the state they had been brought here, neither was fit to travel. Moreover, they were too easily recognizable to get very far. They would wait a few more days then make their move if necessary.

"Three days here," he heard Diego mutter. He glanced over at the young man lying on a pile of straw, staring up at the blackness.

"Three days," he repeated. "Do you think they have stopped looking for us?" The answer was obvious. "Stupid question," he admitted. "I just wanted reassurance." There was no reply. "How long will we have to wait here?" he said for the hundredth time. He didn't wait for an answer. "Doesn't matter. As long as we're safe. With a woman, I could stay down here, like a mole for the rest of my life. It was your friends who got us away," he decided suddenly.

In the time that had passed, Francisco found Diego did not really need answers, his talking was merely a form of mulling over things out loud, and this nervous characteristic, like his muttering in his sleep, was something Francisco had become used to in the past three days.

He liked the actor, who boasted as freely of his cowardice as others boasted of courage. His stories of his life on the roads of Spain, where he had performed with many troupes in the town and village squares, were witty, most times ending in the players being chased out of town because of Diego's amorous or blasphemous behaviour. Yet despite the actor's self-ridicule, Francisco fancied there was a brave man in that brittle body, and the way he had conducted himself at the *auto da fé*, apart from the lapse at the end when the death sentence was passed, he had shown a philosophical courage that matched any Francisco had met.

"It couldn't have been Lopez, the actor you first saw me with," Diego decided. "He's not resourceful. I mean getting the fire pots, the help, the cart and all the other things." He shook his head. "No, Lopez couldn't do that. It must have been your friends." Francisco made no comment. "Your friends are Jews," Diego observed."

"Jews?"

The young man stretched his arm pointing to a corner of the cellar. "Over there," he said. "When you were asleep I did some investigating. I accidently trod on a wooden cover on the ground and when I removed the earth beneath there was a hole. There are religious artifacts there . . . I recognized the Star of David on some of them." He cupped his hands behind his head, then shrugged. "I don't care," he sighed. "They saved us from the fires, so why should I care. Muslim or Jew, I'll go along with anyone who'd save us from cooking."

Francisco rose and made his way through the gloom to the corner Diego indicated. There he discovered the board and the hole, and beneath he found small parcels carefully wrapped in sacking. He took one, unwound its cover, and gleaming in the darkness saw a six-pronged candle holder, on top of it, a star.

"It's solid silver," he heard Diego say. He looked over at the actor who had twisted himself round and lay on his stomach, straw sticking out of his straggly hair.

"If we relieved them of it, it'd fetch quite a few ducats on the market," he suggested.

"I thought you were grateful for being saved," Francisco commented.

"Gratitude's one thing, business quite another," Diego answered simply.

Francisco wrapped the candlestick back in its sacking. Then took another parcel and undid it. There were three small scrolls with strange signs on them, not Arabic, he decided. Probably Hebrew. These people were *conversos* – Jews who had converted to Catholicism to save themselves – but still practising their religion. As a young man he might have been disgusted by their duplicity, their apostasy, but now he just felt a sadness for them.

"Are they *marranos*?" Diego said, using the slang "swine" for those who had converted.

Before Francisco could answer, the door at the top of the stone steps opened throwing a shaft of light into the cellar.

Francisco spun round, and Diego sprang up as two figures came down the steps and approached them.

Francisco immediately recognized one of them, the dark face, hooded eyes, and silks were unmistakable. "Kassim?" he whispered.

"What are you doing!" Leonor's servant demanded.

In springing to his feet, he still held the scrolls, and for an instant felt as though he were a thief caught stealing. "I was just trying to find out . . ."

"Put them down," Kassim ordered angrily. He turned to the older man with him, "Spanish gratitude," he hissed.

His companion appeared a Spanish trader of about sixty, in doublet and hose, with thigh-length leather riding boots. The greying hair was long, his beard carefully shaped, yet the face betrayed no anger at his intrusion into his private life, his dark eyes were more curious than accusing.

"As your friend observed," the man said in a low even voice, "I am a *converso*, like Kassim. A Jew, in my case, following the teachings of the Church to avoid trouble from

150

the Holy Office. Now please put down the Torah in your hand, and replace the menorah!" he indicated the scroll and candlestick.

"We mean no harm," Diego said quickly rising to his feet.

"That's gracious of you," the man replied, "especially considering your position."

"What is our position?" Francisco demanded.

"Precarious," Kassim answered. "This is Señor Juan Mendoza who organized your escape," he glanced at Diego, "and he took you along as we saw you had struck up some friendship with Francisco del Valle. But I might add, I was against it."

"And who financed it?" Francisco asked. "I don't imagine Señor Mendoza is a philanthropist who rescues men from the flames for love . . ."

"Hold your mouth!" Kassim snarled. "If he had not been a friend of your wife, he would never have undertaken such a scheme!"

Mendoza put a restraining hand on Kassim.

"The Marquesa, your ex-wife, financed the scheme," Mendoza admitted.

"And had your family not been under such pressure, there would have been no escape!" Kassim spat. "A Knight of St. John is an enemy to Jew and Muslim alike!"

"We mean no disrespect," Diego intervened nervously, fearing they might find themselves back in the hands of the Inquisition.

"Of course you mean no *disrespect*," Kassim mocked. "Down here in this cellar, at the mercy of . . ."

"It's enough Kassim," Mendoza said, "We only came to tell you where you are and who you are with."

"And where are we?" Francisco asked.

"Two leagues north of Seville," he answered. "And you will have to stay here until the Marquesa tells me it is safe for you to leave. I will arrange for a ship to take you to Sicily . . ."

"Sicily?"

Mendoza smiled. "You wish to get to Malta, don't you?"

Francisco stiffened. Mariana or Leonor had told them more than they should have.

"You will have to get there from Sicily," Mendoza continued. "They are trying to arrange relief for the island from there."

"What has happened there?"

"There is a siege," Mendoza replied. "Thousands of Turks and their allies have invested the island. That is all we know."

"I don't want to go to Malta!" Diego cried.

"You will be released at the same time as Don Francisco," the old man said. "Passage for one will be difficult enough. Suleiman's galleys are patrolling the seas to prevent aid getting through to the island. As a trader, I can promise you little is getting through."

Before either of them could ask any further questions, the Jew and Muslim were making their way up to the frame of light at the top of the steps.

"How much longer will we be here?" Francisco called.

"Until it's safe to leave!" Kassim retorted.

Dejectedly Diego sat back down on the straw, while Francisco began to replace the religious things.

"Ironic," Diego muttered. "In the *autos* I've always performed in, the Jew and Muslim were always the prisoners of the Christians."

"Beyond this house, they still are," Francisco commented.

A long week of irritable boredom passed with Kassim or Mendoza paying occasional visits to them to let them know what was happening outside.

The intensive search had slackened as the authorities began to accept that somehow they had left the city and were now either the problem of another state, or had smuggled themselves aboard a ship for the Indies.

Finally, ten days after their escape, Kassim came to them giving Francisco clothes, a sword and cloak, and to Diego's protests at being left alone, he took Francisco from the cellar, through the darkened house, out to two waiting horses. And without a word, both men mounted. Francisco followed the Moor through the soft velvet night of the Andalusian countryside. He had expected to be taken down to Cadiz, the main port of Seville, but they travelled inland, and within a few hours he began to recognize the countryside he was travelling through.

They were moving towards the ruined mosque the servant had first brought him to when he had met Leonor after his arrival in Seville.

He felt no need to question the Moor, his straightforward sincerity gave confidence. Moreover, he sensed that he was being taken to Mariana. The feeling was different from the first time he had been led to the mosque. Then it was one of expectation, excitement, the sensation that dreams would be fulfilled. Now he experienced sadness, as though embarking on the first stage of a journey whose conclusion was as inevitable as death itself. Only the chinking harnesses interrupted the warm damp darkness that wrapped round them as their horses padded through the groves, silhouetted like the outer defences of an encamped army.

He felt uncomfortable in the silks that Mendoza had provided, and his thoughts were confused. He wanted to see Mariana and yet did not. To lose her again so soon after he had found her cut more deeply. He should have gone straight on to Malta from France. The journey he had taken through Spain had endangered both him and her family. Yet something drove him on to see her, just as it drove him on to involve himself in a battle that was lost before it had ever begun. Destiny? He mused.

No, too grand a name. It was middle-aged romanticism. As Mariana had said the first night he had spent in her house, he saw himself as the shining knight returned to his lady love. And he had indeed expected her to have remained the innocent girl he had brought to the Estremadura, yet so brutally left.

Not destiny, Francisco said to himself, not fate, but arrogance. Arrogance to believe that she would be lost in the limbo of love, waiting for your return. Arrogance to think that you would redeem yourself in the battle for Malta. Arrogance to assume that you could evade the Inquisition throughout the journey. The arrogance of the player, the unsupported self-assurance of Diego who assumed the role of nobleman or Christ when necessary, then played it with the conviction that the *comedia* demanded.

He was closer to Diego's personality than he believed or wanted to believe. But at least Diego had done no harm when he lived his real life. But he himself had wrought a terrible slaughter in the years he had assumed the role of warrior – how had he described himself to the priest – the eternal soldier. No, the eternal *fool*, Francisco, he said to himself, the eternal fool.

Kassim suddenly reined in his horse.

"We are here," he said.

Francisco stared at the Moor blankly.

"The mosque," Kassim whispered, motioning to the rubble in the clearing. "The Marquesa is waiting."

"Why do you do this?" Francisco suddenly asked.

"I told you before," the dark face said. "The Lady Leonor and the Marquesa have been kind to me. They have been kind to Mendoza. That is the reason."

"And that is enough to risk your lives?"

The Moor shook his head sadly. "They call you *el cobarde*," he said staring steadily at Francisco. "You are a heretic, and yet, even in disgrace you achieve fame, and when you are mistreated, tortured, there are those who will defend your name because they believe in your innocence. And if you are killed, perhaps you will become a legend. Good or bad, you will be known. Because even as a heretic you are one of them . . . one of those who took my country . . ." he indicated the ruins of the mosque. "Though your name may be defiled, it will still have significance. But for me and my people, for Mendoza and his people, mistreatment, condemnation, they are as natural to us as breathing. If we are successful in business, it is because we are sly, not clever, and if too successful they destroy us. If we attempt to practise our religion we are burned . . ."

"It is the same for any Spaniard that resists the Holy Office . . ."

"No!" Kassim hissed. "In the wars in the north, you create martyrs on both sides, but when a Jew or Muslim is burned it just creates a corpse." He broke off as if the words were too painful to utter. Then pointed to the nearby mosque. "That is all that is left of us here. The remains of a civilization that practises medicine, while your only resource is the leech; that irrigates deserts while you cannot cultivate fertile land; that explains the stars and the universe scientifically, while you consider those explanations as heresy . . ."

"If you believe all this, why do you help . . .?"

154

"I told you!" Kassim snapped. "Kindness was shown me!" the dark eyes fixed on him. "For me and Mendoza, civility, nothing more, creates an obligation to repay a debt. Civility, which even a Spanish fishmonger takes for granted, is an act of generosity. Despite what you have been through, you cannot know what it is like to be despised from birth." He waved away Francisco's interruption. "Even when you first saw me, it was a shock that a Moor should be sent to help you. You cannot know what it is like to be dressed up like a performing animal . . . it was not Lady Leonor's wish for me to be dressed like this, but her husband's, who wanted to show off another possession . . ." His voice trailed as he smothered the invective. "Go, my Lord del Valle," he muttered. "Bid your wife goodbye, then sail to fight the Muslim, the *heathen*!"

"Suleiman will enslave everyone if he is not stopped," Francisco rasped. "I have been in his galleys. I have seen your *scientists* and *doctors* in a light you could not possibly dream of. No matter how imperfect, I don't want to see the destruction of the Christian civilizations . . ." He broke off. His words were rhetoric. Imbued reactions of a Knight of St. John, and the automatic reflex disturbed him.

Was that what all this had been about? He wondered. Not destiny, nor even something as romantic as arrogance. But the response to the call. The response that had first taken him from Mariana to fight because of duty rather than choice. Did he have so little free will?

"You had better go," Kassim said. "You do not have much time. We have arranged for a ship to take you to Sicily. You will join it at first light." He leaned over and took the reins of Francisco's mount. "No more philosophy, Don Francisco," he stated.

Francisco dismounted and approached the ruin warily. In the shadows of the fallen masonry he saw a cloaked figure, and felt for the hilt of his sword as he closed. Then stopped as the hood was thrown back to reveal Mariana.

The confusion in his mind melted to the warm reassurance of love. He looked around to see if she was alone, almost expecting Leonor to be there as she had been so long ago when they were young lovers. But there was no one else. He rushed to her drawing her in a tight embrace, filling himself with the scent and sense of her, then drew away and gazed at her. Her face was passive, calm, she seemed part of the shadows of the mosque, a tranquil steady permanence, as eternal as time.

There were questions he wanted to ask, should ask, about her safety, the safety of her family. Gratitude for having saved him. But he wanted to hold on to the silence of their being.

Eventually it was Mariana who spoke. "I heard about your ordeal . . . the Inquisition . . ."

"I have known worse."

"Your voice . . ."

"My throat is better. How is it for you and the children?"

"We are safe."

"Are you sure . . ."

"Safe," she asserted. "I am a Marquesa, my son a Marqués, they would not dare touch us," she lied, gazing at the drawn weather-beaten face, so different from the soft smoothness of innocence that had radiated so much here many years ago. She reached up and touched the leather skin, her finger tracing a line over the thick greying beard on his cheek down to his lips. Emotion gripped her at the thought of the wasted years, and she bit back the tears.

"We lost . . ." he began, but the finger pressed on his lips to stop him speaking of the past. He pulled her closer to him, and in the dark folds of his cloak she allowed the emotions to run freely, her body shuddering with each sob that memories, passions and hopes tore from her.

"I will come back," he promised to comfort her. "We shall live the life we were meant to live. You and me, and the children. We'll leave Spain, find somewhere else, and I'll become the farmer I should have been . . ." The words were hollow echoes of past undertakings that disappeared in the vortexes of time.

She gently pushed herself from him. "I weep like a young bride," she whispered.

"You always will be."

"And you always the young Knight of the Estremadura," she answered wiping her cheek. She managed to control the emotions. "I know you will return, Francisco," she said forcing a smile. "This time I'll wait."

"Like a damsel, sewing . . ." he answered.

"Tapestries . . ." she muttered forcing a smile.

"And shall I wear your colours?"

Without replying she took the small gold cross from round her neck giving it to him.

He hesitated a moment, then took it and slipped it into his side purse. He cupped her face in her hands and brushed his lips against hers.

She fought the emotions welling in her again. "Go, Francisco," she whispered. "Please, Francisco. Go," she repeated. "Let it be like this."

"I love you Mariana."

"And I you," she answered thickly. "And I'll hold your image with me, as you are now . . . until you return." She gazed past him at the silver clouds above the hill-tops. Ghost ships of the night, he had once called them, carrying with them the tears of the world. She looked down at the dark earth and stopped herself from looking at him as he returned to the horses.

She heard him mount, but did not look up until the hooves began to pad away over the soft earth. Then through misted eyes she saw the hazy shadows melt into the night.

"God be with you, Francisco," she whispered, as she had done so long ago, tears scalding her as they had done then.

CHAPTER FIFTEEN

The English Knight

Francisco tried to blot out the memories and emotions that threatened to overwhelm him as he followed Kassim through the darkness. In the hour they had been riding, neither had spoken for fear their conversation would arouse the recriminations of the earlier exchange. But as they neared the outskirts of Seville, veering away from Mendoza's house, he became apprehensive.

"Where are we going?" he demanded.

"To a ship," Kassim told him. "A small craft will take you down to Cadiz, and from there you will be taken by galley to Sicily. It has been arranged."

"A generous captain to run the blockade for one soldier," Francisco muttered warily.

"He has been well paid," Kassim rapped. "And he runs supplies for Malta to Sicily. You will just be another weapon he takes."

His look of disdain embarrassed Francisco. It was obvious he was thinking no matter how loyal he had proved, he was still not trusted, and though he wanted to apologize, he felt, that rightly, Kassim would not accept it. So instead he spurred his horse to a trot, until finally they reached the water's edge.

In the mists of early morning that hung over the lapping waters of the Guadalquivir, Francisco saw a small sailing-boat with some men standing near by in the reeds, and he slowly approached them as he recognized Mendoza, protected from the chill by a heavy woollen cloak. Beside him were three men, whom he could not recognize in the gloom, and he dismounted, approaching them cautiously.

On reaching them, he realized two were sailors, and the third, his head hanging in shame, was Diego.

"What's he doing here?" Francisco demanded.

"Don Francisco," Mendoza greeted him. "Everything is arranged, you must take the boat now to catch the early tide."

"What is Diego doing here?" he repeated, glaring at the forlorn figure, already suspecting the answer would concern the actor's indiscreet nature.

"While you were gone, he came up from the cellar," Mendoza sighed. "He went after my maids. I cannot risk him running back to Seville and doing the same thing."

Francisco shook his head in disappointment, eyeing the bedraggled figure. "In the name of Christ," he roared, "I had only been gone a few hours!"

"I heard them giggling," Diego whined, "their voices like angels', light, sparkling, willing, and in the gloom . . ."

"In the boat!" Francisco ordered.

"I don't want to go to Malta and die!" He protested. "I'm a practising coward, Don Francisco. I'll wither like a eunuch's . . ."

"I'll release you in Sicily," Francisco snarled shoving him to the craft. He turned to Mendoza and apologized, but the old man waved it away.

"I know the captain of the galley," he said watching Diego struggle into the boat. "His name is Simon. He'll get you to Sicily. From there you can make your way to Malta." He pulled some papers from his pouch. "You will travel as Francisco Clementes," he jerked his thumb towards Diego. "I've no papers for him."

"He will travel as my servant."

Along with the papers, Mendoza handed him some money. "It's gold from your wife," he explained. "It'll buy you the equipment you need." As with the apology, he waved away Francisco's thanks. "No gratitude," he said. "It's a favour to the Marquesa and her cousin, no more than that. But if you want to show them gratitude, you will not return to Spain again." There was no recrimination in either his expression or tone, the words delivered almost as a lawyer advising his client. "You have a new name, Don Francisco, and under it you can begin a new life. Let those who hunt you forget you.

But the decision's yours," he said wrapping the cloak closer round him against the chill. "God be with you, Don *Francisco Clementes*."

"And you," Francisco called, making his way after the two seaman, now in the small craft and ready by the oars. "Guard against the Holy Office," he cried as they pulled away.

He gazed at the two hazy figures amidst the smoky reeds on the shore, the tall dignified Jew swathed in his cloak and the Muslim in his exaggerated silks of the Turk. And unconsciously slipped his hand into his side-purse and took the small gold cross Mariana had given him. It glinted in the bleak light, and he envied the two men, despite their precarious situation in a foreign land. For they were closer to her than he might ever be. He glanced up again, but the figures had dissolved in the pale mists.

"Better sit, señor," he heard one of the seaman say as the boat rocked in midstream, the current snatching it. He nodded and eased himself beside Diego.

"Your face looks as grim as my stomach feels," the young man muttered resentfully. "It was not designed for the sea. My stomach I mean."

"This is a river," Francisco rebuked.

"It doesn't know the difference!"

"I'll release you in Messina."

"Messina?" He looked down at his stomach. "Do you hear that? We go to Messina. It doesn't believe you," he complained. "It thinks we will die long before we ever reach there."

Francisco ignored him, concentrating on the cross in his palm.

"Battle colours from your wife?" Diego persisted. "Would that the poor and hungry could live such romantic lives."

"You can win your honours by coming with me," Francisco threatened.

The actor shook his head. "Even you might not be going where you think you are going," he said, then indicated the seamen hauling the oars. "They said that over 30,000 Turks have invested Malta, and the island is about to fall. Their galley is taking arms via Sicily. But the Viceroy refuses to send enough help. Do you still wish to go?"

"Why not?" Francisco said bitterly, his mind preoccupied

by thoughts of Mariana standing in the ruins of the mosque. "Lost causes are the only ones to fight for."

"Jesussss," Diego whistled through his missing teeth, "Why has fate cast me with the lead player in this *comedia*!" He rested his thin hand on Francisco's arm. "Don Francisco," he pleaded. "If I have to play second role in this drama, would you mind if I spoke the better lines in that stentorian tone. I've more training than you."

Francisco shrugged the mocking actor off. "Careful," he cautioned.

"No, Don Francisco," Diego answered seriously. "You be careful, I know when I have stepped from the stage and the swords are no longer wood, but steel. You cannot distinguish between the *comedia* and reality." He shook his head sadly. "The heroes the world has been cursed with, the *real* actors, drag us all down in their cauldrons of boiling hate when they make the grand gesture. It's your type that pulls the crowd along behind them like the *chorus*, choosing their sides to die in glory!"

"I've no side," Francisco retorted savagely. "I relinquished commitment many years ago!"

"You have become a heretic, an apostate," Diego challenged. "That is taking sides, that is as much commitment as the Inquisitor General's himself."

"You are too clever with words, Diego," Francisco warned.

"They are my only defence against steel."

"And they nearly lost you your life at the *ventorro* and in the face of the Inquisition."

Diego shook his head. "That was men's ignorance, not my words. I cannot solve the problem of stupidity with words, I can only comment on it."

What he said irritated Francisco, but no more than his own pompous sentiment of "fighting for lost causes" something he had long since abandoned. Yet he did not want to discuss either himself or his motivations with Diego, and if they were to travel to Sicily it would be better to clear things up now, before the young man provoked him as he had done the seaman in the *ventorro* when they first met.

"I am a simple man, Diego," he said quietly. "I can just about read, know little of the arts and less of philosophy," he

161

paused staring into the pale eyes fixed on him. The mocking humour was gone from them. "My profession was thrust on me by fate," he continued, "and I am neither proud nor ashamed of it. But simplicity enables me not to shrink from its demands. If I ever lose that simplicity, I will become vulnerable and die. In my profession, Diego, a man can never give a bad performance, there is no second act to return and improve. Do you understand me?" The nod confirmed it. "No man can practise my profession when his mind is encumbered by the confusions of right and wrong. That hampers judgement, and already I have found my judgement impaired," he glanced at the cross in his hand. "Don't confuse me with your remarks, Diego, the complications of right or wrong already concern me. And don't provoke me for both our sakes. Is that clear?" Francisco turned from him to the cross.

Diego studied the broad face, its scar and creases revealing a troubled past he could barely conceive. The head with its thick grey hair and beard rested on his chest, as the dark eyes concentrated on the cross, tiny in the huge palm. In the past three days, he had felt this giant man just another actor ready to seize the chance to play the lover or hero when occasion demanded. But here in the lace haze and liquid metal waters, he felt a presence that made him uneasy, as though the giant transmitted not only the years of darkness he had spent in battle, but experiences beyond that time, before he was born, in the future, and long after they were both dead. And for a moment, that awful sensation emptied his mind of words. Care, Diego, he warned himself. You let the scenery and props carry you away. Play the role passively. This will only last till Messina, and then you go off-stage.

Yet as the oars dipped and splashed, a strange foreboding came over him.

Francisco boarded the galley, and memories of his capture on such a vessel returned as the stench of decay rose from the wretches chained six to a bench. Their hollow yellow faces gazed emptily at the deck as their bodies draped over the massive oars like flimsy rags left to dry.

He looked up at the bows, where on the *rambades*, the raised platform of the crews' quarters, he saw sailors lashing the cargo to be taken on to Sicily.

The short powerful figure organizing them, jumped down and bustled over to him, barging a deck officer out of the way as he did so. "Simon," he announced reaching them. "Captain Simon. Who're you and what d'you want?"

The dark bearded face, blackened by the sun, reflected both the harsh life of a galley captain, and the irascibility of a master readying his vessel. The salt stained doublet and yellowed ruff hanging loosely round his neck looked out of place aboard the spartan conditions of the ship.

"I am Francisco Clementes," Francisco said using the alias Mendoza had given him. "This is my servant Diego." He handed the documents the Jew had given him. "Juan Mendoza sent us."

"Sail within the hour," Simon growled, pushing away the documents. "You sure you want to go to Sicily?" Francisco nodded. "You know Dragut's corsairs are sweeping the seas," Simon stated. There was no reply, and he shrugged. "You live up there, on the *rambades* with the crew," he said pointing to the platform. The short powerful arm then swung aft to the stern, the poop deck, by a dirty canvas awning. "Officers' quarters. Need me, that's where I am." Diego looked along the narrow vessel, thinking there was hardly anywhere else he could be.

"I don't know what you're wanted for," Simon continued, "an' don't care. But another pair of hands to wield a weapon is useful." Without waiting for a comment he pushed past them waddling down to the poop deck.

Francisco made his way for'ard to the bows, the dejected Diego shuffling after him, glancing apprehensively at the human debris chained to the oars.

The sailors scuttling around the ship paid scant attention to them, concentrating on getting the vessel ready and avoiding the rage of the two deck officers.

"The most passive audience I've ever played to," he said to Francisco as he settled alongside him on the planks, and gazed down at the rows of soulless faces and thin bodies hanging over the oars.

Francisco did not answer, but felt an affinity to those who

163

would have to drive themselves for ten- or fifteen-hour stretches, becoming so burned by the sun it would be difficult to distinguish between Moor and Christian. These, he reasoned, as on other galleys, were probably a mixture of prisoner and captured slave, as he had been. Their sustenance would be bread soaked in sour wine, and unless freed by battle or ransom, they would spend what few years they had dragging the poles they were fettered to. "Do all galleys smell like this?" he heard Diego ask. "Like a rotting corpse," he said unconsciously. "Yes. But the breeze will ease it when we move. If not, I'll get tobacco to plug our nostrils."

Diego looked across the bay where carracks and caravels rested. Their tall masts and high stout castles giving them a solid more dependable appearance than the fragile galleys around them. "Why couldn't we travel on one of those?" he complained.

"They're massing a fleet for the Indies," Francisco answered. "They won't waste them running the risk of Dragut's raiders in the Mediterranean."

"Who is Dragut?" Diego asked, not really sure that he wanted to know the answer as he became convinced that any question would only be greeted with bad news.

"Dragut's a corsair, a pirate, raiding out of Barbary, and at eighty he's the best admiral in the Mediterranean. His vessels are fast, his men well trained, only Romegas can match them."

"Romegas?" Diego echoed despite himself.

"The Admiral of the Knights' fleet. His galleys are sleek, with a shallow draught, and can spin in their own length."

"Like this one?" Diego muttered hopefully. Francisco's grin told him they were nothing like the vessel they were on, and he wiped the sweat from his brow with a shaking palm. "I'd sooner risk the flames," he mumbled.

"You might have to," Francisco replied indicating the tall imposing figure in velvet doublet and soft hat being led towards them by an officer.

"The Holy Office," Diego gasped. "I take back what I said about the flames. Holy Mary, I take it back!"

But the baggage being dragged behind the stranger by one of the crew, suggested another passenger. And from his clothes and appearance he looked a northerner.

"A companion for you," the officer growled on reaching them, then motioned that the stranger should take his place up alongside them.

The man climbed on to the *rambades*, took his chest from the seaman, hauled it up, then settled beside them. "Sir William Howard," he announced as he sat.

"Don Francisco Clementes. This is my servant Diego."

At the term *servant* Diego raised an eyebrow, but resisted comment. Francisco studied the lined face. It was pale, almost delicate for a man who must have been at least fifty. The short pointed beard and pepper hair were neatly trimmed, and the clear blue eyes showed no threat.

"You travel to Sicily?" the stranger asked, his Spanish laced with a thick accent. "And I," he said in response to Francisco's nod. He shifted uncomfortably on the hot planks.

"An uncomfortable trip for two *gentlemen*," Diego observed.

"Few vessels travel the Mediterranean," Sir William answered, addressing Francisco.

"Because of Dragut's galleys," Diego suggested remembering Francisco's earlier words.

The stranger nodded, still ignoring him and referring himself to Francisco. "The Turk is a deadly enemy to all true believers," he sighed. "The Turk and heretic. Was Christianity ever so plagued with a more dangerous pestilence?"

The mention of *heretics* shook Diego. Their position was precarious enough without reference to that subject. "The Muslim is a far worse enemy," he blurted. "At least the heretic can be converted back. I mean he is close already . . ."

His voice trailed off under the cold blue eyes on him, and Diego turned his attention to the slaves.

"I see you are plagued yourself . . ." Sir William smiled at Francisco, "with a talkative servant."

Francisco nodded.

"My master . . ." Diego began.

"I had thought of having his tongue cut out," Francisco interrupted, "but then I wouldn't enjoy his cries for mercy when I beat him," he muttered pointedly. "How long have you been in Seville?" he quickly asked Sir William, wondering if the stranger had attended the *auto da fé*. The answer of two days relieved him, and he watched the stranger whose interest was now taken with the crew raising the lateen sail up the short mast. "Have you travelled on a galley before?" Francisco asked.

"Why?"

"Your accent is northern, English I think, and these vessels are only suitable for the calmer waters of the south. Only a galleon or a carrack can negotiate the northern seas."

"I am half-English," he admitted. "My mother was French, and I live in Provence. England has been no place for those who believe since she broke with Rome. And yes, I have travelled in galleys before."

Francisco glanced down at his hands. They were hard and broad and he fancied beneath the velvet clad sleeves there would be equally muscular arms so different from the narrow delicately lined face that now fixed on him. The pale eyes showed a brief hint of recognition that made him wary, worse it was followed by the inevitable question of whether they had met before.

"I doubt it," Francisco quickly answered. "I have never been outside of Spain other than the Indies."

Sir William slowly shook his head. "No," he said pensively, "I have never been there."

"All men look alike," Diego interrupted, as anxious as Francisco that this stranger had not heard of *el cobarde*. "I am . . . or at least *was*, an actor. And in the *comedias* I learnt that a mask, a tint, a trick of the light, can so blend a face that Jesus, Mary, or the Devil resemble one anoth . . ." he checked under the stranger's glare at his blasphemy. "I mean in features," he added hastily.

"I told you his tongue needed cutting out," Francisco muttered.

"It surely does," Sir William agreed turning his attention to the preparations for sailing.

The short lateen sail flapped feebly in the gentle breeze. The air was suddenly pierced with a shrill whistle followed by another as the signal was given for the slaves to take up their oars.

Chains clanked, men groaned, and blocks and cordage creaked as the two deck officers cracked their whips, the oarsmen swung into action.

The human appendages to the huge poles leaned forward in drilled unison, a foot on the stretcher, another on the bench in front, then with a moan drawn from the depths of despair, they heaved on the oars, easing the galley from the harbour, gradually beating a rhythmic metre that increased as the vessel pulled out into the glittering blue expanse.

Diego gaped at the rows of filthy naked human pendulums swinging back and forth, powering the galley through the calm sea, his heart jumping each time the lash ripped through the air landing on a man. "Better the flames," he muttered. "And this time I mean it."

"Perhaps you're right," Francisco agreed.

Sir William watched both men gazing at the misery below them. He had long become inured to the sight having served in the caravans of the Knights of St. John under La Valette and Romegas. "Your compassion does you credit," he observed, surprised by the large man's reaction. The Spaniard had the appearance of a fighting man, he thought, and would surely have been familiar with the galleys. But there was no reply to his comment. "They're slaves," Sir William asserted. "Some captured Turks who would offer us no better if the position was reversed."

"Then God help us both," Diego whispered.

In the days that passed, Sir William told them he was a Knight of St. John on his way to Sicily to join a relief force that the Viceroy had planned to send to the besieged island. And from the news Admiral Romegas' galleys smuggled past the blockade, he had learned that Grand Master La Valette had prepared well for the siege, having had the defences of Grand Harbour rebuilt and strengthening the three forts of St. Elmo, St. Angelo, and St. Michael to compensate for the lack of the defenders' manpower.

Sir William estimated that about 600 Knights were being supported by less than 10,000 soldiers and Maltese, while Suleiman had amassed an army of more than 30,000 trained men, including Spahis from Anatolia, Karamania and Romania, Iayalars from the Balkans and thousands of levied troops spearheaded by the best of them all – 6,300 Janissaries. Their armada consisted of nearly 200 ships transporting siege guns, food, ammunition and supplies as there would be nothing to sustain them on the arid sandstone rock of Malta.

He explained that he himself had been living in France as it was no longer safe for Knights of the Order to live in an England ruled by the Protestant Queen Elizabeth, and that many Knights had left at the time of her father Henry, to seek refuge in Rome, when the King broke with the Pope, their lands like those of the monasteries seized by the crown. Now, like others, he was answering the call that had gone out to aid the Order.

And in the four broiling days in the confines of the galley they talked of where they had been, wars they had taken part in, with Francisco maintaining his battle experience came from serving with the *tercios*, the Spanish regiments, in the Indies. His story was that he had only just arrived back in Spain when he heard of the Knights' intended defence of Malta, and as a true believer he wanted to join the relief. Yet he was sure the Englishman was not convinced.

During this time Diego lived in a moaning misery as the fierce heat, stench from the vessel and its continuous motion plagued him. He hardly ate, and when he did his stomach rejected the food. And on the second day out, when they had sighted a galley on the horizon, he added fear to his list of miseries.

Though the vessel made no attempt to challenge them, Diego's fears were increased by the Englishman changing into an Italian corslet of armour and Francisco donning a brigantine – a leather jerkin – and drawing a broadsword from the supplies the galley took to Sicily.

Francisco's battledress increased the suspicions the Englishman had of him. The dark brooding face, long greying hair and beard and powerful frame implied more than just the paid trooper he said he was. His aura was that of the individual, not that of a faceless ranker in King Felipe's *tercios* who was of no more consequence than the powder and shot he used.

And in the passing days, he remembered a story of a rogue Knight who had shown cowardice in battle and been expelled from the Order. He recalled the man had disappeared for a time, later to re-emerge in France and the low countries as a mercenary on the side of the heretics. He had also heard stories, in Spain, of how this man had mystical powers given to him by Satan. It was possible that the heretic and the man he sailed with were the same. But on a galley in the middle of the sea, it was unwise to make accusations. There would be opportunity enough in Sicily.

In the sweltering heat of the fourth afternoon at sea, Francisco lay on the blistering planks of the *rambades* only vaguely aware of the splashing oars as aching bodies dragged them through the waters. He wanted to close his mind to his surroundings and let it take him to the peaceful stream where in the cool of the Andalusian evening he had lain with Mariana. He wanted to ease himself into her to smother his doubts, confirm his existence with her love.

There is only you, Mariana, he said to himself, then there is nothing. No light, no warmth, just a void of pain. I will never leave you again. If I live through this one last ordeal, I will be with you always. Will you take a man whose soul has almost been taken from him by barbarism? Will you take this scarred body and heal it with your love? Bathe it in your kisses? He looked at the cross in his palm as though it would provide an answer.

The look-out's call jolted him.

"Galley! To the west! Galley!"

He scrambled to his feet to join Diego and the Englishman already concentrating on the distant threat. While around them the crew scurried, and the deck officers lashed the slaves into extra effort.

Screwing his eyes up against the glare, Francisco made out the unmistakable lines of a high-prowed Turkish raider. Around them, men were loading the bowchaser and smaller cannon, making ready the ballistas to catapult coals and stones, and the smell of charcoal filled the air as a brazier next to them was lit for incendiaries. Francisco watched half-a-dozen men fumbling with arquebuses, muskets, which would be useless against the fast-firing Muslim bowmen at close range. He glanced at the broad lateen sail hanging dry and limp, the first target for fire arrows. "Get that damned sail down!" he yelled at some seamen scuttling to the prow. "Get rid of those sails or we'll burn!"

169

"Get shields from the cargo," the Englishman shouted to a sailor passing. "We'll need cover from fire arrows!"

"Who's giving orders on my vessel! Who d'you think you are giving orders on my ship?" Simon roared hurrying to them. "Leave it up!" he roared to the men lowering the sail. "We'll outrun her!" His next order was stifled by Francisco grabbing his collar.

"You can't outrun a corsair in this tub!" he snarled. "That's not a lumbering galleass, it's a *galliot* out there. Half the weight and twice as fast. She's rigged for war, and trained for the chase!"

"Listen to him," Sir William shouted. "Your only chance is to surprise her. Close in and throw everything you've got. I've sailed under Romegas in the Knights' caravans; this bucket has no chance in a race!"

Simon looked at the steady progress of the galleass as she made for them. His passengers were right, he decided, they stood no chance against that sleek hull. "What d'you suggest, *admirals?*" he mocked.

"Slow down," Francisco advised releasing him. "Let her close. Then make your left bank of oars back-paddle and your right bank pull hard to turn on her. If we surprise her, we'll shower her, burn her out of the water!"

"Do what he says," the Englishman snapped. "It's your only chance."

Without waiting for Simon's agreement, Francisco ordered a fire-party. "Soak everything in sea water," he ordered. He caught a glimpse of Diego, petrified at the engagement. "Diego! Go with the fire-party. Fill everything with water. Drench anything that ignites. And don't panic!"

"Too late," Diego retorted, "I'm panicking now!"

"Manoeuvre us out of the sun," Sir William ordered the deck officer. The man merely looked to Simon for confirmation.

"Do as he says!" the captain roared, the conviction of his two passengers persuading him they had more experience against corsairs.

"Concentrate your missiles on her awnings aft," Francisco ordered taking his broadsword from the deck. "That's where her officers are. Without them order will disintegrate. Do you understand!"

Before Simon could answer, the Englishman was at him. "Have you Greek fire, Trumps, *Sachetti*?" Simon's silence told him he had not.

"In the name of God," roared Sir William, "this *is* a galley, isn't it!"

"Use coals, anything that will burn," Francisco said. "You've four barrels of brandy. Combine two ballistas, wrap lighted rags round the barrels and fire them. They'll ignite."

"Fire *brandy*?" the captain echoed incredulously.

"Within an hour you'll have no ship and be dragging one of those oars on the corsair if you don't!" Francisco roared, steadying himself as the galley lurched to the oars that now pulled her round out of the glaring sun.

The Englishman looked at the corsair bearing down on them, gliding through the waters steadily like a giant sea serpent. He estimated she was making four knots, a good battle speed. "God, they know their business," he muttered.

"So do we," Francisco answered. "Keep seven good men on your vessel and stay with them, captain. Don't let them board the corsair, and make sure you protect those slaves!"

"Compassion!" Simon sneered.

"Battle is a state of mind, captain!" Francisco roared. "If your slaves feel vulnerable you won't be able to control them. They must be convinced we'll win, or they'll panic and revolt!"

"D'you want the bow or stern?" Sir William asked Francisco drawing his sword.

"You can have the honour of the officers in the poop," Francisco answered. "I'll take her bows. Pick eight men, I'll take the rest." Now, he could clearly see the scarlet silken awning over the poop deck which shielded her officers from the sun. Emblazoned on it was a white-pointed star and crescent.

He also became aware of the rhythmic splash of her oars hitting the water in perfect time to the sound of the overseers' gong. Shrill whistles punctuated the air as she thrust at them. But now she was further to their stern as they shifted position, and had lost her chance of ramming.

The manoeuvre Francisco made them execute was the classic Knights' feint in turning on their pursuers. In a

171

shallow draught galley with a trained crew there would be no problems. But Francisco could only guess what might happen with untrained men. He glanced at the strained sweltering bodies being driven by the lash. "Let them rest!" he ordered. "They'll need their strength to turn her. Just hold course and drift!"

Behind he heard the Englishman instructing the sailors how they would board the corsair and where. He exhorted them to fight threatening the terror of the galley if they did not, and promising riches if they did.

The cracks of whips had ceased, the sails lowered, their oarsmen held the course. Francisco prayed the Turks did not expect them to take offensive action, and were overconfident and reckless. Suddenly he heard her bowchaser roar, the ball passing harmlessly over them and crashing into a fountain of spray ahead. Smaller cannon shots crackled, but the missiles fizzled either side of them. They were lucky, he thought, the corsair was eager, her marksmanship slack, and head on, her armoury counted for little. It was only broadside on that she could be totally effective in fire power. Perhaps they think we are going to surrender, he mused, or maybe anticipate an easy prize and want us intact.

He eyed her until she was five boat lengths away, then shouted to the deck officers. "Ready?" The left bank of oars rose. A shot blasted into the planking splintering the decks and gunwales, but there was no panic. Francisco pointed his blade at the officers. "Now!" he roared. "*Now!*"

Furiously the slaves began to row, the lash flying across them as they heaved on the giant poles. "In unison!" Francisco urged. "In unison!"

He had underestimated the will of frightened men. The ploy was working, slowly the galley turned in the calm waters. A quivering hiss filled the air as a cascade of fire arrows were released, soaring into the clear skies, then plummeting, peppering the decks. The Turk knew they would fight, he thought "Fire-party!" he called, and was relieved at the speed the decks were drenched in hissing seawater. Sporadic fires were doused as they made the turn. Now they faced the corsair.

"Row alongside her!" Francisco ordered. "Get right alongside her!"

"Gunners!" Sir William ordered. "Catapults!" He eyed the men on the anti-personnel weapons. "Wait till we're alongside!"

Missiles still rained, while their slaves dragged on the oars until a boat-length away they heard the yells of the corsair's crew, and saw the rushing midships in confusion at their tactics.

"Fire!" The Englishman roared. "Fire!"

Ball, shot, and incendiaries poured from the galley with the two barrels of brandy hurtling ablaze like meteors, crashing into the awnings, spraying flames, devouring the scarlet silk into an inferno.

"Grappling hooks!" Simon yelled to his sailors.

"Draw your oars," Sir William ordered the deck officers. "Draw your oars!"

Through the choking smoke, hooks were slung across hauling the galleys towards one another.

"Board them!" Francisco roared. "Those with me for'ard!"

"Aft!" Sir William cried. "Get their captain!"

Amid the slashing confusion, screams and cries rent the corsair as steel scythed through flesh and decks drenched crimson. Francisco became numb, his body impervious to pain, oblivious to anything but the drill of swinging the double-handed blade, to lunge, chop, parry, and wield in lethal slicing arcs that a lifetime of experience had ingrained.

Diego watched in horror from the decks of the Spanish galley, as men flung themselves at one another fears and emotions submerged in blinding ferocity. And cutting his way forward he saw the giant figure of Francisco del Valle. His sword wheeling and swinging as though it had a life of its own, the man holding it merely hanging on to prevent it flying from him to wreack its own path of destruction. Francisco had been wrong, he thought, when he told the captain that war was a state of mind. It was the suspension of being!

In the still, azure expanse a black pall of smoke hung over the crematorium which had once been a ship. Their own galley, littered with exhausted broken bodies eased from her. No triumphant cheers, no excitement in dividing the spoils, just

173

the oppressive stillness of the aftermath of battle. Francisco stood on the poop deck gazing at the black cloud that marked their *victory*. "It worked," he heard the Englishman beside him say. "They didn't know what hit them."

"Is that how it always is?" Diego asked sadly, still dwelling on the gruesome end when the prisoners were executed.

"Always," Francisco muttered.

"For what!" he cried.

"Survival," Sir William asserted as he looked at the blood-stained brigantine Francisco wore. "You know your trade," he said admiringly.

"I'm a good butcher," Francisco answered trying to shut his ears to the moans of the wounded.

"When I was in France, Spain, and even Malta," Sir William commented, "I heard of a soldier, a mercenary who fought with the fury of ten and wielded a broadsword like others handle a sabre. There must be few who could handle such a weighty cumbersome weapon like that." Francisco did not answer. "This man," Sir William continued, "the man I heard about, wasn't in the ranks of the *tercios*, but an individual warrior. They said he was a heretic, an Antichrist."

"What about him?" Francisco growled menacingly.

"Malta would welcome such heretics," the Englishman smiled as he made his way back to the bows.

Diego still gazed at the burning boat now fading into the distance. "Will Malta be like that?" he asked Francisco.

"Worse," he sighed. "Much worse."

CHAPTER SIXTEEN

Torture

Alonso de Rojas gazed out across the valley at the soft undulating hills surrounding the Marquesa's *solar*. The late afternoon sun had ripened the textures of the Andalusian countryside creating a blend of deep colours radiating a warmth so foreign to someone from the north.

"I'm waiting for your answer," he heard Mariana say behind him. "Why have we been subjected to these constant harassments?"

"Your countryside is enticing," he said ignoring her question. "There is a starkness of light in Avila, where I come from. Both in summer and winter there are contrasts, clear contrasts . . . but here there is a blend." He heard Mariana sigh impatiently, but continued. "In the north, there are clear definitions, in colour, ideas and beliefs. Here, everything merges. Moors mingle with Christians, Jews with Moors, the *conversos*, the converted, are indistinguishable from true believers." He shook his head sadly, "It must be the languid climate." He smiled as he turned to her, "Don't you think so?"

She had already gauged the significance in what he was saying in his convoluted manner but determined not to be lured.

"Are you telling me that you have decided to live here, general?" she asked. "And this visit is to let me know that you are to be my neighbour?"

His smile persisted. "I am talking about the nature of the people who live in warm friendly climates. But the purpose of my visit is to let you know the progress your ex-husband, Francisco del Valle, has made . . . he paused but there was no response. "A *familiar* . . ."

"An informer of the Inquisition?"

"A *familiar*, friend of the Holy Office, had an acquaintance near here, a servant girl . . ." he motioned towards the eastern hills, "Over there, on the estate beyond those hills . . ."

"Is the story to be long?" Mariana interrupted.

"The girl, the servant, mentioned that her master had a strange guest staying in the villa . . ."

"The Andalusians are very hospitable," Mariana cut in.

"Hospitable indeed, Marquesa," he agreed. "So hospitable that they would take in criminals and heretics!" He paused again, but if the woman felt anything she masked it. "However, this *Andalusian*, was a *converso*, a Jew!"

Mariana remained composed though it was obvious they had Mendoza, but there was no point in saying anything until she knew more. Soon after Francisco had boarded the galley Mendoza came to assure her Francisco was safe. But now her concern was for her friend and Kassim who helped him.

"The name of this *converso*," de Rojas continued, "was Juan Mendoza. Do you know him?"

"If you mean have I seen him, it is possible, if as you say he lived over there."

"We took him a few days ago," he said staring hard at her.

"Mater Deus, ora pro nobis," she muttered.

"A prayer?" he said in surprise, "for a *converso!*"

"For anyone who becomes a prisoner of the Holy Office, it is no secret that it is a death, or living death."

"Not for the innocent!"

"And who decides their innocence, general, you?"

"Your compassion is misdirected, Marquesa. The faithful are safe."

"No one is," she asserted.

"Mendoza was interrogated, Marquesa! He told us of a galley that left ten days ago. Aboard it two men, one of them Francisco del Valle. He admitted everything!"

Mariana tightened her grip on her emotions forcing her attention on the blazing colours of the hills.

"He told us of a Moor who had helped him smuggle del Valle and his accomplice on to a vessel!"

She tried to blot out his voice so as not to be provoked into an outburst which would entrap her. As she concentrated on

176

the changing patterns emblazoned on the vineyards and groves, she wanted to merge herself into them, let them scorch out the fear she felt for her family and the Jew, and Kassim and all those involved.

"Would you know such a Moor!" de Rojas roared.

Slowly she transferred her gaze to him. "I have three Moorish servants," she admitted calmly. "I know many who have a large number. Did you not know, general, Seville was a Moorish city, and their numbers abound. Perhaps if you told me the name of the servant I could help you."

"His name," de Rojas smiled. "We have his name."

She waited.

"Mustapha Saud!"

She stared at him dumbfounded desperately trying to smother her relief and pity for the Jew who must have been taken to the limit of endurance when he finally blurted out the bogus name. He must have gone beyond what friendship asked to make de Rojas believe this figment existed. "You will have to look elsewhere," she suggested quietly. "We have no servant of that name."

"And what of Juan Cortez?" de Rojas pressed.

"Juan Cortez?"

"The man who organized del Valle's escape. His friend from the army!"

"I have never heard of him," she said honestly realizing Mendoza had compounded the story by adding another fictitious name to make it convincing.

The general sensed there was something wrong. There was just the merest hint of relief in her expression. He looked at her hands clasped in front of her. The knuckles white from pressure. "Perhaps the Jew lied," he muttered.

"It's possible," she agreed. "Under torture one would say anything, I have no need to tell you that." She forced the words, "Why not proceed with your tortures, see if the infliction of even greater pain produces greater truth or greater lies."

"The Jew is dead," he said carefully. "Unlike *el cobarde* he could not withstand the excruciating agony . . ."

"General!" Mariana snapped, aware of his goading, "If you have no respect for your rank or yourself, at least have some

177

for me!" The fury mounted. "I suggest you find the men Mendoza named and rack them. Find them. Use the *toca*, the *bastinado*!"

The flood was unstoppable as tears welled in her eyes for the man who had died under such hideous conditions. "Use your torturers and executions in the name of God, and in His name leave me and my family alone. You have harassed us and done everything save accuse and arrest us, because you have no proof other than fifteen years ago I was married to Don Francisco!" Her voice rose hysterically. "I am petitioning the King to help me be rid of your persecution. I swear de Rojas I will not let this rest until he imprisons you!" Hot tears rolled down her cheeks and her voice carried across the hills. "This obsession will consume you. It will burn you up as sure as your fires consume!"

She broke off as someone rushed up to her. It was Ruiz.

"Leave my mother alone!" he cried. "Leave us all alone. Take your soldiers and get off our land!"

For a moment de Rojas stood motionless, gazing at them in the flames of the setting sun, then relented. "When you write to the King, Marquesa," he said in an even tone, "tell him he will find me in Sicily where del Valle's galley was bound. You may also tell His Highness I will run *el cobarde* to the ground, and this time there will be no ceremony when I kill him!"

Mariana pulled Ruiz tighter to her, but said nothing.

De Rojas brushed past them as he strode on towards the *solar*. And neither spoke for moments after the spectre had disappeared, then Ruiz broke the silence.

"Why has he gone to Sicily?" he asked releasing himself from his mother's arm.

"Your father is joining the Knights to fight in Malta."

"Francisco del Valle, *el cobarde*?"

"Yes," she sighed. "*El cobarde*." She waited tensely for the usual reaction from him and his denial that Francisco was his father, but there was none.

Ruiz stared at his mother, her face taut, ready for his reaction, but determined to retain control. He had heard what de Rojas had put her through, and in the past days had sat tight lipped while his aunt, Leonor, had recounted the story of how his mother had brought him from the Estremadura to

178

Andalusia, and though he had preferred not to believe it, part of him yielded. Too many had been willing to sacrifice themselves for the powerful stranger that had visited them those fateful days, and though he found it difficult to accept, he understood that whether Francisco del Valle was his father or not, he was at least a man to respect. When they had tried to humiliate him by making him wear the *sanbenito* at his trial, it was his judges who had lost respect in the face of his silent dignity. And the story Leonor told of his supposed disgrace in Tripoli no longer rang true with the simple story played out in the *auto* which described his part in that war. Whoever del Valle was, he thought, he was not a man to be ashamed of. Especially now as he had gone to fight the Turks in Malta.

Tentatively he put out his hand, and his heart stopped. For a terrible moment he thought his mother would refuse it.

Then slowly she took it and squeezed it.

Neither spoke as they made their way back to the house.

CHAPTER SEVENTEEN

Sicily, Messina

Francisco lay on the straw mattress in the bare room he had rented in a *pensión* on the fringes of Messina. The heat of the afternoon had silenced everything. Man, animal, and insect had disappeared to avoid the relentless late June sun that beat like a hammer on an anvil during the day, trebling its strokes as the hours wore on.

He had spent nearly three weeks on the island waiting, like many other volunteers, for the vacillating Viceroy of Sicily, Don Garcia de Toledo, to give permission for ships and men to sail to the relief of Malta.

Francisco had kept in touch with what was happening through Sir William Howard whose respect and confidence he had earned in the action against the corsair, and from what the Englishman told him there appeared to be no more than 700 men ready to embark for the beleaguered island. Six hundred infantry, 40 Knights, and an assortment of *gentlemen* and adventurers. La Valette would welcome their help, but it would have no effect on the outcome against the host Suleiman had sent. His 30,000 troops were under the direction of Admiral Piali and Mustapha Pasha; the young Admiral having earned a formidable reputation in raids on Italy and the capture of Djerba, and Mustapha Pasha was skilled in both land and siege warfare. There was also news that Dragut, the Barbary corsair, had arrived despite his eighty years, to add weight with over 1,500 Algerians. But it was rumoured that the old man had been mortally wounded in directing an attack on St. Elmo, the first of three forts to come under assault.

The news was being smuggled from the island by Maltese fishermen who sailed their boats from creeks and coves to the island of Linosa where the reports were relayed to Sicily. Therefore what they heard was days old, and Francisco was well aware a moment in battle could reverse a situation.

Nevertheless, it appeared that the Turks had concentrated their fire on the outlying fortress of St. Elmo at the foot of Mount Sciberras across from the Grand Harbour. In theory the fort should have fallen in eight days, but it had now lasted a month, and Francisco could imagine the privation and suffering there.

Sometimes the wind carried on it the sounds of summer thunder as the guns, thirty leagues away on the island, pounded the fort. The giant basilisks the Turk used so effectively in sieges to powder the walls of defences roared their warning far across the straits to those who thought of aiding their comrades. Perhaps, Francisco mused, it was that sound that held the Viceroy back from sending relief.

Once Malta fell, it would be the stepping stone to Sicily, then Europe. Garcia de Toledo must have been well aware that soon he might need all the supplies and men he could muster to fight a replica of the battle being waged when after Malta the Turks concentrated on his own island, Sicily.

The Englishman had told Francisco that he believed the Turks were tactically naive, attempting to wear each stronghold down one at a time. The battle centred around Grand Harbour with the Turks ignoring Medina the old capital in the middle of the island.

La Valette had grouped his forces in three points. Two thousand men in St. Elmo, and the rest across on the two spurs of land jutting into the harbour, Fort St. Michael on the promontory of Senglea, then across the creek, parallel, on the spur where the village of Birgu was situated, backed by Fort St. Angelo. Thus the defenders had their backs to the sea and faced attacks from the high rocky sandstone mainland with Turks firing down on them.

The prospect was grim with only 500 Knights and a few thousand regulars to defend the position. However, the natives, despite the antipathy of the Maltese nobility for the arrogant Knights who had taken over their island, were supporting them against their traditional enemy, having been subjected to constant raids and pillaging over the centuries.

181

As Francisco lay mulling over Sir William's information, it was the thought of never seeing Mariana again that disturbed him more than the dangers and privations ahead.

He held up the small cross which he seemed to have spent all his time gazing at as though it radiated her warmth. And as he stared at it, he could see the images of the formal party in which he had first been introduced to her.

Her family, Leonor, his father, were all in a large room in her house in Seville. Everyone restrained, forcing polite conversation, imprisoned by the stifling traditions of *visiting* that conversation demanded. Mariana quiet, but exchanging amused glances with Leonor, while her father and his spoke of *matters of importance* without ever mentioning a contract of marriage between their children. Francisco wondered if that image, of the petite girl whose hair shone like silk, and eyes reflected her bright intelligence, had been the one he had carried with him for all those years. If it had been, it was now replaced with that of the mature woman whose gentle compassion infused him with love and mellowed the savagery that had infused him in fifteen years of war.

"I want to come back to you, Mariana," he whispered gazing at the twisting gleaming cross on the chain. "Ease the violence and pain from me. Let me live as I had hoped, as a man, not a war machine, an appendage to a scything blade." The wasted years had produced nothing but blood to irrigate lands that had absorbed more than their share of it, he thought. And as he looked at the cross he saw the scar that ran from his wrist to his arm. He tried to remember when and where he had got the wound. He could not. Like others on him, he could only vaguely guess what caused them. But he had forgotten what *issue* was being fought over at the time. He had pitched himself into battles whose reason he had either ignored or couldn't remember. And from it all, only fragments of images remained. A victim's expression reflected in flames; processions of ragged people emerging from smoking ruins; the shriek of a mount as it fell; hiding in reeds from a hunting-party . . . just a confusion of events that stained the soul and steeled emotions to the most terrible of Man's excesses.

Yet now he prepared to follow the same course. Cut down

men hardly different from himself. Take part in another cause he barely believed in. Had it not been a Muslim and Jew who had helped him escape?

A knock on the door interrupted his thoughts. He got up and opened it. It was the Englishman. Francisco acknowledged him, walked back to the mattress and wearily sat down.

"This heat is as bad as Malta," Sir William complained wiping rivulets of sweat from his face and going to the window which offered no relief. "Have you seen anything of Diego, your man?" he asked looking out.

"Since I gave him part of the prize from the galley, he has disappeared."

"If you see him, tell him to be careful. My sources tell me there is an Inquisitor-General on his way here from Spain. He'd apparently tried to sail earlier but couldn't get a vessel."

"Alonso de Rojas?"

The Englishman nodded. "But take comfort; we have four galleys under the command of Don Juan de Cardona, and our force will be landed under the command of Chevalier de Robles, a good man, I've fought alongside him."

"And will they protect me and Diego from de Rojas?"

Sir William smiled, "There is no need to. We sail tomorrow." Francisco's anxious expression surprised him. "What's wrong? I thought you would be pleased after these three weeks."

Francisco got up and walked over to the window by him. He looked out at the green mountains that swept up from the sea. "I'm no longer sure I have the conviction."

"Pope Pius has granted plenary indulgence to all those taking part in this war!" Sir William exclaimed. 'Whatever your crimes this will mean you'll be beyond the powers of those who condemn you, don't you understand?"

Francisco remained silent.

"Don't you realize that no one will be able to threaten you again, if you come through Malta?" The Spaniard's reticence irritated him. "Look, I know it's not fear for your own safety that would change your mind . . ."

"How do you know?"

"From your action on the galley. Perhaps you lack conviction in the cause. But you must believe in your own future if God grants one, and your participation in this war will assure it."

"Do you know what they call me?" Francisco challenged.

"I don't want to." The older man retorted not wanting confirmation of Francisco's alleged heresy. "Three weeks ago we became brothers in arms. For me, your existence began then. What happened before is of no concern to me. And what happens in the future only concerns you!" He glanced at the cross that dangled from his hand. "And the one who gave you that cross you so often hold." He went over to the door and opened it, "Your name is registered with the relief force and you can join the galley whenever you wish. Take this opportunity to rid yourself of the past and help raise the spirits of those who are doomed without us."

"You think 700 will make a difference?" Francisco said grimly.

"In numbers, no. But our brothers live suspended between existence and non-existence, and I believe you, more than any other, know what that means. So you can gauge what can be gained from realizing you are not alone, and that the sacrifice was, and will be worth it."

There was no response.

"Within four days, Don Francisco, it will be the Feast of Corpus Christi, a day especially sacred to the Order of St. John. Be with us on that day. Be with us in body and spirit!"

The mention of the feast prompted memories of obligations undertaken so long ago in his past. "You will fight with the English Langue," Francisco asked almost grudgingly, realizing that he would never again be able to fight alongside the Castilian Langue, yet surprised the thought troubled him.

Sir William shook his head.

"I told you, my father was English, my mother French. I will fight under her name alongside the Knights of Provence. This is a time for all of us to adopt new lives . . . even at our age." He said as he left.

He watched the door close, then crushed his hand hard round the cross in his palm, and as he turned he saw the large double-handed sword in its scabbard by the mattress. His stomach churned. In the silence of the room his ears rang with he chant of *el cobarde* hurled down at him like boiling oil from the parapets of the garrison at Tripoli. "I owe them nothing,' he muttered, "And yet I go. There was never any doubt. Why? To fulfil a vow? Is it really to fulfil a vow? Do I still value such obligations?" He closed his eyes as beads of sweat trickled into them, stinging them like tears. "And yet I join them . . ." he whispered. "Why . . .?"

The following day he walked as if in a dream through the narrow empty streets towards the harbour, the island pink in the setting sun. He could hear Mass being celebrated in the churches he passed, but did not go in. Instead, he continued on down to the shore where the swish of the waves and call of the gulls created a peace that belied the storm raging just beyond the straits. He stopped some way from the assembly point where the four shallow draught galleys swayed empty in the lapping waters guarded by a few soldiers. None of the men moved or spoke, appearing lost in the thoughts that preoccupied men from the time they took weapons to wage war with their neighbours.

Their helmets, cuirasses and tall pikestaffs burnished by the dying rays, human torches flaring their warning of the fires to come.

From the small church near by he heard voices straining *Gloria in Excelsis Deo*, but he knew that in the hearts of those that sang, the communion they experienced was that of man with himself. A special communion known only by combatants about to join battle, where Man reached deep into himself searching for answers that only the clash of arms could provide. And no other experience would create that sense of total isolation. Christian and Muslim might believe in the Paradise of an after life, but it was at moments like this when the conviction quivered under the scrutiny of the eve of battle.

He took a deep breath, then ambled towards the soldiers. "Francisco Clementes," he announced approaching the officer of the troop, "A volunteer."

The man gave a cursory glance to the list in his hand, then motioned towards a galley.

There was no need for a careful check, Francisco thought.

185

The names of the volunteers had been registered earlier, and those who wanted to go along with them would be welcomed

He made his way on to the vessel and settled on the platform of the *rambades* where soon he would be joined by hundreds of others to experience the full impact of Suleiman's wrath.

A few hours later Francisco was staring at the dark sea separating the two islands. The galley was crowded with troops whose subdued voices blended with the whispers of the waters and splash of the oars. The lights of Sicily were gradually swallowed by night and now he tried to isolate himself from his surroundings to mentally prepare for what lay ahead. His survival in the past had always depended on his ability to detach himself from what was round him and fight in that numb state of reaction which created a sense of invincibility.

However, before he could reach that state of withdrawal he heard a familiar voice that startled him. "Don Francisco?" it called. He turned to see someone working their way through two burly soldiers to get to him. And emerging from them in an ill fitting cuirass and lop-sided salade, the po-shaped helmet of Italian soldiers, he recognized the thin pallid features of Diego. The sad face forced a wan smile.

"What in God's name are you doing here?" Francisco hissed as he reached him.

"Being sick."

Francisco dragged him closer.

"Where did you get the cuirass, the armour?"

"Bought it!" he retorted indignantly, "Just as you bought that . . . that . . ."

"Brigantine," Francisco told him, supplying the name of the heavy leather-armoured jerkin he wore. "But what the hell are *you* doing here?"

"I wonder myself now," he answered as his stomach convulsed.

"I gave you 300 ducats as a share of what we took from the corsair. Have you spent it already?"

"I used it for my needs," he replied as he hauled himself

the gunwale in case of an emergency. "The religious fever on these galleys is unbelievable," he gasped as the galley rolled.

"Everywhere there are men leaning over the side saying 'Oh God! Oh Jesus!'"

"It's no joke," Francisco hissed. "What have you done with the money?"

"Most went on wine and women, the rest I wasted."

Francisco shook his head in disappointment. Somehow he was pleased to see the actor again, yet felt he was an added responsibility. "You do know where we're going?"

"Malta."

"Then why are you here?"

Diego tried to rub his stomach through the metal cuirass. "You do not have a monopoly on valour, or duty, *señor*," he protested affronted. "There are *others* who are willing to sacrifice. Just look around you!"

The outburst appeared sincere, but out of character.

"I even went to Mass before we sailed," he asserted. "Did you?" Francisco did not reply. Perhaps, he thought, Sir William was right. This was a rare opportunity for men to change their lives if they survived what lay ahead, and Diego might have seen that himself.

"It was a moving experience," Diego added, "the Mass I mean. After I had played God so many times in town and village squares, I thought I would go to His house to see if He approved." He turned from Francisco and stared at the sea, now phosphorescent in the moonlight. "Besides, I have lived my life as a coward, a profligate, and now the Lord has seen fit to allow me to take part in one final drama which will herald the rebirth of His prodigal son."

Francisco was stunned. It was as if he had read his mind.

"Can I not walk hand in hand with my brothers through the shadow of the valley of death?" Diego said dramatically.

Francisco was not sure whether he was giving a performance, or echoing a sermon he had heard at Mass. But he had never thought of Diego *walking* through the valley of the shadow of death. *Running* perhaps, but not *walking*!

"Mark me, Francisco," Diego continued. "It shall come to pass that a man shall see his brother . . ."

It *was* a sermon that had influenced him, Francisco decided, it must have been. But before he could comment on the miraculous transformation, a booming voice interrupted them.

"Hey, Diego. D'you feel better?"

It came from a sergeant of the Imperial Spanish Guard, who clasped a massive hand on the young man's shoulder, almost felling him.

"I think you have the wrong person," Diego mumbled, looking away. The rebuff only made the sergeant grin even more broadly. Then he called back to some comrades. "He's sobered up!" A guffaw of laughter greeted the announcement, and the actor avoided Francisco's glare.

"They got you drunk," Francisco said despairingly. There was no answer. "Your conversion came in a *ventorro* over wine!"

"Brandy," he answered staring at the sea.

"And they rigged you out in that ridiculous uniform and got you to sign up for the relief force?"

"Elegance in war is of no consequence."

"Did they tell you that?" Francisco sighed. "Did they tell you that where we are going you will be expected to fight all day and night if necessary in sapping humidity, and you will have to wear that outsize cuirass and salade to protect you from ball, arrow, spear and splinters. Have you *any* idea of what we face?"

"I'll stand as well as any man!" he responded angrily.

"I've no doubt about it," Francisco said quietly. "But are you prepared to *fall* like most will?"

Diego looked back at the sea, his stomach convulsing yet again. But this time not from sea-sickness, but the thunderous rumble that rolled across the dark waves.

"It's St. Elmo," Francisco muttered, as around him the soft mumbling became an urgent babble. "The Turks must be investing the fortress . . ."

"And the noise?"

"Basilisks and bombards so large a man could sit in their barrels . . . they fire stone and marble to pulverise defences. That's what you heard." Francisco noticed him grip the side to stop himself from trembling, and he shook his head sadly. "Oh Diego, you're so stupid. With all your clever words, you have no sense."

188

"I will face what's coming," he protested weakly. "I will . . . will . . ."

"What?" Francisco asked. "Watch the jaws of hell open, and look down into them?"

The comment was swallowed by another deep rumble that rowled across the sea.

CHAPTER EIGHTEEN

Malta, Mdina and Birgu

From the battlements of the old city of Mdina, Francisc
watched the thousands of camp fires glowing in the langui
night far into the distance, encircling the promontories (
Senglea and Birgu by Grand Harbour, where the defender
had established the fortresses of St. Michael and St. Angelo.

The old city of Mdina had been left untouched since th
siege had begun one month before, its temporary security du
to its position on high ground overlooking the surroundin
countryside. Here the original aristocratic families of Malt
remained along with the population, some Maltese militia an
a force of cavalry which had orders to attack small parties (
Turks, but not meet the enemy in full force.

As soon as they had arrived in Mdina, they heard that S
Elmo, the fortress below Mount Sciberras, had fallen. An
though it was a severe blow, the relief force was grateful tha
they had managed to slip past Admiral Piali's galleys an
land on the northern island of Gozo, then make their wa
through Mustapha Pasha's land patrols to the high citadel (
Mdina. The feat adding to their conviction that God was wit
them in their bid to aid their brothers.

The news of the fall of St. Elmo was kept from Juan d
Cardona who had orders to return with the relief to Sicily
the star fortress capitulated. But Chevalier de Robles, the
land commander was determined to bring whatever aid h
could to the besieged. Their transports had returned to Sicil·
so now they were cut off, their only hope was reaching th
main fortresses of St. Michael and St. Angelo.

As he stood on the battlements watching the flashes an
listening to the boom of cannon not two leagues awa·

Francisco shivered. St. Elmo had cost the Turk 8,000 men, and 1,500 had died in its defence. Atrocity was conducted on both sides, the Turkish Admiral Piali ordering the decapitation and crucifixion of all Knights, save for a handful held for ransom, and having their bodies floated across Grand Harbour to Birgu in a demonstration of what La Valette could expect. In retaliation, the Grand Master had Muslim prisoners decapitated then fired their heads from cannon. And even here in the relative calm of Mdina, the Governor, Don Mesquita, was hanging a Muslim every day from the battlements.

The pattern was so familiar, Francisco thought. Each side was obeying the conventional rules of siege warfare. Once the attackers received a refusal to surrender, any barbarity could be practised. And yet in Rhodes, forty-three years before, de l'Isle Adam had surrendered to the young Suleiman, and the city and population had been spared. But when the Knights had left there, it was years before they were offered Malta as their last refuge. From here they had nowhere to go, and without a base, the Order would disintegrate. So there could be no acceptance of terms, and no quarter given.

He wondered if at Rhodes someone like him had stood looking out at the Turkish fires, dwelling on what would happen once the battle had been resolved. But of course nothing had been truly resolved, that's why he was here looking out at the sons of that same force that had attacked the sons of that same enemy nearly half a century before. The thought was depressing.

Beside him, Diego moved in his sleep, and he glanced down at the actor propped up against the parapet. He looked too young to be involved in the carnage that was to come. But then there were children in Mdina, Senglea and Birgu. Nothing and no one was spared. It was the same in the wars with the Catholics when Christian butchered Christian with the same relish that both hacked at the Muslim. It was just in the barbarous nature of Man.

Haven't I spent the past few days here teaching Diego how to load and fire a musket, stab with the pike, slice with the sword, ignite a hoop to burn his fellow man, he mused. And against his protests that he couldn't kill anyone, haven't I stressed that when the time came, he would become the same

191

steel-clawed animal more savage, more destructive and with less compassion that any of those in any jungle. He shook his head sadly. "Diego, you cannot conceive of the fury that lies ahead," he muttered.

Yet even in his heavy brigantine and morion – the traditional Spanish helmet which replaced the uniform the soldiers had got him, Diego still seemed too slight to play the part of warrior at the ramparts. As he stared at him the memory of Miguel de Rojas returned. He could see the boy sleeping just before the attack on the Tripoli garrison. But he was jolted by the sound of someone climbing the stone steps to the battlements. He unsheathed his sword, but it was Sir William, who approached stepping over the outstretched legs of Diego to join him.

"Your servant doesn't take guard duty seriously," he commented glancing at the sleeping young man.

"He's not my servant," Francisco answered, "and he shouldn't be here anyway, he was tricked into coming. But when are we leaving for Birgu?"

The Englishman shrugged.

"Will there be an attack here?"

"No," said Sir William, "Mustapha Pasha, the Turkish general, and Admiral Piali have created the old problem of divided leadership. Our spies tell us that Mustapha wants to spread the attack, but Piali wants to concentrate on Senglea and Birgu first. You know of course that Dragut was sent to co-ordinate their strategies, but he's either in a coma, wounded, or dead. He hasn't been seen." He looked out at the flashes in the distance. "Their guns look down on Senglea and Birgu from the heights of Mount Scibberas the tongue of land jutting out into Grand Harbour and from three other positions. But as you know, those flashes are just a reminder that they are there. Once they have dragged cannon around to the heights of Corradino, and the landward side of the harbour, and sailed their fleet from Marsamuscetto into Grand Harbour, they will have completely encircled Senglea and Birgu. Then they will open a torrent of fire such as you or I have never seen."

Francisco studied the narrow face, wet from the evening air. The sad eyes, patrician nose and grey pointed beard gave the Knight a benign look. There was nothing about him that indicated the warrior, and the destruction he was capable of as he had seen on the galley. Even the slight frame, padded with armour though it was, denied the fury that could be unleashed.

"Why do you stare at me?" Sir William asked, still concentrating on the spread of fires that glowed beyond the arid plains.

"I was wondering what makes us do this," Francisco answered.

"To defend the faith," he retorted.

"That's *why* we do it. It doesn't answer the question *what makes us do it*."

The Englishman moved from the parapet towards the steps, "Don't dwell on that problem too long," he said. "We are here and no one else is. That's all you need to think of, because nothing else is relevant until we leave."

"When is that?"

"When conditions permit," he called, making his way down the steps and disappearing into the darkness.

"A righteous man," he heard Diego say, now awake. "The Englishman," he said, "a true and righteous man. The world is filled with the righteous and unrighteous," he sighed. "But why is it the righteous who decide who and what is righteous?"

"Because we let them," Francisco replied leaning on the damp stone parapet watching the distant camp fires.

His memories of Mariana returned, as he lay with her on the trip up to the Estremadura from Seville. They had stolen away from their servants and escort where they had lain on a grassy slope clasped tightly to one another, sweet sexual tensions liberated in the abandonment of making love under the sky only released.

And as they lay together, staring down at the camp fires of their escort glowing through the night, they talked of the eternity of their love. So many plans, so many vows, he thought, words and love protecting their naked bodies from the chills of the night. The passions of youth needed no fires to warm us, Francisco mused. We take our warmth from the sun in the day and the stars in the evening, Mariana had said. And so they had. But now those same stars had descended to the earth spraying the dark plains beyond the citadel with a burning passion so different from those so many years ago. And now he felt the chill of night slice through him like a blade.

On the sixth night of their stay in Mdina the Sirocco, the hot humid wind that blows from Africa, carried in a dense sea mist blanketing the island. De Robles, their commander, was quick to take advantage of it and under its cover the force drifted like phantoms through the wet limestone rocks and crags of the bare countryside, hidden from Turkish patrol, their padded footsteps and chinking armour muffled by the fog.

They met no living thing as they worked their way down the west of the island behind Turkish lines. People, livestock, and produce having long been gathered in behind the walls of the fortresses.

In years of experience in siege wars, Grand Master La Vallette had learnt that the fire and fervour which initially burned within the defenders of a city soon became extinguished by pangs of hunger. So while Suleiman prepared his armada, the Grand Master had reinforced his defences and as soon as the Turkish fleet was sighted, everything was brought in from the countryside, wells poisoned, and anything that could offer sustenance to the enemy, destroyed.

Thus as the small force slipped across Kalkara Creek to the small town of Birgu pressed against the shores of Grand Harbour they found a welcoming population far from demoralized and starving, but confident and hopeful.

Though disappointed at such a small force, the fact that they had slipped through the enemy's lines was seen as a victory over Turkish incompetence.

They were soon warned about the courage and determination of their enemy with the Turk's vast losses at St. Elmo being quoted as an example. As a Knight told Francisco, even if the leaders, Mustapha Pasha and Piali were bad strategists, the men who served them had proved why they were the most formidable soldiers in the world and had conquered throughout Europe. Despite losing 8,000 taking St. Elmo across the harbour, they still numbered some 20,000 to 30,000 camped in a steel crescent round the strongholds of Senglea and Birgu.

Francisco and Diego were allowed only a short rest then

despatched with others from the *Piccolo Soccorso* – the Small Relief – as they had become known, across a bridge of boats that linked Birgu with the promontory of Senglea and its fortress of St. Michael.

They made their way through the narrow streets of Birgu where the town thronged with activity as women and children repaired damage to the defences wrecked by sporadic bombardment. It seemed that no one slept regardless of age, as though the entire population of the island had converged in this one tight corner in a feverish effort to construct some vast machine, Francisco thought. But of course, they had. This was the one situation perhaps the only time, when Man could co-ordinate and co-operate to channel his efforts in constructing an efficient machine to wipe out others of his species. And in his short grim history on the planet he had progressed from the spear to arrow, arrow to gun, gun to cannon, and cannon to basilisk. Francisco wondered how far they could be from creating a machine with such destructive powers that it would be inconceivable even to those who made it.

Diego beside him was overawed by the activity and damage from missiles that surrounded them.

"What are you thinking?" Francisco asked.

"I was thinking of the contradiction of *making* things to *destroy*."

"But the generals think they're destroying to make."

Diego looked puzzled.

"They think they're destroying the bad to create the good."

"How do they know what's bad?"

"They don't. But they establish the rules."

"And what right do they have to do that?"

"The right we give them," Francisco smiled, "like the righteous, we spoke of before."

As they reached the short bridge of boats by the smoky creek that would take them across to Senglea, Diego looked back. The town was half-hidden by the dense mist, but still its feverish industry clanked and rumbled across the bridge.

"So this is war," he muttered.

"This is its preparation," Francisco answered. "The sporadic fire just a reminder that the enemy is out there. The fighting is yet to come."

Diego did not answer, but followed the others across the unsteady pontoon bridge to the promontory of Senglea in a land he knew nothing about, nor had ever thought of. About to fight for a cause which he knew even less about.

In Senglea half of them were ordered to the harbour area behind two giant windmills, while Francisco and Diego were told to go with some others to the walls on the landward side.

Diego made his way after Francisco up the ramp to the parapets then hesitantly looked over. Below him he could just make out a sheer drop into a man-made ditch which through the swirling mists looked like an empty moat.

If it had not been for the precarious position they were in, he thought he might have found the situation romantic. Defending the faith alongside the men lining the walls in their armour and scarlet tabards emblazoned with white crosses. The unseen enemy ahead, hidden in the mists. The perfect state for an epic. Yet there was a gnawing doubt that things were not going to be as he imagined. Before he could dwell on it, he heard Francisco instructing him.

"To our left is Birgu, and the creek we crossed; to our right is French Creek. La Valette has put palisades there . . ."

"Palisades?"

"Stakes in the sea, to stop the Turks landing," he explained. "Behind us is Grand Harbour, heavily defended, and ahead of us the enemy we concentrate on . . ."

"Do I need to know all this?"

Francisco looked at him for a moment, wondering if Diego really needed an answer to that question. His expression told him he did. "You must know exactly where you are in battle," he sighed. "Or you might find yourself marching shoulder to shoulder with the Turk." Francisco wondered if his nerve would hold on the first shock of the attack. "Do you remember what I told you about the arquebus, the pike and sword?"

He nodded, but was convinced he would not be able to use them even if attacked. He had never even hit a man let alone killed one. He gazed around him. The mist was slowly lifting from the harbour but still lay thick on the hills in front of them. It was now early morning and he felt cold and hungry.

196

It was getting lighter and he looked along the broad walk where grim faced soldiers lined the parapets. He noticed the assortment of armoury, besides weapons, that was piled at regular intervals near the soldiers, and the man-sized barrels that seemed so out of place there. "What are they for?" he asked Francisco pointing to one.

"You see those poles?" Francisco said indicating a pile of long hollowed-out tubes, "and those clay pots? Both contain wildfire, inflammable mixtures of sulphur, pitch, resin and turpentine. The cords round the pots are soaked in sulphur. In an attack grab one, light it from the braziers over there, and throw it." Diego stared in silence, his eyes wide in the same horrific awe that Francisco fancied he must have shown when first instructed in the armoury of battle, and had now become so impervious to. He put his hand on Diego's shoulder, to steady him. "I will be beside you, that you can count on."

The words were of no consolation, and his expression showed the full horror of what was about to befall them. But Francisco knew at this moment no sentiments could offer relief, there was only the job at hand, as it had been for him when he had experienced that first savage clash. His tone became factual again. "Those poles are called Trumps, because they snort like animals when lit. You hold one tight, light it, and flames will blast from it for a time." He motioned to the hoops a few paces from him. "Those hoops are also combustibles, you light one and fling it down on those climbing the walls. The barrels are filled with salt water. The Muslims prefer *Sachetti*, like those fire grenades Kassim threw into the streets when we escaped in Seville. They do the same thing as our Wildfire pots . . . if one explodes near or on you it will burn. Jump into one of those barrels and douse yourself." He gripped the young man tighter as he paled and swayed.

"Why do you think I said you would feel as though the jaws of hell had opened?" Francisco said. He pointed back across Grand Harbour where the mist had almost cleared. "That smouldering ruin below Mount Scibberas was St. Elmo. The Turks took it six days ago, yet it still burns."

"I can't stay here!" Diego exclaimed backing away, "I can't do it, Don Francisco. I just can't . . ."

197

Francisco held him firm, his gloved hand a vice on the thin shoulder. "You *will* stay!" Francisco hissed eyeing the men near them watching the scene. "There is nowhere else to go. Run and you'll be drawn and quartered as an example." He released him, "There is more character and courage in you than you know yourself, and you will dig deep into your soul and find it," Francisco muttered gently. "You may mess yourself, but you will do it quietly. And when you scream from fear, you will make it sound like the battle-cry of the hardened warrior. And you will carry that weapon with honour, Diego. Not a man here, including me, doesn't share your fear. There is not a man here who does not want to run and bury himself." His voice trailed as Diego's eyes stared past him, like saucers, gaping beyond the walls at an awesome sight. Francisco steeled himself, and without looking he could imagine what filled the young man with such horror. He quelled his own pangs of fear, and slowly turned.

The early morning breeze had now blown the mists from the hills and there, not a thousand paces from them, beyond the deep ditches and trenches, spread like an enormous oriental carpet across the barren landscape thousands of tents and pennants shimmered in the sunlight.

Sweeping the crests of the hills down to the Marsa in the bay, in scintillating silks, jewels, brandishing weapons, was the host of Suleiman.

Iayalar, Berserker, Algerian, Spahi, Mameluke and Janissary lined the brow in a massive demonstration of strength.

Diego gripped the parapet for support expecting the army to swarm down on them crushing defences and defenders, throwing them back into the seas behind them.

"Diego!" Francisco cautioned. "It's just a display to frighten us!"

"They've . . . They've succeeded," he stammered.

"They won't attack now, they won't attack before a bombardment. When they do, and we've driven them back, as we surely will, you'll have faced their worst and *survived*! And *nothing* will ever frighten you again!"

The words were distant echoes in his ears. All he heard was the thumping of his heart, all he saw was the blinding brilliance of colour that threatened to engulf him.

"They won't attack," Francisco assured him. "It's just a human rainbow in the sun . . ." His words were lost in clear voices calling across the hills. The rainbow sank to the earth as the host knelt responding to the call of the Mullahs.

"They're taunting us!" Diego cried.

"They're praying," Francisco answered. "Praying to be welcomed into Paradise if they die."

"I'll convert," Diego said weakly.

"At this moment many would follow you," Francisco smiled grimly.

That evening they heard the trundling of carts, snorts of oxen and the moans of slaves as the Turks hauled giant cannons over the rocky slopes to the Corradino Heights in preparation for the pounding that would soften up the defenders.

But the expected bombardment did not come. And as the sun rose, Diego and Francisco wrested themselves back from the sanctuary of sleep waking to the sounds of trumpets, not cannons.

Soon the air filled with a strange melodic music coming from the drums, cymbals and stringed instruments as the host assembled and began to march to battle. High on the crest of the hills black-frocked imams exhorted the faithful to fight and die for the glory of the Prophet, while behind the stone parapets men crossed themselves, some uttering the last prayers they would offer in this life.

"Francisco . . ." Diego whispered nervously.

"I'll fell you if you even think of running," Francisco hissed as piercing screams shattered the air and the slopes burst into an iridescent flow that swept down at them.

"Algerians," the soldier next to Diego muttered.

"Algerians?" he echoed blankly.

"Came in with Dragut. Untried troops showing their mettle to their Turkish masters," he spat.

"Showing their mettle," Diego repeated again in a daze as the wave rolled into the ravelins and ditches below them.

"Do up your helmet!" Francisco ordered him. "Tie the scarf under your chin . . . remove your scabbard from your belt or it'll impale you!"

Behind them they heard the rapid crackle of fire as muskets opened up on galleys that had been dragged overland into Grand Harbour to attack the seaward defences behind them. Francisco caught sight of de Robles, who had led them to Malta, high on a bastion, directing cannon fire into the ranks of Muslims. Roars now split their ears mingling with the screams of wounded as grape-shot peppered Turkish ranks and chain whipped paths of destruction. But the blasts did nothing to deter the inexorable waves that rolled on and washed the walls breaking against them.

Sulphur and chemicals choked the air as hoops, Trumps, and Wildfire hurled down and cauldrons of pitch and oil were tipped over exploding in a fierce inferno as the jaws of Hell opened. Ladders jammed against the walls. Algerians escaladed hurling *Sachetti* that burst into clinging inflammable sprays. The soldier who had spoken to Diego roared into a human torch as a pot shattered into him.

Diego gaped in terrified panic while the world around him melted in the boiling turmoil of battle as Christian and Muslim clubbed, hacked, and stabbed in atavistic savagery.

Beside him, Francisco had reverted into the threshing-machine he had seen in the galley. His eyes slits, mouth drawn back in a wolf's snarl, the giant blade in his hands resuming a life of its own, only reflexes directing it.

A turbaned head suddenly appeared just above the parapet. Diego froze.

"Get him!" Francisco screamed. "Get him!"

Diego lifted his sword, transfixed by the dark brown head that grew hands as it clawed for leverage.

"The scabbard!" Francisco roared as he cut into a man. "Pull the damned blade from the scabbard!"

Diego could not move. Suddenly the head exploded into a fury of scarlet as Francisco sliced across it. Simultaneously he barged Diego out of the way, grabbed a Trump, ignited and blasted down on those following. The tongues of yellow flame thundered from the tube incinerating attackers. Diego retched as the sweet smell of burning flesh drifted up. He turned to run, but a fist cracked across his jaw felling him.

"They'll hang you!" Francisco roared as he spun hurling himself at the bodies scrambling over the walls.

Maltese women left the cauldrons, picked up weapons and fought as savagely as the men beside them.

Diego's senses returned and he found himself looking up at a burly red-eyed Maltese woman lashing at an Algerian, the short battle-axe in her hands wheeling arcs. The attacker lunged, his blade driving in her, she screamed, doubled and fell beside Diego. Blinded by fury, he grabbed the axe she dropped and leaped, hacking at the dark bearded face. Chopping till the man fell at his feet. He swung round as a scimitar flashed, severing the arm that held it; then crouched, a cornered animal, snarling, vicious, ready for the next assault.

Behind them, Knights and soldiers poured a withering fire into the boats that tried to land from Grand Harbour, and those Muslims reaching shore met the same ferocity as those scaling the walls of St. Michael.

Reinforced by troops that crossed the narrow creek from Birgu, and protected by the palisade of stakes to prevent landings on their flank, the defenders gradually forced back the attack to the parapets, and then to no-man's-land beyond.

The first wave had been repulsed.

Francisco listened to Sir William Howard as he talked to him in the shadows of the parapets that evening.

The Englishman had come over from Birgu with the force that relieved the hard-pressed garrison on Senglea. And while men and women cleared the bodies inside the stronghold, he had talked of deeds that had taken place and names of the fallen, some of whom Francisco recognized. But there was no pride or glory in his tone when he referred to this action or that Knight. The comments were delivered in short factual statements with long pauses between as his weary brain tried to recall the events. Francisco hardly commented. Once a battle was over, there was little he wanted to say or remember about it. Instead he gazed at the windmills that stood facing Grand Harbour, so incongruous amidst their charred bloodied surroundings.

"We lost 250," the Englishman said. "Zanoguerra, the commander of that point," he waved his finger, "led a counter attack with Fra Roberto . . . the priest cross in hand rallied men round him . . . Zanoguerra was killed."

"It was his bright decorated armour," Francisco mused. "Must have been a target for every musketeer they had."

"He was a brave man," Sir William challenged.

"So was he," Francisco answered indicating the partly charred body of a soldier a few paces away.

The Englishman looked down at his dented stained cuirass. "Don't know if the blood's mine or Turkish," he muttered dabbing at the dark brown smears. He felt his neck and arms. "Must be Turkish." Francisco looked at the exhausted Diego who sat numbly propped against a barrel. "They lost 3,000," Sir William continued. "Nearly a thousand blown from the waters when they tried to land below Fort St. Angelo . . . right in the face of de Guiral's battery . . ." he shook his head in wonder, "Couldn't have known it was there . . . ten boat loads of Janissaries . . . nine sunk."

Francisco said nothing.

"Frederic de Toledo, the Viceroy of Sicily's son, was lost. He was a novice in the Order . . . left by his father, Don Garcia, in good faith that he would send a relief force."

"He kept his promise and sent it," Francisco commented acidly, "it was us."

The Englishman nodded.

"Maltese swimmers fought off an attempt to dislodge the palisade in French Creek," he muttered. "Fought the Turks in the water . . . they're still in the water now . . ."

"The Turks?"

"The swimmers . . . stripping bodies of jewels . . . these Muslims came in dressed up ready for Paradise . . ."

"Like us."

"Us?"

"Zanoguerra . . . his armour made him a target."

Sir William wearily pushed himself up with the aid of his sword. "Going back to Birgu," he said. Francisco watched him make his way to the ramp and down to the littered compound crouching to avoid Turkish snipers.

"He enjoys this," Diego murmured resentfully. "That old idiot enjoys this . . . he mulls over it, analyses it, talks about it. Jesus, didn't he have enough!"

"Perhaps it's his way of getting rid of it," Francisco answered. "Washing it out of his system."

Diego spat. "I can still see the face of the first man I killed."

"But d'you remember the faces of the second or third?" Francisco asked.

Diego did not answer, but stared at the destruction and broken bodies round them. "So *this* is war," he muttered.

Francisco shook his head. "This is *battle*. War is the glorious design in generals' minds. Battle is the stench and death and the memory of the first man you killed." As he moved his arm to shift his position a pain shot through it. He glanced down. His shirt had been burned through and the top of his arm scorched. He stared blankly at the wound, partly covered in a dirty makeshift bandage. But he could not remember when it had been burned or when he had tried to dress it. Like all the other scars on him, they just appeared as though dents and scratches on his cuirass.

For a moment he tried hard to recall when he had felt the pain of the wound, but couldn't. Yet at this moment, it seemed the most important thing in the world to remember. It was his *arm* not his breastplate. It was part of *him*. Living flesh, not dead metal. For an instant he thought he remembered. It was when he had killed the Muslim in the green jacket. That was it. The sword had gone in, stuck, and as he dragged it out, there was the searing pain. That was it! No! He'd wrenched his arm drawing the sword out. This wound had occurred when . . . but he couldn't remember. He *had to* remember! His body was more than a piece of waste metal to be tossed in a cauldron. He was more than that! He was a *man* not a *machine*! His eyes began to mist.

"I'm a man," he whispered to himself. "I'm a man, not a machine."

"Francisco!" Diego called.

He swallowed hard and looked over to him.

"Francisco . . ." he repeated searching for words. "Let's . . . let's get some food or something," he said quietly.

"Where?" he replied looking back at the wound.

"I don't know," he sighed, "but let's get away from this filth."

CHAPTER NINETEEN

Messina

"I *must* get to Malta!" Alonso de Rojas demanded.

The Viceroy, Don Garcia de Toledo, nodded wearily, though he continued to look out of the window at the blue stretch that separated Sicily from the besieged island where he had left his son as a guarantee of his return.

Since the relief force had departed twenty-two days before, he had himself been besieged by other Knights of the Order pressing him to arrange a second force to aid their brothers. But the situation was more complex than they imagined. The Knights were no subjects of the King of Spain, as he was, but owed their allegiance to the Pope in Rome. Yet that was a minor consideration in the face of the military problem of committing thousands of troops to a cause which might be lost, when those same men and materials might be needed to defend Sicily herself if the Turks took Malta.

He had instructed Commander Cardona not to land if St. Elmo had fallen, but despite his instructions, Cardona had done that. Those 700 men could now be considered as lost. And though the Knights' galleys under Romegas were intercepting Turkish supply vessels, the armada Suleiman had originally sent was provisioned to last well into the winter. Besides, he reasoned, Admiral Piali's galleys would not be so sluggish next time to allow a second relief to get through. Maltese fishermen that managed the blockade, brought news that Birgu and Senglea were under constant bombardment awaiting a massive assault, and once they had fallen the island was lost. So another 6,000 men would find themselves as trapped as those in those towns. Besides, he had ordered La Valette two months before to send Romegas' galleys as transports for a relief. But La Valette had ignored him and sunk those same galleys in Grand Harbour, hoping to refloat them once the siege was over. Now it seemed the Turk might be refloating them after his victory and adding them to Suleiman's considerable fleet.

"What about my transport!" de Rojas insisted impatiently.

The Viceroy turned to him.

They had once met at the court in Madrid when de Rojas was gaining a reputation as the Inquisition's most feared officer. But then, he had a cold incisive personality that bred its own brand of terror. Now he seemed hysterical. Thinner, more hawk-like than before, and certainly more agitated. However, that could have been due to delays he had in reaching Messina from Syracuse which lost him his chance of capturing Francisco del Valle who went with the relief force just a day before de Rojas reached the capital.

"I understand your urgency to join your brothers fighting the infidel," Don Garcia said quietly, aware that his obsession had little to do with helping the Order. "But you must understand that I cannot allow such an important officer of the Holy Office to be put at risk in some small Maltese fishing-boat."

"Don't worry about my safety!" de Rojas rapped.

"But I must," Don Garcia replied calmly as he moved over to his desk and sat down. "Should you meet any accident, or worse be captured by the Turk and displayed in Constantinople, it is *I* who shall have to answer the Grand Inquisitor!"

"I will write a letter relieving you of all responsibility," de Rojas immmediately offered. "I will say that . . ."

"As Viceroy I am expected to make decisions, general!" Don Garcia shouted indignantly. "Shall I answer the Grand Inquisitor with a note, like an erring schoolboy, explaining why my lack of judgement cost the Holy Office such an important person as you!"

De Rojas studied the long aristocratic face glaring at him for his insult. He could not be certain that the Viceroy himself might not be in league with *el cobarde*, or at least had not become bewitched by his sorcery. "Have you ever met Francisco del Valle?" de Rojas demanded. "Met him personally!" For a moment Don Garcia was taken aback by the question, and the insult it implied. But he said nothing, not willing to dignify the question by answering it, his outrage, nevertheless, evident.

"Perverting the course of justice," de Rojas threatened, getting up, "especially that of the Inquisition could cost dearly, your Excellency!"

"The course of justice," the Viceroy echoed in mock surprise. "I thought you wished to join your brothers in the Order. I imagined all this haste to reach Malta concerned vows which you once took to defend the faith."

"Your Excellency," de Rojas said in a low menacing tone. "We all serve the faith in our own ways. You by *not* sending a relief force, for I am sure good reasons, and me by hunting down those who would undermine our beliefs either in war or peace."

"Are you referring to anyone in particular?" Don Garcia snarled, himself rising from his chair. "Because I warn you, general, his Holiness Pope Pius has given a plenary indulgence to all fighting for our cause in Malta. Moreover, if say, a personal quarrel arose between two men, and one were to abuse his office to revenge himself despite His Holiness' remission of the victim's sins, then that official would be guilty of corrupting his office."

"But theologians would decide whether a remission of sins had been granted. And I would remind you, Excellency, that that is the province of the Dominicans . . ."

"And the Dominicans *are* the Inquisition," Don Garcia added wearily. "It would be an interesting problem, General de Rojas," he said gesturing to the door. "But meanwhile I have other interesting problems to consider. I am sure you saw the group of Knights waiting outside to press me, as you are, to send a force to Malta. You have my word, you shall be on the first galley of the relief when it sails."

"And when is that?" de Rojas demanded leaning across the table, resting his knuckles on the outspread map.

"When I, His Majesty's Viceroy to Sicily, decide it is both safe and expedient!"

De Rojas spun round, muttering, and the Viceroy watched him stride from the room and slam the door.

Quite mad, Don Garcia silently observed, quite insane.

But he breathed deeply, composing himself, ready to tackle more urgent problems than de Rojas' obsession, and he glanced down at the map of Malta the general had been leaning on.

The soft parchment still showed impressions of de Rojas' knuckles, the marks covering the spurs of land jutting into Grand Harbour where Senglea and Birgu were about to bear the brunt of the Turkish attack.

CHAPTER TWENTY

Massacre at the Marsa

Francisco and Diego huddled under fallen masonry as the night flared and trembled rent by the bombardment from the guns on the heights of Scibberus, Corradino, Gallows' Point and Mount Salvatore, and in the deafening noise Diego felt as if Birgu and Senglea would be pulverized to powder from the iron, stone and marble missiles crashing round them.

For three weeks, since the first attack, the Turks had intermittently pounded the positions then assailed them. Nothing had escaped damage nor anyone wounds. The hospital was overflowing and the streets littered with the dead. Yet crumbled walls had been repaired by men, women and children. Blocks of stone raised in the streets by slaves, for protection, and though hungry, no one starved, nor died of thirst as the water supplies, buried deep beneath the earth, had withstood the shattering impact of the giant missiles that rained. La Valette's preparations had been as thorough as Suleiman's and his generalship better than that of Piali or Mustapha Pasha. Nevertheless, the siege had dragged into its third week, and with each onslaught the number of defenders was depleted.

The air was now thick with powdered stone and smoke belched from the fires around them as they crouched in their shelter. Their bodies shook with the earth as each smashing ball tore into it.

"They've increased the bombardment!" Francisco called.

"Is it possible!" Diego answered. "I thought they'd plucked the stars from the skies as ammunition. I don't see any up there. Do you?"

Francisco gazed at him, crouching in the shadows. His eyes

had become stark, like those of all the others in the strong-holds. Weary from lack of sleep and meagre rations. Exhausted from fighting off attacks on the battlements, moving rubble to repair damage, and numb to the horrors each successive onslaught brought. He had been wounded from cuts and splinters, but since his initial baptism, three weeks before, he had not flinched nor shirked any responsibility asked of him. "How's your woman?" Francisco called, remembering the girl he had met a week before. Diego shook his head sadly indicating she was killed. "When?" Francisco asked.

"Four days ago ... five ... I can't remember. In a bombardment!"

"Why didn't you tell me?"

"You never asked," he answered blandly.

"I'm sorry."

Diego shrugged philosophically. "Hundreds have been killed."

He quickly pressed himself hard against the rock as a ball screamed in, erupting in the ground. Diego scrambled closer to him as a salvo roared past them blasting a cannon, flinging its barrel and wheels in all directions like a toy.

Francisco watched a wheel bounce high in the sky and saw the first glimmer of morning as its background. He became apprehensive as the strands of light streaked against the black clouds of smoke rising from Birgu.

"That's the worst attack yet!" Diego called. "There'll be a massive assault soon." He had become seasoned to the pattern of bombardment followed by waves of Muslims rushing in. The worst had been five days before, yet Francisco's expression told him that this one could be even more terrible.

They sat quietly watching the dawn break as the cannons died down, their fire becoming sporadic until fading like a storm rolling off in the distance. It took minutes before they could adjust to the silence, their fraught senses, as after previous bombardments, needing time to react to the temporary release. Both of them trembled like bowstrings in the dusty makeshift shelter, as muscle and sinew eased. They sat not saying anything, imbuing the precarious lull, treasuring it in anticipation of the next bombardment.

Soon the stillness was interrupted by the sounds of men hurrying to the walls. They stumbled over debris and through the dust, cursing quietly as they made for the ramparts. They did not move in the usual rush to repel an attack, but as though spectators hurrying to their seats in an arena.

Neither said anything as they emerged from the masonry and followed the others up the ravelin to the walls.

The smoke and dust were rapidly clearing, and as the blanket disappeared it revealed the massed armies of Piali and Mustapha Pasha.

"Jesusss Chrrissst!" Diego whistled through the missing teeth.

The brows of the sandstone hills surrounding them had grown a forest of glinting steel in the storm of the Turkish cannons. This time there were no throbbing prayers or exhortations from the Turkish Mullahs, just a frozen silence that struck every defender as he stood fearful of the gales that would blow those steel leaves across the pitted ground to engulf them. Time passed with no one uttering a word as they gazed at the spectacle.

Diego swallowed hard. "What day is it?" he whispered to Francisco.

"He shrugged. "It's August."

"It's not the tenth of August, is it?" Diego whispered anxiously.

"I'm not sure, why?"

"I think my birthday is the tenth of August."

"It's the sixth or seventh, I think," Francisco answered.

"Good. I didn't want to spend my birthday like this."

Francisco did not answer, but remembered how he had asked the same question at the *auto da fé*, only then it was May.

"When's your birthday?" Diego suddenly asked in a tremulous voice.

"In March," Francisco answered, his eyes fixed on the forest as it began to move.

"Spring," Diego said. "That's a good time to have a birthday."

He glanced at the giant beside him, his matted beard and hair now completely grey, eyes deeper set, face burned dark from the sun, under its dust and grime. In the past weeks he

210

had grown to love him as he would a father if he had one. And for the first time in his selfish life he was more concerned about another's survival than his own. A dozen times a scimitar that should have ended his life had been blocked by the blade of the broadsword, before it eliminated his attacker. A dozen times the incendiary that landed at his feet threatening to devour failed to claim him as Francisco barged him from the flames. He lost count of the times that growling bear's voice had cajoled and coaxed him back from the depths of hopelessness. And looking at him now, gazing impassively at the overwhelming force that threatened them, it seemed impossible that as a young man he had been labelled *coward*. Equally as impossible to imagine him as a young man. He seemed neither old nor young, but somehow permanent, ageless.

"God be with you Don Francisco," he heard himself say unconsciously. Francisco turned to him. "And you, Diego," he smiled.

The young actor suddenly felt sheepish. Embarrassed by his own words. "With *all* of us!" he heard a gruff soldier's voice cry beside him as the steel forest on the crests suddenly erupted.

Crashing down the hills, spearheaded by the Janissaries, the host swept up to the walls and through the breaches blown by cannon and basilisk. Their sheer weight of numbers forcing the defenders back, incendiaries and shot making little difference to their progress.

Diego hacked with the short axe taken from the Maltese woman three weeks before. Francisco scythed with the double handed sword. But as each attacker fell, two took his place. Again the air clouded with the stench of burning flesh, and the ground became slippery with blood as the Turks used their comrades' bodies as stepping stones to victory; while Christians used their own dead and wounded as protection from the relentless force pressing in on them from every side.

Muslim banners and pennants began to replace Christian flags on the parapets of St. Michael as the furious attack pressed hard on the crumbling defences.

Diego parried, lunged and chopped with the short axe, slowly being drawn away from Francisco by the mass. He caught glimpses of the double-handed sword swinging its lethal arcs. Then it disappeared. As men fell beside him, he realized that St. Michael could no longer be held. Their only hope was that Birgu and St. Angelo had not succumbed. But in the midst of their total capitulation a miracle happened.

Above the roar of battle, trumpets blasted the air with a cry so urgent that the Turkish vanguard checked. The soldiers gazed at their enemy in amazement.

The trumpets blared incessantly.

Turkish officers screamed for their men to turn. Defenders gaped as the seething mass reluctantly sacrificed its hold, turned and raced back towards the hills. No Christian followed, either suspecting a trap, or dumbfounded by the retreat.

Diego, inexperienced as he was, knew that whatever happened to force the retreat must have been of major significance. His ears were suddenly assailed with the triumphant roars of the defenders as they rushed back to the parapets, tearing down the banners of their attackers, screaming derision at them as they retreated and hurling incendiaries and ball after them.

But Diego stood for moments among the mass of dead and wounded stunned at having been spared.

Soon he became aware of the terrible moans and cries of the Christian and Muslim injured and quickly looked round for Francisco. But he was not there.

He began to run wildly among the piles of bodies, rolling men over, prizing apart those locked in the embrace of death, but could not find him.

Frantically he searched all morning, turning over corpses and severed torsos until in fearful desperation he stood screaming,

"Francisco! *Francisco!*"

But in the eerie peace that had settled over the compound, only the sounds of the dying answered him.

Amid the bright sunlight and scented blossoms of the Andalusian countryside, Francisco saw Mariana with María Teresa and Ruiz by her side.

The boy showed none of the hostility of before, nor the little girl her prim off-handedness. All three were smiling, waving at him, beckoning him to join them.

But he could not escape from the damp darkness that held

him. He struggled violently to break from its hold, to escape from whatever bound him but was unable to.

He knew if he were to remain where he was, his chances of being with them would be lost. He threshed against the invisible bonds holding him, called to them to wait. But they didn't hear and began to walk away.

"Mariana!" he roared. "Mariana!"

His perspiration mingled with the damp darkness of his surroundings and with a surge he ripped himself free from the force and began to run through the void to where they were.

Still they retreated, ignoring his pleas, he forced himself on until finally he found himself less than a hundred paces from the sunlight and trees.

"Mariana!" he screamed.

She stopped and turned, as though suddenly recognizing his voice. "Francisco!" she called, "Don't! Don't come!"

He stopped.

Between them, separating his darkness from her light, was an endless swirling vortex that spun away to infinity.

"Don't!" she warned. "To cross is death!"

"I want you!" he cried desperately, "I want you!"

"It means death, Francisco!"

He tottered at the edge of the darkness, his head swimming. She turned with the children and began to run.

He felt his foothold giving. He was slipping into the vortex. But as he fell a hand grabbed his shoulder dragging him back. "Francisco!" someone called, "Francisco!"

As he opened his eyes, he saw the pale sparsely bearded face of Diego staring down at him.

"Francisco!" Diego called. "You're awake! You're alive!"

Around him he became aware of the cries of others, but he was not in the field of battle, he was in a large evil smelling hall.

"Where is this?" he whispered as he moved. Stabbing pains split his side and head.

"Keep still," Diego pacified. "You are in the hospital in Birgu."

Francisco shrugged off his restraining hand and forced himself upright.

Crowded around him was a mass of humanity with every

213

conceivable wound man could sustain. And moving between the sprawling bodies were monks and Maltese women offering food and care to the conscious. He glanced at a severely burned soldier beside him.

"Some soldiers found you and brought you here," Diego said. "I searched for almost a week before . . ."

"A week!" Francisco exclaimed. "Is Senglea lost!"

Diego shook his head "As you fell, the Turkish attack was called off. It was a *miracle*. We were lost, when suddenly they retreated." Francisco stared incredulously. "Their camp at the Marsa, where they had left the wounded, was attacked. Chevalier Mesquita, the Governor of Mdina, sent in a Knight, de Lugny, I think his name is, with a hundred cavalry from Mdina. Mesquita saw our plight, and sent cavalry to destroy the Turkish camps. The Turks, believing it was the relief force rushed back!"

A ball outside crashed near the hospital, shaking the walls, sending dust cascading down. Within moments the Maltese women moved among the patients brushing them, clearing the dust. A few patients cried out, but there was no panic, everyone inured to the bombardments now.

Diego looked round the huge stone hall and watched the nurses as they cleaned up the mess. "They really look after this place," he muttered. "It's the most sanitary on the island."

"It's a hospital."

"I've seen hospitals where rats crawl among the patients, and not in war conditions."

"The Knights are a Hospital Order," Francisco said. "Some are dedicated to helping the sick, not fighting." He rested back as the wound in his side burned into him, and listened to the distant sporadic roar of cannon and eruptions as the missiles landed. But the firing was less intense than it had been.

"They're running short of ammunition," Diego said reading his thoughts. "You can hear how they conserve their shot. An officer told me that they are plagued with disease, most of those killed in the Marsa had dysentery or worse." He glanced round him. "Maybe these conditions have saved us from that."

Francisco felt the large swelling at the back of his head. It was that wound which must have knocked him out.

"I heard La Valette speak," Diego suddenly announced.

"The other day he came down himself. An imposing figure. A determined expression, clear of voice. He could have been an actor. He told us we were servants of the Lord fighting for Liberty. That we must die rather than yield. That he would die in a soldier's uniform rather than submit to the disgrace of capture . . . I wish you had been there, Francisco. In the smouldering rubble, with torches illuminating the square, he delivered words with an emotion that bound us regardless of rank or sex. It was inspiring . . ." His voice trailed as he saw the concern in the dark eyes.

"Diego," Francisco hissed. "I have heard La Valette's words a hundred times in a hundred battles when a commander rallies weary and hungry troops. At present brave words are needed. But don't get caught by their sentiment . . ." he paused as two women came over to the burned soldier next to him, wrapped him in sacking and struggled with him to the door. "That's the result of brave words." Francisco continued in a whisper. "You once told me that even cowards have more fame than the peasants who till the land. Even as a coward people will talk about you, write plays, discuss the arguments of your case . . . even follow a cause for or against you. You're not stupid, Diego. Don't be caught up like chaff in the wind, and be blown in whatever direction the blast of words takes you!"

He ignored the young man's pained expression. "Diego, you have fought bravely. This is your moment of glory, and if you get through, savour it in the future. Tell your children you were at Malta. But live long enough to have them!" He winced as the passion of his words ripped at his wound. "Don't relive this moment in a thousand other battles which lose their significance, as the scar tissue creeps across your body like a stain on your soul." He grit his teeth as pain seared through him. "Don't waste your life in the midst of death . . . I never heard a commander's speech that talked of *living*. Only the sacrifice of *death* . . . The moment the siege is ended . . . I vow I'll never kill another man . . ."

Diego rested his hand on Francisco's shoulder. "Rest . . . the wound will burst . . ."

"I'll never take another life, Diego," Francisco whispered desperately. "To be a hero . . . you must be a butcher . . . do you understand me . . .?"

The young man nodded and rose from the floor. He looked down at the haggard face and dull eyes staring up at him.

"I will join you on the walls, soon," Francisco promised, his face contorted with pain. "But after this . . . no more killing . . . I vow . . . no more killing."

Diego turned and picked his way through broken bodies that littered the floor like carcasses in a slaughter house, and in the flickering flames of the oil lamps he saw mutilations that just a few months before would have made him retch until he fainted. Now he had become hardened to the sight. He had once seen men decapitated by cannon-ball, limbs severed as though torn from a rag doll, skin liquify in fire, and it no longer affected him. He had looked long and hard into the cauldrons of hell, and what he saw no longer made any impression.

His senses had become tempered so that the deaths of women and children around him no longer penetrated beyond their acknowledgement. Even fear, that treasured quality which protected life, had deserted him. He no longer craved sex, and the joys of blaspheming had vanished.

So why had La Valette's words stirred him? He wondered. And as he walked from the hospital into the narrow streets of Birgu now shrouded in the humidity of night, he realized La Valette's word's had affected him because they embroidered the hideous horrors of reality with a golden thread of dreams. They wove a fine mesh of ideals over terrifying scenes binding them together. They had been urged to dedicate themselves to *death*, not *life*, as Francisco had said, asked to dedicate themselves to a struggle, which in the end would merely be another incident in Man's terrible history. Francisco knew this and had known for God knows how many years.

That was why he did not want him to become inspired by the *glory* and *sacrifice* of the struggle. That was why he could make the distinction between *battle* and *war*. He stopped and looked round him.

In the shadows of the night weary and exhausted people sat staring or sleeping amongst the rubble that had been a town. Every action had become an effort, every lull in the fighting a chance to recover the little strength they had. They no longer spoke, but muttered, as though saving their strength for that

216

last desperate scream when they were struck. Battle had drained them all, no one had been left unscathed either physically or mentally.

His eye caught sight of a small bare foot protruding from the rubble. It twisted at such an angle, that the child it belonged to would have been screaming if it were not dead. He moved to go over, but checked himself.

Suddenly the foot, the fires of the torches, and people misted as tears streamed down his face and his body shuddered as the emotion choked from him.

In the sweltering heat that even the thick white walls of the hospital could not keep out, Francisco lay listening to the roar of battle that raged out just beyond the city by the Castilian lines defending Birgu.

In the two weeks he had spent in the hospital since being wounded, it had been comparatively quiet, and in dozing semi-consciousness he escaped from his surroundings and strolled with Mariana and the children across the soft hills of Andalusia. And when his wounds ached, he closed his eyes and she was there, soothing, easing the pain. He had lost count of the number of times he had ridden north with her to his own estate, only this time, not as newly marrieds, but as they were now. She with the children, he, vindicated and without the stigma that had plagued him. Ruiz was no longer hostile, but responsive and as they rode he taught him the lore of the countryside. María Teresa no longer stiff and formal, but bubbling, inquisitive and excited as a child of seven should be. And Mariana had abandoned the stiff tight silks and satins she wore, exchanging them for loose woollens and linens that flowed in the wind as she rode. And at each stage of the journey back their love grew pushing back the past as it unravelled the untroubled future.

But consciousness always brought with it the reality of the present, and now as he lay, he became aware of the sounds of an attack which seemed to be growing to the same scale as the assault on Senglea had.

He had heard that the Egyptian miners the Turks had brought with them had managed to penetrate the hard rock beneath the defences both at Birgu and Senglea, and had managed to blast breaches in the walls, but the roar that had heralded this onslaught indicated a large section had been brought down.

He struggled to his feet, flung on his brigantine and binding his belt tight round the wound in his side, he grabbed the broadsword and hobbled out into the streets.

The stark sunlight blinded him. But he focussed to see panic. Desperate pleas and screams mingled with the furious cries of the Turks at the Castilian lines. There was an ominous tolling of the bells of the Conventional Church which the Knights used as their religious centre.

He barged through groups fleeing towards Grand Harbour away from the fighting, and stumbled on towards the parapets where the Castilian line was barely holding.

The walls had been blasted and had slipped into a deep hole mined by the Egyptian engineers. Pouring through it like the sea through a breached dike, were the white-robed fanatical Janissaries, forcing defenders back as the scent of victory gave the attackers a crazed irresistible impetus.

Nothing that could stem the flood, he thought, but better to die there, than be butchered in a hospital like those sick Turks in the Marsa.

He gritted his teeth against the pain and forced himself forwards screaming obscenities at his enemy.

At the same time, converging on his objective, he saw a group of Knights led by an old man, wielding a sword running as though each step trod away the years his hoary face reflected. As Francisco caught up with the party he realized that this was the Grand Master, La Valette.

Swarming round them now came defenders who moments ago had fled. Such was this man's charisma, that the position almost lost, was consolidated, strengthened, then swung from defence into so savage an attack that even the spearhead of the Muslim fighting-machine began to wilt. A grenade burst near them, and the old man stumbled as splinters tore into his leg, the Knights round him constantly forming a human wall which Francisco found himself joining. They eased back as more soldiers rallied and the white wave of fury was enveloped by the scarlet tabards of the *tercios*.

218

Gradually Francisco found himself backing from the conflict with the other Knights, protecting La Valette, half-dragging, half-carrying the septuagenarian Grand Master.

As they reached the safety of the town, Francisco became aware of the blinding pain of his wound. He hauled himself from the group round La Valette to rejoin those beating back the Turkish stragglers on the parapets. But he only managed a dozen paces before a void opened and swallowed him.

He woke to see a kindly face peering down at him through the cavorting shadows thrown by oil lamps. The watery eyes, drawn cheeks and grey beard were familiar, but he could not put a name to the face he tried to move. Something sharp stabbed into him. It was the wound.

"Lie still," the old face said. His hand stretched out to restrain him. "Your action opened the wound you sustained earlier."

He pushed the hand aside and forced himself into a sitting position. He was in a large quiet room, furnished in heavy oak, and realized he had been lying on a table. Everything was covered in a coating of fine dust which had fallen from the ceiling and walls during the bombardments, yet miraculously, the furnishings, paintings, even the lead-cased windows, remained intact. "You'd better drink this," the old man said. Francisco stared at the clay vessel in his hand. "It's water," he assured him in Spanish fringed with an accent similar to Sir William Howard.

"Where is this?" Francisco asked.

"You are in the Grand Master's quarters," the old man answered. "I am Sir Oliver Starkey, the Grand Master's secretary."

Francisco shoved his fingers into the bandages binding him, withdrawing them he saw they were black.

"It's a fungus," Sir Oliver told him "It's from this island, it will both heal and cleanse."

Francisco tried to push himself from the table, when the slim hand restrained him again. "Please wait," the Englishman said. "The Grand Master wishes to see you."

He now recognized the secretary. He had seen him many years ago when he had been a Knight, and had caught glimpses of him during the siege. Besides Sir William Howard, who fought alongside the Langue of Provence, this was the only representative of the English Langue since the country had turned from Rome.

"How long have I been here?" He asked.

"A day . . ."

His answer was interrupted by the door at the far end of the room opening to reveal a Knight who stood stiff while a slim erect figure limped past him. The full pointed beard, hooked nose, and dark eyes were unmistakable. It was La Valette.

He approached Francisco, stopped a few paces from him, then studied him. The Knight who had opened the door brought a chair.

"Leave us," the Grand Master ordered in a gravel voice.

Sir Oliver began to move. "Not you," La Valette said. "Please stay Sir Oliver," he said easing himself into the chair.

The yellow flames from the oil lamps twisted shadows that danced on the stone walls enlivening the images in the paintings and tapestries around them. In the far distance the thunder of the Turkish batteries rumbled and Francisco felt as though he were to undergo the trial he experienced in the garrison at Tripoli.

The dark eyes fixed on him betrayed neither compassion nor the savagery that the Grand Master was capable of, as his retaliation to the Turkish atrocities bore witness. Yet his expression did not show the anger or contempt of Juan d'Omedes who presided over his trial fifteen years before. There was a searching curiosity that was perhaps even more disturbing.

"You are a brave man . . . Francisco . . . *Clementes*," the Grand Master finally said, stressing the assumed name Francisco had taken when he joined the relief force. "You came with Chevalier de Robles' forces, *requiescat in pacem*. A brave man."

Francisco was not sure whether he was repeating that *he* was brave or de Robles, for whose soul the Grand Master prayed, the Knight having fallen in a previous attack. But he made no comment.

220

"I heard you came from the hospital, wounded," the Grand Master continued, "to join your brothers at the parapets . . ."

The tone indicated he wanted confirmation, but Francisco gave none.

"Then you rallied round your wounded commander in the face of a Janissary assault, Sir Oliver tells me."

Francisco still remained silent. Old age, he thought, could dull the senses or hone the intellect to the sharpness of a scimitar. In this case the old man's intellect was incisive. He stared into the unblinking eyes trying to penetrate his mind.

"We have met, Francisco *Clementes*," La Valette suggested, still emphasizing the alias. "We met many years ago when as a novice to the Order you were part of an exchange of prisoners . . ."

The Grand Master recognized him and there was little doubt that he was aware of Tripoli and his defection in France and the low countries. Anxiety crept through him. Despite any heroism he had shown, La Valette was deeply religious, committed to defending the faith regardless of a man's merits. And Francisco was aware of the fate of de la Cerda, a Knight who in the early stages of the battle for St. Elmo insisted to La Valette that the fortress would not hold more than eight days, then slightly wounded found himself in the dungeons of St. Angelo for his faint-heartedness, only able to redeem himself by dying in battle.

"Do you remember *me*, Francisco *Clementes*?" he asked.

"I remember you," Francisco answered calmly.

"He bears a striking resemblance to a disgraced Knight called Francisco del Valle," La Valette said to his secretary standing beside him. "One or two Knights from the Langues of Castile and Aragon have also mentioned it. But del Valle's name was vilified, and the man himself would have been executed by Juan d'Omedes, the Grand Master at Tripoli, had it not been for the fact that he was attacked during his trial. It was also said that de Valle joined the heretic forces fighting the faith declaring himself an *apostate* . . ."

"I am Fran . . ." Francisco began.

"You are Francisco *Clementes*, I know!" La Valette asserted before Francisco could make his admission. "But I was commenting on how looks can deceive," he continued. "As far

221

as I know Francisco del Valle is dead. Why his wife, I believe, even married a Marqués soon after he died." The eyes now showed a trace of amusement as though the old man were sharing a joke. "You were kept here so I could thank you. I wanted to tell you that your name, the name of Francisco *Clementes* will be recorded along with those of others who have been in this siege. I wanted to ask you to join us, and as Chevalier Francisco Clementes, help restore the prestige and honour so nearly lost when we were driven from Rhodes, and like beggars made our way to this island." He waved away Francisco's interruption. "Make no mistake, when this is over; when they find out how we stood against the most powerful forces Islam could muster, the name of the Order will resound throughout the world, and go down through all time. If you join us, you will gain more than riches, you will become part of posterity."

Francisco eased himself from the table and painfully made his way past the Grand Master towards the door.

"Where are you going?" Sir Oliver demanded.

"To my post on the parapets," Francisco answered, leaning against the door for support.

"You may join the Langues of Castile or Aragon," the Englishman said.

Francisco shook his head wearily. "I will join Diego on the walls at Senglea."

"Diego?"

Francisco tried to remember Diego's family name but couldn't. "Diego," he just repeated. "A nonentity, who came here by accident, and whose name will not be added to the rolls for *posterity*. A nameless, faceless, shameless actor, who without realizing it, is giving the greatest performance of his life . . ."

"And why did *you* come?" La Valette asked not turning to him. Francisco shrugged.

"I thought it was to repay a debt I owed for being saved from the tortures of the galleys . . ." he shook his head in disappointment. "Now I know it was a desperate need to regain the honour and respect of those I deemed peers and masters." He smiled ruefully, "God help me in my arrogance I craved recognition through redemption. And yet now, each

222

time I swing my sword, each time I open bodies, I realize I shame myself, degrade my worth, vilify my own name . . ."

"Be careful," La Valette warned. "It might have been such sentiments which checked Francisco del Valle's valour at Tripoli."

"Perhaps it was," Francisco admitted tiredly. "But he was a young man who did not realize that once the bull is held by the tail it is impossible to release it. A mistake one never makes twice."

"The offer that has been made," Sir Oliver said, "will redeem your name and mean salvation . . ."

"Redemption and salvation," Francisco mocked. "That can only be achieved by man through himself. If the last fifteen years have taught me nothing else, it has taught me that."

"Redemption comes through the grace of God!" La Valette roared now glaring at him.

"Whatever you say, my Lord," Francisco conceded without conviction.

"You will join the defences held by Castile," Sir Oliver insisted.

Francisco pulled open the door. "I will be on the parapets of St. Michael," he replied, walking from the room.

The Englishman was about to call the guard but the Grand Master held him. "Leave him the anonymity he seeks," La Valette muttered pushing himself from the chair. "As *el cobarde* he suffered enough. God will decide his fate, and with His help, let us plan ours."

He walked over to the silver processional cross and stared at it. "The Grand Council wants us to concentrate our forces on St. Angelo," Sir Oliver said. "The Turks are weakened by disease, frustrated by failure, and terrified of returning to the wrath of Suleiman. They have to have victory and we cannot hold them for ever. Shall I order the withdrawal?"

The Grand Master reached out and touched the silver cross. "There will be no withdrawal," he sighed.

"Excellency, the Council believes that if we take the holy relics and . . ."

"No withdrawal," La Valette repeated quietly. "I will not crowd my forces into one space where they could be blasted from the earth. We will stand our ground where we are now.

The holy relics, including the hand of John the Baptist in the Conventional Church will remain where they are. There would be total demoralization if we moved them."

"And the archives?"

"They will remain where they are as well. Nothing will be moved. No one will leave their post."

"Do you think Don Garcia will at last send aid?"

"The Viceroy of Sicily will do what is best for him," he said. "We stopped relying on Don Garcia de Toledo three months ago when we accepted we were on our own." He listened for a moment as the Turkish bombardment intensified. "When we came to this island thirty-five years ago under Grand Master de l'Isle Adam, we knew we had nowhere else to go. It was live or die here. This great Order has been decimated by international politics, attacked by the Muslim, and weakened by its loss of faith. Here in Malta we establish ourselves or die in the attempt. This I announced to the Council when the siege began. We rely on no one but ourselves."

He hobbled past Sir Oliver and stared out of the window at the night sky lit up by the flashes of the Turkish cannon. "I will order the bridges linking Birgu to Senglea and St. Angelo to be blown up," he said. "Regardless of what the council wishes. We are all on our own now, and may the Lord help us."

CHAPTER TWENTY-ONE

Release

Diego pressed his head back against the charred cracked limestone walls, above him the stars glittered in the clear September sky. He wanted to think of something, anything, to close himself from the stench of the putrefying bodies in the ditches below them, and the misery of the men, women and children in the city of Birgu. But he had found it difficult to think of anything for a time recently as the oppressive conditions closed in like a death shroud.

"How long can it go on?" he mumbled to Francisco beside him. "You should've taken La Valette's offer and joined the Knights on the Castilian line," he said without waiting for an answer to his first question.

"Why?"

"Because . . ." his voice trailed off and he shrugged. "When did they destroy the siege towers?" he asked, forgetting his last comment and vaguely recalling the two large siege towers being brought down.

"Few days ago."

He licked his dried cracked lips and tried to swallow. Now, more than ever since the siege began, water was becoming scarce.

"That was when the Englishman . . . the one we knew . . ."

"Sir William Howard."

"That was when he was killed, wasn't it?"

"He was killed on the day La Valette made his offer," Francisco muttered staring at the still bodies strewn around the compound. "Nearly two weeks ago."

"Two weeks ago," Diego mused. "What date is it?"

"September the fifth or sixth, I think."

"It's not the tenth?"

Francisco shook his head.

"My birthday's on the tenth."

"You told me it was the tenth of August."

"Did I?"

He nodded.

"I was lying," Diego muttered, "I don't know when it is." He turned to Francisco, "When's yours?"

"I told you," he sighed. "In March."

Diego's face must have aged twenty years, he thought. His eyes wore the same stark expression as the others. His hair and beard were matted, his armour no longer recognizable. Even he himself had changed out of all recognition. His hair and beard were completely grey, and once, when he had caught sight of himself in a cracked window, the reflection that gaped back was that of a dirty starved beggar.

"How's your wound?" Diego asked.

"Better," he said automatically, not having bothered to look at it for days. "How's your arm?"

Diego glanced disinterestedly at his limp arm which had been lifeless since being cut in an attack. He vaguely remembered the anguish he had felt when he realized he had lost the use of it. But in successive attacks, the attempt to survive had overridden everything. "It's still there," he said, then thought for a moment, there was something he wanted to tell Francisco. He remembered, "Sir William, the Englishman is dead."

"I know," Francisco replied patiently.

Diego's conversation had sometimes been incoherent over the weeks. His words often having no pattern to them, answering questions asked hours before, or offering information, as just now, that he had been given moments ago.

"What will you do after this?" Diego asked.

"After the siege has ended?" Francisco said as though there were some given date when it would finish. "Go back to Spain I suppose. Go to Mariana."

"I'm staying here. Here on the island. I have a right to don't I?" Francisco nodded. "I will fish," Diego said firmly. "There are coves to the north a Maltese told me. I'll go up to one of them. Live there. Take a boat. Fish. Live quietly, in peace."

"And catch mermaids," Francisco teased, forcing a smile.

"Mermaids?"

"Women who live in the sea."

"Mdina was attacked," Diego said ignoring the remark. "The Turks sent a force. But the Governor dressed women and children as soldiers. Put them along the walls. Piali withdrew. Thought he faced another St. Elmo."

"I know," Francisco said. He had told Diego the story himself the previous day.

"God those ditches stink!" Diego hissed. "How many more can they lose!"

Francisco did not answer. But he estimated that Mustapha Pasha's army still numbered at least 10,000 against their meagre force. Yet it seemed impossible that any enemy could suffer such terrifying losses in each attack, and still fill the crests of the hills to launch another. It seemed equally impossible that they themselves could withstand the assaults and still find men to defend. Yet since he had left the hospital two weeks before, there had been five major attacks taking a terrible toll on both sides.

Their supplies were all but exhausted, and the Turks couldn't have been any better off. The Knights' galleys had completely cut their supplies from Algeria.

Both armies now lurked like wounded animals, he thought, lashing out to dislodge one another, inflicting deeper lacerations, neither yielding nor gaining any advantage, each praying the next attack would inflict the final blow, then reeling back to lick wounds, regain confidence, and strike again.

Nevertheless, the Turks had the advantage of outnumbering them, and if they wanted to risk Romegas' galleys, could get reinforcements. But they would need to decide soon. It was now September, the last month they could keep this battle going. Once winter had set in, they would have to harbour their fleet safely, then find ways of living on an island that offered neither food nor fuel.

If I survive, he said to himself, I'll never become part of any war again, regardless of its significance. The moment this is over, I'll never harm another being again. What we are doing defies reason. Each time I raise my sword, it is as

227

though I kill part of myself. His fist tightened round the small gold cross which he had come to grasp day and night regardless of whether he fought or slept. It was more than a talisman, it was all that bound him to life. It had become part of Mariana for him. She was reality he told himself, the rest sham, a mirage which he drifted through along with the other phantoms that haunted the city and hovered on the walls in the roaring flames dissolving into nothingness in the rage of battle.

"They say a relief force has landed in the north," Diego suddenly said. "A soldier told me . . ." he paused as he tried to remember, "yesterday . . . I think he told me yesterday . . . No, no it was the day before . . ."

Francisco nodded, but took little notice of the information. For weeks rumours circulated that a relief force had landed, but none materialized. Perhaps, he thought, the ghost force needed to exist in people's minds to keep them going on. There was nothing else to. Even the reasons for the struggle itself had probably been forgotten by everyone on both sides save the generals.

"There are thousands of them," Diego mumbled as he fell into the twilight world between sleeping and consciousness where dreams are controlled and images shaped. "They're sailing through the shallow clear waters of the creeks. I can see the men pouring on the shore . . . scarlet tabards . . . like poppies spreading across the rocks . . . thousands of them . . ." he whispered as his voice trailed into sleep.

Francisco closed his eyes too; but he saw no relief force, only the image of Mariana standing among the ruins of the mosque. Her long satin cape folded round her, her eyes reassuring. He held on to the image desperately, fearing that to let it go would allow the evil nightmares to invade his mind bringing with them the dark spectre he had seen so often in the past weeks. In swirling mists he saw the same shadow thrusting at him with a sword felling him, swallowed by the darkness.

Gradually exhaustion forced him to release the tenuous hold he had on Mariana's image and the mists crowded in.

* * *

He woke to the disheartening sound of the batteries opening up growling and roaring their proclamation that the Turk still had ammunition and was willing to contest the few hundred paces of land until the bitter bloody end.

Around him people were shouting and he roused himself quickly, automatically unsheathing his sword to face another onslaught. But as he looked over the parapets, the enemy was not there poised for an attack. For moments he stood bewildered, wondering if he were still asleep. Then saw people flooding down towards Grand Harbour, not shouting, but *cheering*!

He screwed up his eyes in the brilliant light and saw the familiar lines of Christian galleys, their pennants flapping against the turquoise sky, their guns roaring a salute to the ruins of St. Elmo and the resistance of St. Angelo. Pacing themselves steadily beyond the range of the Muslim guns, they glided through the scintillating waters booming defiance at Piali's fleet in the harbour, daring them to come out after them.

He looked down at Diego, who lay very still.

"Diego," he whispered, "Diego, it's Christian galleys."

The young man did not move.

For a moment he froze, not knowing whether to touch him or call, then grabbed him.

"Diego!" he roared.

Diego flung out his right arm shoving him away instinctively as though being attacked, then reached for the short axe.

"It's me, Francisco!"

Roused from his deep sleep, he looked bewildered as he struggled to the parapets obeying instincts ingrained over the past months. Francisco clasped him round the shoulder relieved that he was alive and turned him towards Grand Harbour. "Galleys," he said. "Christian galleys."

Diego stared at them perplexed, then as the realization seeped in, tears filled his eyes and flooded down his cheeks. "It's over," he whispered. "It's over."

"Stay at your posts! Stay at your posts!" Knights and officers roared up to the defenders at the parapets. "They might attack!"

229

"But it's over!" Diego cried.

"It's a precaution," Francisco soothed. "It's just a precaution."

"The relief has landed," Diego said. "I saw them . . . I . . . don't know where, but I'm sure I *saw* them . . . *somewhere!*"

He turned back to the arid hills. His heart sank at the sight of the Turkish tents and flags still there, still menacing.

He swung back to see the galleys turn making their way out to sea, their prows rising and dipping in the sparkling waters as they returned to Sicily.

"In the name of God! Aren't they going to land? Aren't they going to help us?" he cried.

"There's only four of them," Francisco said. "But the Turks took no action, something must have happened. Perhaps the relief has landed in the north, and they're conserving their ships for evacuation."

"And the galleys?" he asked dejectedly.

"Maybe on their way back for more troops." Francisco clasped him firmly. "We wait now, Diego," he said. "Now we stay at our posts, and wait.'

That night the small town of Birgu burst into a flood of illuminations as oil and torch blazed the revived flame of life that the celebrations brought. The phantoms that only a day before had haunted the streets, regained their souls as the shroud of imminent death was lifted. Food and wine which had been conserved was broken out to feed not only physical appetites, but the spiritual ones of those who had known nothing but despair in the grim months which ravaged them.

On the ramparts soldiers ate the food and drank the wine which had been brought to them as they watched the city rejoice in its salvation while at the same time keeping vigil on the fervent activity they could hear beyond the hills.

In the heights around them the steel crescent which had gleamed so brightly at its inception, now cracked and crumbled as though it had been hacked against unyielding rock. And its disintegration could be heard across the dark valleys of the dead, as snapping whips, creaking transports, and the

230

moans of slaves echoed while they dragged basalisks and cannon from their positions to embark on retreat.

Dawn broke in the brilliant gold of the September sun, as Francisco and Diego gazed at the deserted Grand Harbour. The mass of masts, fields of silken canopies, and banks of oars had evaporated with the night. Across the charred and bloodied hills nothing remained of the vast army save the dead, their loose robes flapping in the dust and silence.

All along the parapets men shuffled to haul themselves or wounded comrades to their feet to see the miracle of the empty hills and waters.

None spoke for fear of disturbing unseen elements, provoking the fire and fury that had rained down on them for three months. And in the stillness they heard the forgotten sounds of birds singing, insects buzzing and the breeze whispering along the high walls. Only in this calm did they become aware of their wounds and of the enormous cost in life and destruction. No one and nothing escaped unscathed, and from what had been houses, a mass of people emerged, drifting through the rubble of their shattered town on to the gates and beyond. From across the creek, the bells of the Conventional Church of St Lawrence rang, not to call men to battle, but to proclaim its end.

To the north, round the village of Naxxar, Ascanio de la Corna, the commander of the relief force, watched uneasily from the heights as the Turkish galleys swung off their original course and began to make their way back to the island. He could only guess that Mustapha Pasha and Piali had decided that their own vast numbers were match for the 8,000 soldiers landed.

De la Corna held his Knights, *tercios* and Maltese militia from Mdina, until the galleys pulled into the bay and began to disgorge their troops. From his high vantage point de la Corna waited until his impetuous men, inflamed by stories of the destruction and sacrifice they had heard in Sicily, were at last given the order to attack.

Iayalars, Berserkers, Mamelukes and Spahis were cut down under the blazing fire and savage charges mounted by the enraged Knights. The Janissaries who had originally formed a bridgehead to cover disembarkation, now found themselves fighting a rearguard action to protect their troops struggling through the waters in retreat. Demoralized, confused, and exhausted by disease and privation, Suleiman's army no longer had the will to face fresh troops driven by passions of revenge, and it was only the brave action of small pockets of Turks that saved the rout from becoming a massacre. Within hours of the attempted landing, the battle abated leaving in its wake a scarlet sea washing in the corpses of hundreds who had died in the fierce fighting, a battle as devastating as it was unnecessary.

Less than two leagues away in Senglea, unaware of the battle in the north, Francisco watched bewildered men, women and children wander beyond the gates over those few hundred paces of rock that would have meant certain death to those venturing there a few days before.

Methodically and dispassionately they began to strip the bodies of the Turkish dead. The spoils of this war would be rich, he thought. But none he had ever fought alongside were more worthy of those gains than those bedraggled figures drifting slowly up the slopes, for the first time in three months able to breath air free of sulphurous incendiary fumes, hear sounds other than those of cannon roaring.

He watched ragged children cling to exhausted mothers, still apprehensive, staring wide-eyed as men flipped over bodies in their search for valuables. Yet some just knelt in silent prayer amongst the arid rocks which had become the last resting-place for so many Muslims who with the declaration "*Ashhado an la Ilaha illa Allah*," There is no other God but Allah, had finally entered Paradise.

The bells of the Conventional Church clanked again.

"It's Mass," Diego, beside him, said. "I'm going. It's the Feast of the Nativity of the Virgin." He saw Francisco's surprise that he knew which feast it was. "A soldier told me," Diego muttered sheepishly. "Will you come with me?"

Francisco shook his head. "I want to go down to the sea to cleanse myself," he said, "if there's enough water."

"Wait until Mass is over. I'll go with you."

232

Francisco agreed, then watched the slight figure, leaning to one side to compensate for his paralysed arm, shuffle down the dusty ramp.

He crossed the compound to join hundreds of other weary men, many supporting wounded comrades as they made their way to the smoking ruins of Birgu. And as he looked down into the ditches of the rotting dead below the parapets, and up at bodies that littered the hills, he felt an overwhelming sense of shame.

The sea hasn't enough water to cleanse me, he thought.

They sat on the hot rocks in the late afternoon having hardly exchanged a word all day since they had bathed in the pale blue waters swirling into the small bay near Birgu.

For the first time in months Francisco felt again that he had become part of what existed around him. The rocks, pink in the late afternoon sun, the tough scrub quivering in the breeze and the sea fizzing as it swept in. Yet something was missing, then he realized that for the only time in his adult life he was unarmed, and for the first time it did not worry him. He felt completely at peace, as though he had experienced a complete transformation yet sensed there was one more step to take to complete a journey begun so long ago in the smouldering ruins of Tripoli.

"I'm going to stay here," Diego said interrupting his thoughts. "I'm going to stay and become a fisherman."

"Are you sure that's what you want to do?"

He nodded. "There's no demand for an actor with only one good arm, and even less for one who can only utter brave sentiments without conviction."

He studied Francisco. When he had first met him his hair had been black and grey, now it was grey and white, his face had become hollow, and yet despite that, he exuded a tranquility with a strength more formidable than that of the warrior. "What will you do?" he asked.

"Return to Seville and Mariana," he replied without conviction.

"You have someone to go to," Diego said, concerned about the emptiness of Francisco's answer.

"You will find someone."

"A mermaid?"

"With the breasts of a Madonna," Francisco smiled.

"Don't blaspheme," he rebuked.

Francisco sighed staring at the sky as shafts of orange cloud jutted across it. "I am pleased you have found your faith again," he said gently, "but keep a sense of proportion, or you'll become as arid as those who created the hell we've been through."

The reference to his rebirth prompted Diego.

"At Mass this morning, when La Valette read the sermon . . ."

"I don't want to hear it," Francisco said quietly. "I just want to breathe this peace, not words which are as ephemeral as those changing clouds."

The short battle-axe clanked against the rocks as Diego pushed himself to his feet, irritated in his misunderstanding of Francisco's sentiment. "You are as narrow-minded in your apostasy as those who believe," he snapped.

"I'm as limited as my experience," Francisco answered as he rose and began to walk down to the shore.

Diego watched him for a short time then made his way amongst the rocks up to the slope on the plain, hurt that his new found faith was rejected by one closer to him than any other had ever been.

He glanced back. Francisco was standing on the strand of shore staring at the sea. He had discarded his brigantine and the leather jerkin was swallowed up by the swirling water. His hair seemed even whiter than it had a moment ago, blending with his linen shirt rippling in the wind. He appeared transfixed by something he could see far out on the horizon.

"He's a better sense of drama than I have," Diego muttered irritably. He started back for Birgu, kicking stones and swinging the short axe at any object along its path. "You're more prejudiced than you realize, Don Francisco," he muttered as he walked. "You see the things you want to see and nothing else. You once said you were no philosopher and barely literate. How right you were . . . How right you were . . ." But as he walked mumbling angrily to himself, swinging the short axe the thud of hooves snapped him from his thoughts. A hundred paces to his left he caught sight of a rider, standing in his stirrups, scanning the shore, his long dark cape flowing in the wind.

He stopped and watched him. There was something vaguely familiar about the tall gaunt figure that searched so intensely.

Then, he wheeled his animal round and began to make his way towards the beach. His silhouette in the crimson sunset was menacing, and as Diego screwed his eyes up and watched him force his animal down beyond the ridge, he *knew* there was something formidably familiar about him.

"Francisco del Valle!" Alonso de Rojas called to the solitary figure standing by the lapping sea.

Francisco turned to the dark figure on the rocks some distance from him.

"I've travelled from Sicily for you," de Rojas snarled dismounting. "I once told you there would be nothing you could hide from me!"

He hurried down until a few paces from Francisco.

"I've been waiting for you, Alonso," Francisco said quietly.

"Waiting?"

"I've seen you in my dreams every night," Francisco answered quietly.

"Then where is your weapon?" he challenged, drawing his broadsword from its scabbard.

"Weapon?" Francisco repeated, then shook his head, "I have no weapon. But I have this," he said holding up the small gold cross that spun on its chain.

"It's not enough to save you from God's judgement!" de Rojas roared closing in on him.

"God's judgement?" Francisco smiled. "Is that what you are doing here? Executing His judgement. Is that how you found me here, by divine guidance?"

"You are a large man, *el cobarde*. Big in body, short in courage as Miguel witnessed. You were easier to find than that day in Tripoli."

"Still Tripoli," Francisco mused. "Still seeking vindication for your own hesitation that day."

"For you, there will always be Tripoli!"

"For *us*, Alonso. For *us*! For men like us, there will always be Tripoli. The suffering, the waste, and the degradation . . . for

235

men like us, there will always be Tripoli." He stared calmly into the dark glaring eyes. "Will my death quell the doubts you have about your own courage, Alonso?"

"It will satisfy many crimes you have been guilty of!"

"Then so be it," Francisco said spreading his arms.

De Rojas hesitated, disturbed by del Valle's composure. It was as though he welcomed death.

"Strike, Alonso," he said. "There is nothing to fear. The dreams I had of domesticity with Mariana were no more than reveries of a weary soldier dozing at his post. You won't harm me, Alonso, you will release me."

As de Rojas gazed at him, he felt as though he were somehow bound up in an inevitable sequence of events of which this were only part. The clam face, crimson in the scarlet rays, was not that of Francisco del Valle. The long white hair and beard, deep eyes and hollowed cheeks, were not of *el cobarde*! Unconsciously he tightened his grip round the hilt of his sword to stop himself trembling.

"Why do you hesitate?" Francisco said.

It was del Valle's voice, de Rojas told himself. Yet unarmed, he could infuse him with fear. Fear of an unarmed man! Was there ever clearer evidence of his satanistic powers. Even as he looked at him, his appearance altered. It was witchcraft!

Their shadows grew longer as the sun touched the horizon. Perspiration ran down into the general's eyes. He was losing control of his senses. Del Valle was stealing his spirit. Something flashed brilliantly blinding him. It was the small gold cross dangling from his fist, ablaze in the rays of the setting sun.

"*Die!*" he screamed, savagely thrusting at him.

Francisco dropped to his knees, his muffled cry lost in a roar that came from the brow of the hill. Swinging round de Rojas saw a wild-eyed demon rushing at him, the short axe in his hand searing in the fires of the sun. He dragged his sword from Francisco, but his surroundings became a blur of terror, and dropping the weapon he fled to the sea.

"*No!*" Diego screamed hurling the axe, felling de Rojas as it lodged in his back.

He ran to Francisco, cradled him, and eased him to the ground. Francisco stared up at the tear-stained face hovering in the red haze of evening.

236

"Mariana . . . love . . . Mariana," but the words would not come.

His body was numb, and Diego's words were echoes in his mind like the sounds of the sea as it washed against the shore. All he saw were the red mists that floated, gradually obscuring Diego's face until sleep released him.

In the shadows of evening Diego gazed down at Francisco's body wrapped in the blue cloak of a Knight of St. John, nestling in the small boat. Round his neck the gold cross gleamed in the moonlight.

"Find a place to rest, Don Francisco," he whispered as he pushed the boat into the splashing waters. "There across those seas, with the Knights of the caravans you will find the peace that none gave you on land." He pushed the boat into the darkness, the waves washing round his waist as he watched the current draw it towards the silver waters.

CHAPTER TWENTY-TWO

Malta, 1570

Mariana stood with Ruiz by the dock of Grand Harbour and stared across to Mount Sciberras where once Turkish guns poured their murderous fire down on St. Elmo and Senglea. The heights had been levelled and now boasted the white walls of a new city being built there – Valetta.

The blue waters of Grand Harbour bustled with craft, yet she felt a strange peace on the spot where so many thousands had died. She looked across the small creek to Birgu, nearly restored by aid the island had received after its heroic struggle.

"We must enrol Ruiz in the Order," Diego said to her, looking at the tall young man who stood beside Mariana. He wondered if he resembled Francisco when he had been that age. "Do you remember me?" he asked.

"You came to our *solar*, soon after the siege," Ruiz replied.

"Five years ago," Diego said. "It's still a dream. No, a nightmare." He pointed to the Corradino Heights. "Guns," then to hills beyond Senglea, "cannon," and over on Gallows' Point, "basilisks," he shook his head in disbelief. "Everywhere, every day, bombardments, then attacks . . ." his voice trailed. "Francisco and I fought there," he said indicating the crumbling parapets of Senglea. He sighed. "But you don't want to hear that . . . I ramble like an old soldier . . ."

"I want to hear about it," Mariana said. "I want to visit all the places you told me of when you visited us."

He nodded. "I'm married now," he suddenly said. "I live in the village by Salina . . . I'm a fisherman . . . oh, I told you before."

"Is your wife Spanish?" Ruiz asked.

"A mermaid," he said.

"Mermaid?"

He shook his head. "It is a joke I share with Don Francisco."

"You speak as though he's alive," Ruiz said.

"He is," Diego answered staring at the silver waters. "Sometimes I go to the parapets where we stood and talk to him. And sometimes down to the bay where . . ." He checked himself, "where I last saw him. And we talk. No one died," he said. "And when the bells of the Conventional Church in Birgu ring, for those of us here, we see them. Two years ago Grand Master La Valette chose to sleep," he indicated the new city of Valetta. "He's over there in the chapel of the Blessed Virgin, Our Lady of Victory."

He shrugged off the painful memories. "I will take the Marqués to the Convent, where he can enrol as a novice. His background will allow him to enter the highest Orders, the Military Knights, or the Knights of Justice and then . . ."

"I am entering as a serving brother," Ruiz interrupted. "I will enter under my father's name!"

"The Marqués d'Olivera?"

"Don Ruiz del Valle," the young man said.

Diego took Mariana's arm, but she stood still, staring at the parapets, her eyes brimming as an image gazed back at her. The tall grey bearded man, in his unmistakable brigantine, leaning on the huge broadsword smiled in a peaceful contented way she had never known. She moved to rush across the compound to him, but Diego gripped her arm tightly.

"I know he is there, Mariana," he said softly. "For you, he will always be there, whenever you want him." Gently he eased her away. "Come," he said to Ruiz. "Let us visit the places where Diego nearly fled from battle, cried like a baby, and killed the *only* man who deserved killing." He pulled Mariana. "Come," he said. "We can return whenever you wish."

Epilogue

On 18th May 1565 a Turkish armada amassed by Suleiman the Magnificent, and estimated at over 200 vessels, invested the island of Malta under the commands of Mustapha Pasha and Admiral Piali. Their force was between 30,000 and 40,000 strong and it was believed that within a few weeks they would be able to finally destroy the Order of the Knights of St. John of Jerusalem, who had been constantly raiding their ships throughout the Mediterranean. But in fierce resistance, 541 Knights under the command of their Grand Master, Jean Parisot de la Valette, and with 9,000 Spanish, Maltese and foreign troops, resisted until September when relief was sent from Sicily.

Less than 10,000 Turkish soldiers returned to Constantinople when the siege had ended, while 7,000 defenders had died. Of the 541 Knights who fought, 250 perished, and the remainder were too badly wounded or crippled to bear arms again.

In July 1568, La Valette died of a stroke, but he lived long enough to see the city which bore his name – Valetta – built on the slopes of Mount Sciberras. Two years before, in September 1566, at the age of seventy-two, Suleiman the First Sultan of Turkey died while besieging Szigetvar in Hungary.

Though the siege of Malta did not break the power of Turkey, its effects on its military prestige were deep and lasting. And six years later, in October 1571 two adversaries who were in the siege, El Louck Aly and Chevalier Romegas were again in confrontation at the battle of Lepanto where under Don John of Austria the Turkish fleet was outmanoeuvred and routed.